Vengeance in the North Woods

VENGEANCE IN THE
NORTH WOODS

Randy Peters

authorHOUSE®

AuthorHouse™
1663 Liberty Drive
Bloomington, IN 47403
www.authorhouse.com
Phone: 1-800-839-8640

First published by AuthorHouse   09/21/2011

ISBN: 978-1-4567-9891-8 (sc)
ISBN: 978-1-4567-9892-5 (ebk)

Library of Congress Control Number: 2011916506

Printed in the United States of America

To my loving wife Donna
for sticking by me despite the hardships
along our wonderful journey through life.

.

CHAPTER 1

The pack moves through the night, silent as ghosts, in snow halfway to their bellies. Thor runs in front; lean and fast, he leads with an uncanny intelligence. The woods around them are a mixture of spruce, fir, and hemlock. Their senses stay peaked; it has been days since their last meal. The smell of food mingles with the cold, pitchy scent of trees. They know what kind of food too, cattle. These penned animals make easy prey; however, eating their kill before a farmer runs them off poses a challenge

The tantalizing scent leads them to a large, flat cornfield. On the far side-200 yards away-stands a muddy barnyard surrounded by a four-strand, barbed wire fence. To the right sits a big, red barn. Straight ahead and ten yards further, a two-story farmhouse watches over everything. On the clearing's outskirts, Thor turns toward his mate. Athena carries one of their two, surviving pups by holding the scruff of it's neck gently clamped between her teeth.

"The food lies close by. Find a hiding place for the little ones and leave Nikita standing guard. I'll locate our meal, then explore our surroundings." Thor whispers.

Athena's St. Bernard father gave her the genes to become the biggest in her pack. She inherited his muscles and her wolf mother's brains. She turns to Nikita, smallest of the adults, who holds the other pup, "Thor wants us to find a hiding place for Harley and Ella, you'll be standing guard."

Nikita nods and follows Athena into the underbrush. Soon they come upon some deadfall with small, softwood trees growing all through it. The saplings hold up a blanket of snow, creating an almost invisible cave.

"Nikita, you'll have to put both babies in there. I'll never fit in that tiny hole."

Athena keeps watch as Nikita stows her puppies in the heart of the jumble. With her youngest children safely tucked away, Athena returns to find Thor and Bandit in their usual argument.

"Dammit, Bandit, don't defy me. We need food. We're all hungry and the puppies are weak."

"You take too many chances, Father. Raiding a farm is far more dangerous than running down a deer."

"We need food so we can build the strength for running down a deer. We are barely strong enough to catch rabbits."

"I should lead this pack. We'd be much more prosperous."

"Any time you think you're wolf enough to take over, you go right ahead and try." Thor curls his upper lip; a low growl starts deep in his chest. He crouches, ready to knock some sense into his son, yet again.

Shiloh, Bandit's mate, steps between them. Her pure white coat shines in beautiful contrast to her love's coal black one, "Stop this, you two, please. If you spend all your energy fighting, we'll starve, and the babies will die first."

Thor straightens and lets out a long sigh, "You're right, Shiloh. Bandit, we'll finish this discussion later."

While Thor walks away, Shiloh nuzzles Bandit. Her presence calms the rage burning within him, "Please, Love, be still. It **is** dangerous, but we must eat. We've had little since the humans drove us from our home. Damn them, I hope their dens fall and crush every one of them."

"For you, My Dear, I will do anything. The day approaches though, when I will take my father's place as leader."

"I know, but now is not the time."

Beyond a small, spruce thicket, Thor paces. Athena stands close.

"Dammit, Athena, what's wrong with your son? He has no sense."

"He's your son too, Thor, and he acts more like you than you wish to admit. In his own way, he wants what's best for the pack. Unfortunately, you two have different ideas of what that is."

"I am leader of this pack, and until I am unable to do my job, he will do as I say." Thor storms off, looking for a way to calm down before the hunt; if he doesn't have all his wits and composure, someone will die.

Later that night, clouds disperse and reveal a full moon, thus making their hunt more treacherous. Wolves don't need the light to see their prey, but farmers need it to see them. Even though he knows he should wait, Thor can't. Ribs show in every member of his pack.

"Aright, everyone listen carefully. I don't like the conditions, however, I don't think we can chance waiting for Brother Moon and the weather to favor us. I'm afraid we'll lose the little ones if we do. Our meal sits penned up next to that barn. We'll circle in and drive them back toward the woods. This will gain us some time before noise alerts the farmer. We must kill quickly, then everyone grabs a piece and runs. In and out, quick and clean. Mother and I will take center, Bandit and Shiloh go right, Demon and Avalanche left. When we close for the kill, concentrate on calves. They're easier to catch and they taste better. Understood?"

Each wolf voices a low, undulating growl of consent.

"Good, let's go."

Their wraith-like movements barely disturb any snow as they make their way—single file and low to the ground—across the windswept field. A sudden change in wind direction alerts the cattle of impending danger and they mill around in fear. As Thor's pack circles them, the herd of thirty or more becomes increasingly agitated. When everyone finds their place, Thor gives a short yip and his family ducks under the fence. The herd panics; they rush to the barnyard's far end where they're stopped by more barbed wire. Thor charges and his pack follows. They take down three calves with an efficiency that rivals trained assassins. Working as a unit, they push the cattle back toward the house to avoid being trampled in a melee while making off with their supper.

Inside the dwelling, Bob lies in his warm bed under a heavy quilt Emma Jeanne and her mother made. He had protested at first, saying it was too girly a thing for him to use. He didn't want any flowery shit in his bedroom. Now he's glad he lost that argument, their quilt works just fine on a chilly night like this. The sound of panicking cattle shatters Bob's cozy slumber. Terrified moos from his bovines rip him out of bed.

Emma Jeanne rolls over, her bleary eyes trying to focus in the dark, her voice sounds like she has a mouthful of cotton, "What's goin' on?"

Bob lifts a pair of overalls off the floor and pulls them on over his long underwear, "I dunno, somethin's got the cows spooked bad. Could be coyotes. I'm gonna go check."

"Well, be careful."

"I will."

Bob creeps down well trodden, wooden stairs in his stocking feet. Being as quiet as possible, he makes his way to the front door and slips on his green, rubber barn boots sitting to its left. Hinges creak when he eases open the closet door. "Damn, I gotta get around to oilin' them things." Bob reaches in and pulls out a .32 Winchester his dad gave him when he was a boy. Leaving the closet open, he sneaks out, crosses his gravel driveway and edges toward the barnyard; what he sees inside gives him a jolt. Bob has heard about wolves moving into the area, but until now, he's never seen any. He'll sure as hell thin a few out, though.

Thor's jubilant lupines zip about, in a hurry to get away with their kills. Once they reach safety, they can eat. No one senses the farmer creeping inside the fence. The tall, lean, hardened man draws a bead on Thor. A black blur flies at him and he fires. A bullet hits Bandit square in the chest, tearing out part of his spine on exit. Thor turns in time to see blood explode from his son's back; Bandit's body slams into Bob, knocking him down.

Thor cries out, "No-o-o! Bandit, no-o-o-o." he coils the muscles in his hind legs, ready to attack.

Athena charges in, head butting her mate in the shoulder, turning him toward the woods, "That human already rises with his killing stick, Thor. We must run. Now!" She keeps pushing him to get him started.

Thor races across the field fueled by fury. Athena reaches the trees moments later. Her mate's eyes glow red. She knows a word from anyone will bring on a fight, so she joins him quietly. When she sits beside him, he growls, "I'm going to kill that human bastard. I shall revel in the sound of his scream just before I crush his throat."

Knowing Thor needs time alone, Athena leaves to check on her puppies. She finds them happily chewing on the carcass Demon and Avalanche managed to get back whole.

They jump up and bounce excitedly as soon as they see her, "Mama, Mama, look what the twins brought us. Where's Daddy?"

"He'll be along." She looks at her white friend who stands close by, "Shiloh, I need to talk with you. Alone." They walk a few yards away and stop on the backside of a fallen tree. Athena turns and faces Shiloh; tears stream down her face, "Bandit didn't make it. He jumped on the farmer to save Thor and that two-legged bastard shot him."

A pointed stick of pain stabs Shiloh in the heart. Her chest crushes under the weight of denial. "No, you lie. My Bandit can't be dead, he was right behind me."

"I'm sorry, Shiloh." Athena doesn't have strength enough to look her son's mate in the eye. She snuggles close and they cry together; their tears mingling in the snow.

Athena lets her family eat their fill before calling them together and telling them of Bandit's sacrifice. The news strikes like a boulder dropped from the sky, leveling the wolves souls under intense misery. Reality sinks in as slowly as spring run-off. In tear soaked voices, the pack sings; bone chilling sounds from their funeral song echo throughout the night.

Thor sits on a knoll overlooking the farm. He can't join his family, too much fury courses through his veins. He stares at the bloodspot where Bandit died. A snarl trembles on his lips and tears burn in his eyes, "You will pay for what you have done to my son, human."

Early the next morning, Athena rouses everyone, "C'mon, let's go. We need to scout around and find a more suitable place to hole-up. Nikita, guard the babies. Thor, are you coming?"

"No. I'll be watching the farm. Alone."

"I wish you would come with us, Dear."

"Leave. Now."

"Very well." Athena hangs her head and walks away, shoulders slumped, heart withered.

The pack begins its search; sadness pierces their hearts like a dull knife. Thor returns to his lookout point and glowers down upon the barnyard. In a few hours, he watches Bob—rifle in hand—following their tracks.

A toothy smile filled with joy and hatred spreads across Thor's lips, "That's it you stupid creature, come into my domain."

Thor slinks off the hill and heads for his children's hiding spot, placing each step with precision to avoid alerting his quarry. When he's almost there, he hears Nikita's warning growl. The human must be close. Thor runs all out, dodging branches and jumping deadfall. He arrives in time to see Nikita holding a defensive stance at the entrance of their wooden cave. Inside, his pups whimper in fear. Fury boils up inside Thor as the farmer raises his rifle, oblivious of the one hundred and fifty pounds of hatred moving in on his left, all focus set on the menace facing him.

Bob's mind swims in plans of destruction, "Once I kill this damn wolf. I'll set fire to that deadfall, see if there's anythin' besides pups in there."

Thor gets behind his enemy and lets out the kind of snarling growl that turns men's blood to ice. The farmer's heart stops and his stomach drops to his feet; he turns toward the source of that terrifying sound. He comes face to face with the most vicious looking wolf he has ever seen. His eyes bulge from their sockets, his jaw drops, his fear numbed arms slowly lower his weapon, and a strangled cry whispers past his lips. Thor leaps—white teeth glistening in the sunlight—onto Bob's chest, knocks him down and pins him to the ground. The wolf's sharp canines tear through the man's throat like a butcher slicing steak. Blood sprays Thor's fierce face as he shakes his head, tearing Bob's windpipe free. Standing on his prey, the metallic tang of blood and victory clinging to his tongue, Thor tips his head back and releases a long, triumphant howl. A twig snaps behind him. He spins and looks in Athena's horrified eyes as she steps from the brush into the carnage her mate created.

"Oh, Thor, what have you done?"

"I have avenged our son and protected our pups, the way any father should. This human," he spits the word out as if it taste like poison, "will take no more children from us."

"But, My Love, others will come. They always do. We must leave before they discover this one."

Thor lifts his head and sniffs the air, "Heavy snow approaches. We shall go during the storm, it will fill our tracks and we can disappear."

Before long, Athena gathers her pack around their leader as a thick sheet of snow blocks out the noonday sun. The corpse under Thor's feet will soon be covered. He addresses his family from the grisly podium, "Alright, I want Mother and Nikita behind me carrying the pups, Demon and Avalanche next. Shiloh, you watch our backs. We're moving out fast."

"Where are we going, Father?" the twins ask in unison.

"I've heard stories of a place in the west where buffalo still live and humans are scarce. Maybe we can start a new life there. Come, let's leave this ugly place behind." Thor lifts his leg, urinates in the farmer's face, then leads his family into the blizzard.

Emma Jeanne stands staring out a double pane, insulated window, framed by white curtains decorated with pictures of blueberries. Her typical, country kitchen feels empty. A knot of worry builds in her stomach as she watches snow fill her husband's scant tracks, leading across their cornfield and into the woods. It's milking time and he's not back yet; something must be wrong.

"Damn him," she mutters to herself, "I told him to wait until Adam came back from spreading manure in the East Meadow. It's dangerous going after wolves alone. I better send Adam after him."

Emma Jeanne throws on her old coat and rubber boots. She crosses their yard at a trot and opens the milk-house door. Noise and heat from the barn slap her face. She walks alongside a huge stainless steel, bulk tank. Out of habit, she places a hand on the smooth, shiny tank, assuring herself that its refrigeration unit continues keeping the milk inside cold. She passes through a narrow doorway into a milking parlor where six cows line up (head to tail) down both walls, with railings all around them. In a concrete pit running up the center, Adam—a brown haired bull of a man—works amongst a jungle of hoses, preparing to start the evening chores.

"Adam, I want you to go look for Bob. He's been gone a long time and I don't want him chasing those darn wolves through the woods after dark. I'll take care of the milking."

"Sher thing, Emma Jeanne. I'll grab muh .30-.30 outta muh truck and take Festus wit me."

Adam climbs five, steel-grate steps out of the pit and hustles outside. He snags a lever action, .30-.30 Winchester rifle off the gun rack in his rusty, blue, Chevy pickup, gets a box of bullets out of the glove-box, loads his rifle, and snatches Festus' leash off the seat. He slams the door with his elbow while chambering a shell then walks to Festus' temporary dog house (a big, plastic igloo normally used for housing calves) beside the barn. A young bloodhound springs to his feet when he hears the cocking Winchester; he knows it's hunting time.

Adam hooks on Festus' rugged, leather leash then leads him to Bob's half filled tracks, "Awright, Festus, let's go find Bob, then you an' me cin have a beer."

Festus yanks against his restraint; if not for Adam's bulk, his dog would drag him across the field. They make a quick beeline across the opening. The bloodhound has no doubts about where the trail leads. At the tree line, Festus slows, growling. A strong wolf smell burns his nose. Fine hairs on the back of Adam's neck stand on end. The woods lie silent, creepy silent. His heart skip every other beat as his dry throat constricts. Something horrible lurks in the air. Twenty yards in, they find a strange looking lump in the snow. When Adam dusts off Bob's corpse, his stomach rolls at the sight beneath.

"Shit, Festus, lookit what they done ta Bob." He heaves a strangled sigh and searches the area with a fire building in his belly, "From the looks a them tracks, they ain't been gone long. If'n we hurry, we cin git some payback. Hunt boy."

Festus yanks the leash out of Adam's hand and disappears into a spruce thicket; his braying bark echoes through the trees.

"Hellfire, I better hustle or I'll lose thet damn dog fer sher."

Thor hears a deep throated bark and stops to determine its location. His ears prick and hackles raise. Softwood trees grow dense here, distorting sound direction. The scent of cold pitch mixes with a sour odor of man.

"C'mon, everyone, I smell human following that dog. Let's try avoiding them."

Thor leads his pack up a steep ridge, hoping higher ground will give them a better vantage point and maybe some idea where their pursuers are going. If they see man and dog trying to cut them off, they can change course and get away. The pack's adrenaline pumps through their veins in hot, energy charged pulses. The dog closes on them. Thor knows wolves have much more stamina than dogs; they just have to keep moving. Thor charges across the pinnacle and suddenly breaks out of the brush into a small clearing. In a panic, he locks up all four feet, skidding to a halt. Athena slams against him from behind, almost knocking him off a forty foot cliff.

"Damn," Thor yips as he watches a snowball off his foot shatter upon the rocks below.

He takes a few steps left and finds another drop off. He turns, trots the other way, and discovers a deep void. They face cliffs on three sides and a dog with its human behind them; Thor must take action.

"We can't backtrack now, we'll have to make some sort of a stand here. Athena, you and Nikita hide the puppies in that thicket on our right. The rest of us will try scaring off the dog before his human catches up."

Athena and Nikita slip into the bushes. They nestle under a pile of deadfall then lay atop the puppies thus keeping them warm and quiet. They become invisible to their pursuers, yet can see the entire clearing. Their remaining family members form a half circle along the cliff edge; Thor at center, Demon on his left and Avalanche to the right. Shiloh hovers in a thicket near their flank. Festus bursts from the underbrush and slides to a stop inside the ring. Shiloh appears behind him, blocking his retreat. Thor steps forward, ears laid back, lip curled, and growling. After an initial cower, Festus regains composure and assumes a defensive stance. Thor struts within biting distance, trying to stare the bloodhound down. He can smell the young dog's fear; a sense of power invigorates him.

Thor speaks in his deepest, most ominous voice, "Pack law keeps me from killing you outright, Cousin. I must allow you the chance to flee. Do so now, and save your life, as well as your human's."

Festus' pounding heart drives icy blood through his body. Chills make him shiver uncontrollably. He tries keeping his bladder in check, but a drizzle of urine betrays him. He crouches, preparing for a fight he knows he can't win. The frightened dog gathers all the bravado he can scrape together from hidden corners in his heart.

He looks Thor square in the eye, "Listen to me, Wolf. My human will be here any second. If **YOU** leave, you can save **your** life and your pack's. My human is angry over you murdering his friend. He brings his killing stick and shall destroy you all."

Adam stands just out of sight in a thicket, blanched from the deadly scene playing out in the small clearing. A gentle wind carries his scent away from the pack, but that could change at any second. He raises the rifle and exhales a long breath to still his shaking hands. He must be quick and accurate to save Festus. He cocks the rifle's hammer with his thumb and slowly squeezes the trigger.

Athena knows she has mere seconds to execute a rescue. The human in front of her will kill her entire family if she gives him a chance. She musters every ounce of strength into her legs and powers forward. She slams her head into the back of its left knee at a dead run. Adam's foot launches skyward, his rifle barrel heaves straight up, and he fires while crashing onto his back; air leaves his lungs in a painful whoosh. Athena's pack flinches at the shot and whirls toward the bushes. Festus sees a chance and leaps at the lead wolf. Thor steps right, grabs Festus' collar, using momentum to spin his opponent around, and slam him on the ground. Festus doesn't even register the pain before Thor pins him down by the throat. Athena stands on Adam's chest, nose pressed firmly against his. Drool drips from her curled lip into the human's face. Her deep, thunderous growl turns his bowels to water; he loses control of them. Nikita bites onto the rifle's wooden fore-stock, rips it from his hand, trots to the cliff and drops it over. Festus stops struggling for fear Thor will crush his windpipe.

Shiloh walks up and snarls in Festus' ear, "If it were up to me, I would destroy everyone who has any association with the bastard that killed my Bandit. You'd better take your human and leave before I decide to disobey pack law."

Thor releases Festus; Athena steps off Adam's chest then backs toward her mate, growling. Festus rises, coughs, gags, and joins his master's on wobbly legs. Adam stands, weak kneed, hands shaking and breathing as if he's just run a marathon.

Thor looks Festus in the eye, "If you or your human follow us again, I'll kill you both."

Festus swallows a hard lump in his throat. He quivers at the thought of how close he just came to death. One by one, the wolves retreat into the thicket. Adam can't believe his luck. Tears of relief brim his eyes, "Festus, I swear to God, I'll never hunt wolves again. Hell, I ain't even gonna fetch muh gun. Let's git outta here 'fore they change their minds and come back.

CHAPTER 2

The pack retrieves its youngest members, turns west, and hurries off the ridge. Running all out, Thor rushes on, heedless of his surroundings. Emotions swirl in his heart: anger at the traitorous bloodhound (willingly condemning his cousins to death, willingly led by man), fear over their brush with death, the crushing pain of losing Bandit, worry about their future, and worst yet, a gnawing desperation creeps into his gut. His instincts tell him such a bold move West will prove to be a bad idea, but his mind can find no other way out.

Thor pushes his family for two days, hoping he can get them as far from humans as possible. On their third morning, they reach the edge of a swamp. Coarse, light green grass grows out from the shallows while cattails reach for fickle sunshine. Smells of black mud and rotten wood hang on heavy air. Splashing water marks the wolves' progress as they slog along in this smelly mire. Demon and Avalanche take their turn carrying Harley and Ella. Shiloh runs next in line, with Nikita at the rear. Athena plods through muddy soup beside her mate.

"Thor, I don't think we should be in a swamp. We don't know this territory and if we get soaked at this time of year, we'll get sick. Our babies aren't old enough to stand much sickness."

"We're less likely to come upon humans in the swamp. Right now that's most important."

"Can we at least stop awhile? We've been running hard and getting past this mess will take a lot of strength. We may travel a long way before finding another dry resting place."

Thor rolls his eyes, "Very well. But no longer than necessary. This is no time to be weak."

The pack finds their hiding spot on a wooded hummock. Cedar trees grow thick as quills on a porcupine in rich peat. At the center lies a small, comfortable opening, coated by a thick layer of duff. Shallow water crusting over with ice and black, soupy mud surrounds their haven. Noisy conditions created by ice and mud will prevent any human from sneaking up on them. The wolves curl up and try to sleep.

Harley and Ella, who have been carried most of the way, vibrate with energy. They soon lose interest in chasing their tails and each other. They try to start a wrestling match with Demon. He wakes snarling and snapping; Harley gets a nip on the hind leg that sends her away yelping and limping. Athena watches through slitted eyes. She won't step in on the puppies' behalf just yet; some lessons are best learned the hard way. The tingling numbness from her bite wears off and Harley jumps on Ella. They roll into a small cedar tree, sending an avalanche of snow cascading onto Shiloh. The icy blast shocks her awake, she jumps up with a startled yip. A gob of snow sits between her ears like a pointed hat. The pups laugh and howl in delight.

"I'm going to bite your damn tails off." Shiloh growls in a low, menacing tone as she shakes the cap from her head.

Athena speaks up, "Alright, you two, come over here and lay down. You've wreaked enough havoc for one day."

Harley and Ella know from experience that noncompliance will get them sent to their father for a nipping they won't soon forget. The puppies crouch, tails between their legs, and scurry over to Athena. Shiloh watches; unmasked anger burns in her eyes.

"You know better than to pester wolves while they're sleeping." Athena scolds them, "I taught you better than that. What's wrong with you? Acting so uncivilized. You're behaving like human pups. I've half a mind to make you both run tomorrow. Maybe losing sight of the pack for a day will scare some sense into you."

Fear flashes through Ella's young mind, "No Mama, please don't leave us behind. We'll be good, I promise."

Harley knows her mother won't abandon them, but she also knows when not to push her luck, "We're sorry, Mama. We'll be good, honest."

"Give Shiloh and Demon your apology, they're the ones you irritated most." Grumbles Athena.

Heads down, with tails tucked between their legs, Harley and Ella approach the elder wolves, apologizing to each in turn. They get snarls and growls for their efforts. They realize they've gone overboard then slink toward Thor. Ella's feelings are so hurt, she can't talk.

Teary eyed, Harley looks at her father, "Daddy, everyone hates us now. We didn't mean to make them mad. We were just playing."

His children's innocent sorrow tugs at Thor's heart. "I know, but sometimes you go too far in your play. You forget about other wolves' needs. Right now, we all need some rest. Besides, Shiloh and Demon don't hate you, they're still grieving Bandit. We all are."

Thor can't keep the pain out of his voice. Losing Bandit tore out a piece of his soul. His mind wanders back to their last conversation standing in that softwood forest, scents of cold pitch and tension hanging in the air, "Bandit, we need food."

"Raiding a farm is too dangerous. We should chase down some safer game."

"We don't have the strength to run after any prey."

"I should lead this pack, we'd be much more prosperous."

"Any time you think you're wolf enough to take over, you go right ahead and try."

Harley and Ella snuggle close and break his sad reverie. They lie face to face across his front legs and lean against his chest. He drops his head to nuzzle them, "Don't worry, Little Ones. Given time, Shiloh and Demon will calm down." He refocuses his thoughts on quelling the children's worries, puts on a bright smile and asks, "Now, how about a story?"

The pups jump up and bounce in circles around their father in expectant excitement, chanting in unison, "A story, a story, please, Daddy, tell us a story."

"Only if you lie down and listen quietly."

Harley and Ella race from Thor's rear, along opposite sides of him, toward his front. They turn the corner at his front shoulders and crash headlong into each other. Thor chuckles shakes his head, then begins an historic tale,

"When I was a pup about your age, I lived in a wild, beautiful land. There were ridges and valleys covered in an assortment of trees. Game ran thick: deer, moose, elk, rabbits, partridge, mice, and snakes abounded. My father, your grandfather, Odin, held leadership of our pack. Though small, he demanded respect and quickly put upstarts in their place. Those were good times. We could run for days without meeting any competition. Other packs stayed in their own territories, even catamounts and bears left us alone. Everyone had plenty and fights were uncommon.

As I grew older, things began to change. A new creature showed up in the forest. A two legged beast with no respect for nature. These things were called men. They soon proved themselves the most dangerous creatures of all. They began cutting down trees to build strange dens and feed their fires." Thor looks down with a solemn expression, "Beware of fire, my children, it destroys everything in its path. Man is the only creature who tries to control fire and they sometimes lose their grip on it. When fire gets free, it can wreak as much havoc as Man. Anyway, the more trees humans cut, the more forest animals were crowded together. At first, we tried avoiding people while working around other predators. Then man started killing our prey with wanton abandon. Winters grew lean, as there was less and less food. Many wolves starved during those first few cold seasons. Soon we had no choice; we started raiding human territories in order to survive. Wolves, bears, and catamounts quickly learned how easy man's food was to take. Humans kept their animals in pens or locked dens, so they couldn't escape. For a while, we lived well again, but man is as crafty as he is evil.

First they came into our forest carrying long sticks that thundered and shot flame in a smoky cloud. Out of the fire and smoke flew small metal balls that struck with tremendous force, puncturing our hides and killing us. We called them killing sticks. Man started with just a few here and there. Then they got together, formed bigger hunts and murdered every predator they could find. The catamounts, following their secretive nature, disappeared first; bears left next. Our wits, tenacity, and stealth helped us hold out longest. In response to our ingenuity, humans devised a nasty contraption called a leg catcher.

These merciless things have strong, snapping jaws filled with long, sharp teeth.

In their cruelty, men hung meat in a tree, just out of reach, and put leg catchers under the leaves or snow. They even learned how to use a deer's scent glands to cover their stink. When hungry pack members came upon the meat they would leap for it, then inevitably got caught in a leg catcher. The only escape was to chew their own leg off; a bloody, painful experience. As time went on, a lot of three-legged wolves started running around the forest. They were the lucky ones. Often, humans showed up carrying killing sticks before a trapped brother could free himself. The cowards destroyed any helpless wolf they found. Then those ruthless barbarians peeled the wolves' hides off and kept them as some kind of grisly trophy. Then, to finish their desecration of us, they'd often use the pelts to protect their weak skin from the elements.

Sadly, humans breed and destroy at an alarming rate. Our forest shrank like snow in the hot sun. Rival packs got pushed into each other's territory. We defended our land, fighting wolves and humans both with everything we had. Still, by hiding behind their devices, Man decimated our numbers. Humans proved hard to kill, unless caught alone and without killing sticks; then they are soft, weak, easy prey. We learned that warring against rival packs only causes more suffering for everyone. Instead of battling each other, the remaining wolves came together as one pack. By cooperating, we increased our productivity and knowledge of man. After a few seasons, we became very good at avoiding man's leg catchers and killing sticks. We even figured out new ways to take food away from him without losing anyone. Our midnight raids got more successful than we hoped. Keeping our bellies full became easy once more. For a while, our numbers increased. Under Grandfather's leadership, the pack grew strong again.

Unfortunately, Grandfather grew arrogant to the point of raiding humans in daylight and stealing their pups at every opportunity. He believed that by working as one, we could drive them out of our forest. In response, Man created death meat; a carcass filled with some nasty poison. When a wolf eats death meat, he dies a slow, painful death. Any scavenger who devours his corpse suffers the same fate. One morning our pack came across a dead calf, just inside the woods, next to a human den. Grandfather, being leader, ate first. After a few bites, he realized something was wrong. Humans could cover the tainted scent of death meat, but not its strange taste. Father led everyone away; afraid humans may have ruined the living animals as well.

By afternoon, he was in agony. His stomach twisted and cramped. He defecated a steady, burning, runny stream. He crawled to a brook and tried drinking away his fiery thirst. Water increased his cramping and diarrhea. The pain in his eyes tore our hearts out; we felt so helpless." Thor's throat constricts and his voice quavers as a tear runs down his cheek, "He spent a whole day howling and crying before death came to cure his suffering.

Grandmother was devastated, no one could console her. She and Grandfather had been mated since they came of age. She wouldn't eat or drink and never left Grandfather's body, singing the death song every night. I think she hoped humans would come and end her pain. They never did though, it took Mother two weeks to waste away and die. I guess a broken heart is a slower killer than a broken stomach."

With a heavy sigh, Thor takes a minute to wipe the tears off his cheek then shake old, buried pain from his voice. Harley and Ella look up at him in rapt attention. He looks down at his children, smiles, and wonders how two creatures this small can bring a heart so much happiness, even during a painful trip into the past. Once recuperated, he continues, "Grandfather's brother, Lightning, took over leadership. His mate, Flower, adopted me and treated me like one of her own. They were complete opposites. He was a stubborn fool, she was intelligent, patient, and kind. Lightning lived in such paranoia about keeping his new position, he spent all his time proving his authority. He paced around our pack listening in on conversations, always looking for signs of mutiny. Lightning even bribed wolves to spy on each other so he could dole out punishment for dissidents. He developed a cruel idea of justice. If he suspected a family member of plotting against him, he made that member run a gauntlet. Our entire pack lined up in two rows, facing each other. The accused would then be forced to run between these rows while participants pummeled him with bites and slashes from sharpened claws. When the judged fell, the others tore him apart. If he made it through without falling, Lightning exiled him; doomed that poor soul to live out his days alone and shamed.

As I grew older, I became disgusted with Uncle's treatment of our pack. Whenever he set up a gauntlet, I would leave early on a hunting trip and later feign ignorance of the ritual's time. Uncle spent so much time passing judgment that he neglected most of his hunting responsibilities. Everyone lived in fear and hunger. I wanted to challenge his authority, take my rightful place as Alpha Wolf. I knew I could lead the pack better than Lightning, but Flower kept talking me out of it. 'He won't give you a fair chance.' she would say, 'If you got the upper hand, his followers would mob you. I know I shouldn't speak ill of my mate, but I couldn't stand to see you killed. I can't suffer that kind of pain.' So with growing impatience, I waited.

While on a hunt during the feasting moon that year, we broke out of the thick, softwood brush and found the most beautiful young female I had ever seen cowered under a fallen log; thin, tired and too frightened to come out. Dead, rotting wolves lay all around the small clearing. Lightning said we should leave her. He was busy hunting and wouldn't waste time on an orphan pup. Flower's big heart gave her a fierce determination, to help; she and I stayed behind. Smitten, I stood watch while Flower talked to the frightened female. Standing with my back to them, I kept one ear cocked in their direction. She and I were both in our first breeding season and I wanted to learn all I could about this intriguing female. Finally, she told Flower her story in a low, quaking voice.

Her mother and stepfather were pack leaders. They always tried their best to avoid humans. They knew from the start man was trouble. Her stepfather grew steadily more concerned over gossip from the crows about a brazen wolf pack that raided human territory. Her parents could foresee trouble and were making plans to find a new, safer home much further north when the two legged beasts came.

Dozens of them appeared out of the brush. They were everywhere, carrying sticks that made noises loud enough to kill. The pup's mother hid her under a log, ordering her to stay there until she returned. She then tried leading the humans away from her daughter. That poor, terrified young wolf heard the snarls and screams of her family's decimation buried under ear shattering roars from the humans' sticks. Gray smoke left hanging in the air burned her eyes and stung her nose. After the men left, she stayed under that log-afraid of what she might find-hoping her mother would return. She lost track of how many days went by; throughout the night, nightmares plagued her tortured mind. Pain soaked cries echoed through her memory as she told us of sights and sounds too gruesome for me to repeat.

Even after their long talk, it still took Flower several hours to coax that girl out of her sanctuary. When she did emerge, I knew

I was looking at one of The Great Forest Spirits. My heart stopped and melted into a puddle; I'd just met my soul mate. This wolf was the most beautiful creature I had ever laid eyes on. Despite her bedraggled state, she shone like an exotic treasure. She stood very tall for her age with more brown coloring in her coat than any other. She swayed, weak from hunger, so Flower sent me after food. I dashed off, determined to flaunt my hunting prowess. I returned a short time later—chest puffed out and three rabbits held by the ears in my mouth—to find her fast asleep with Flower curled partway around her in a comforting embrace.

Flower and I stayed there a week, nursing her back to health while we waited for our pack to circle back through the area. During that time, we learned more of her enchanting history, including the fact that her biological father had been a human slave called a St. Bernard who escaped bondage and joined her mother's generous pack and taken by his bold, brave yet compassionate nature, she claimed him as a mate. He was much larger than any wolf, but not suited for life in the wild. That same season, he died of exposure just before she was born. When we discovered her name, Athena, it reminded me of a gentle wind blowing through the softwood trees. As Flower and I earned her trust, I began realizing she had a heart as big as the rest of her; she owned more kindness and generosity than anyone I'd ever met.

She filled out very fast during her recuperation. I showed off my hunting skills at every opportunity, so we had more than enough to eat. She also proved an adept hunter who possessed innovative ideas. Using cunning new techniques from her pack, the three of us were able to encircle an old deer and bring him down with minimal effort. I grew more impressed and in love every hour.

When our family returned, your mother disappeared inside herself. Lightning flew into a rage at the fact we had saved a helpless stranger. He even suggested killing her to cut down on competition for food. He took two strides toward your mother and Flower stepped between them, bristling as she challenged him, 'You will not harm this child. I have adopted her and if she is not welcome in your pack, then neither am I'. Lightning stepped back, so shocked at the sight of his mate with her ears laid back, hackles up and carrying a menacing tone in her voice, that he could only walk away. He never argued against Flower's decision, but she warned your mother to stay close beside her at all times, just in case. Although she loved her mate, Flower knew he could be devious. She suspected that given a chance, Lightning would kill your mother then try blaming humans.

Your mother followed Flower everywhere, and I followed your mother. We grew closer each day; we soon agreed to be mates, keeping it secret for fear Lightning would retaliate. He never softened his position about Mother not being part of his pack. Even when she served a crucial part of a kill, I'd have to sneak her part of my share so she could eat. When your mother surprised me with news that she was pregnant, I was ecstatic, yet, saddened. I knew we must leave for Lightning would not allow our pups to live.

One bright, sunny day, while the pack slept, your mother and I told Flower our secret then said goodbye. My heart tore in two. Though thrilled at the thought of being a father, I knew I'd never see Flower again. She never let her sadness show. Instead, she sent us into the world with her love and a promise to pray for us everyday.

The two of us went east for many days, always holding onto the hope of finding a place we could call our own. Although we tried, your mother and I never did get completely away from humans.

Still, we continued our search until finding a small territory between other packs and man. By that time, most wolves were sympathetic toward strangers. After all, we shared a common enemy. Your mother stayed tough, hunting by my side everyday, ensuring that neither I nor our unborn pups went hungry. Eventually, she grew too heavy for running. She then gave in and let me take care of her; a job I performed with relish.

Three moons later, on a warm, spring day the sun shone and the birds sang while my newborn children mewled and fought to find a nipple on their happy, exhausted mother. I was the proudest wolf in the world. We lived many good seasons after that. Bandit, Demon, Nikita, and Avalanche grew into strong, swift wolves. Shortly after his second breeding year, Bandit found Shiloh, a refugee from yet another massacre orchestrated by humans. Mother and I accepted her into our family without question, treated her as one of our own. We often listened to her horrific tales of a death meat epidemic spread by those two legged beasts. Our hearts broke at the thought of how much pain she carried inside. Bandit watched over her during nightmare soaked days and we began a new vigilance, always watching for mankind. The stress proved rough on Mother, she went through a few barren seasons before getting pregnant with you two ruffians.

A few moons past your birth, our tentative happy time ended. We ran into humans again. It took all our wits to survive them. Mother and I knew about their killing sticks, leg catchers, and death meat. Other wolves weren't so lucky, they died a vicious death. Once more man destroyed our forest, built their dens, and crowded us. We were hungry in no time. We decided fighting new, invading packs and destructive humans would lead to our family's annihilation, so we came south. It seems, there's no place for us here either, which is why we're moving west. Maybe, we'll find a land away from people and learn how to hunt the beast called buffalo."

Thor looks down and sees his babies facing each other lying across his front legs, tight to his chest, Ella's head resting on Harley's shoulder, and fast asleep. Thor's heart swells with pride and love for these innocent little puffballs. He looks up and winks at Athena.

She smiles, "For a malicious killer, you sure have a way with children." She walks over and lies beside her mate; they lean on each other then drift into slumber.

CHAPTER 3

Nightmares from the past plague Thor's dreams. Visions of Odin's writhing, painful death intertwine with memories of Bandit's heroic act. Guilt boils in his gut like a thick, witch's brew. He should have done things differently: listened to Bandit, kept a better watch for the farmer, cured his father, something. He twists, turns, and squirms throughout the morning. Sleep is a fleeing rabbit he can't quite catch. He rises, pacing long before anyone else stirs, watching over the pack, letting them rest until midday. One by one, they wake and stretch; sticking their rears in the air, leaning back to pull kinks out of their front legs, then while holding their heads and chests high, drop their hind ends as far as they can.

Once he shakes sleep from his body, Avalanche pads over to Thor, "Are we going hunting, Father? I'm hungry."

"I want to keep moving. If we come upon easy prey, we'll stop, otherwise, I don't want us wandering around and taking a chance on getting lost in an unfamiliar swamp. They are dangerous this time of year. We can get wet during the day and freeze to the ground at night then if it were to stay cold for a long period, we would starve. Not knowing how big this swamp may be, I want to get us out as soon as possible."

"But, Father, we need food."

Thor bristles and curls his lip, voicing a deep throated snarl. "Are you questioning my authority?"

Avalanche assumes a submissive posture, rolling onto his back and tucking his tail between his legs, "No, Father, I am concerned is all."

"Leave the worrying to me. Now, go carry one of the pups, you'll be safer if you hold something in your mouth."

"Yes, Father." Avalanche rolls over and slinks away on his belly.

Athena sighs then follows Thor out of earshot from the others, "Was that really necessary?"

"What do you mean?"

"Your verbal attack on Avalanche."

"He needed to be put in his place."

"He's young and not used to waiting for his meals. Things were once easier than they are now, that's what he's accustomed to."

"We are on the run. We must keep moving and take what we can get."

"I understand that, but he doesn't. Biting everyone's head off won't improve our situation."

"I suppose you're right. I've just been worrying so much and sleeping so little lately. It doesn't take much to set me off."

"Well please try to hold your temper, there's no point in making the family more miserable than they already are."

"I'll try."

Thor and Athena rub noses and give each other an affectionate lick on the face. He looks deep into her brown eyes, hypnotized by the love he sees there. She still takes his breath away, "What would I ever do without you?"

"You'd be hopelessly lost."

"And then some."

Thor would spend all day engrossed in the bottomless depths of his love's gaze if he could. His heart tells him, "stay, spend some quality time with her." His mind overrules, tearing him away and sending him back to his responsibilities. Thor's heart longs for the broken connection like a bear wanting the honey buried deep in a bee tree. It takes all his resolve to resume the task of leading his family to safety.

"I wish we could spend some time alone, Athena, but we'd better get moving."

Thor's words puncture her heart, leaving a gaping hole in her chest, "Yes, I suppose we should. Seems like there's always something separating us these days."

"I'm sorry, Dear, but I can do nothing about it right now. I swear, once things settle down, I'll make it up to you."

She walks away; sadness weighs her head down. Thor assembles the pack and they splash on through cold water and sticky mud. Saturated smells of wet peat, black mud, swamp grass, cedar trees, and stagnant water hang in the air like fog. The wolves break into a large opening. Water, spotted with grassy humps, stretches as far as the eye can see. Beaver trails interlace the hummocks.

Thor gathers everyone and gives instructions, "Don't step into any of these trails. They're especially dangerous for we can't tell if the water is six inches or six feet deep. A slip could mean a wet paw or a complete dousing. If we get soaked, we'll wind up catching a killer cold."

Using grace and caution, they jump from hump to hump. Deeper in, soupy, black mud gets closer to the water's surface.

By evening, a thick viscous muck takes over; chilled air smells black and dirty. Hummocks get larger and flatter. Thor finds a dry place covered in high, sharp leaved, swamp grass. When the wolves walk on it, this floating island tips and rolls like soft ice on a spring lake. A quick scout reveals some high traffic, beaver trails surrounding their haven. Thor posts hunters around the perimeter; each lies low in the grass, just far enough back from its edges to conceal themselves.

Soon, Shiloh sees advancing ripples disturbing the alleyway's mirror surface. A beaver barely keeps his head above water as he slips along his silent path. Shiloh's body tenses. She must catch this food; it could mean the difference between life and death. She strains to subdue stressful thoughts, needing a clear head in order to hunt well. The beaver lazes along in front of her. Shiloh leaps out of the grass like a savage jack-in-the-box and catches him in a flash. It's not an instant kill, though, and the beaver gets a chance to slap its tail on the water, warning others of danger.

Two uneventful hours later, Thor calls an end to the hunt, "I think our luck has run out. Let's eat then get some sleep, we'll start fresh in the morning."

Shiloh sits in front of him with her head hung low, "I'm sorry, Thor, I should've made a better kill."

"Don't worry about it, Shiloh, at least you got one. Let's enjoy what we have."

The wolves split Shiloh's kill, savoring every bite then settle into an exhausted sleep so deep, no one even twitches for three hours. They quiet night gets ripped apart by the high pitched barks of hunting coyotes. The pack leaps into high alert. The adults have no fear for themselves, but their pups could be in danger from their vicious cousins. They stand rigid; ears pricked, and hackles up. Thor searches the darkness, trying to pinpoint their rivals. Athena slips in beside him and whispers in his ear, "Are you thinking what I'm thinking?"

"We may get a better meal yet. We'll let the coyotes do the work for us then take their kill."

Athena joins Harley and Ella who lie snuggled together in the pack's protective center, "You two listen and listen good. We need every family member to steal that meat away from the coyotes. Therefore, you will have to stay here alone. Keep huddled together for warmth and lie low in the grass. Don't move or make a sound until I come back for you, understood?"

The puppies look at each other then at their mother with big, teary eyes, their jaws hanging open. Ella breaks their terrified trance, "But, Mama, you can't just leave us. We're not big enough to defend ourselves. What if a fisher cat shows up? Please, Mama, don't leave us."

"I don't have much choice. That sounds like a large bunch of coyotes. We'll need everyone in case they feel brave and a fight breaks out. Stay quiet and out of sight, you'll be fine. If a fisher cat shows up, howl like crazy and we'll come running, o.k.?"

"Do we have to?" whimpers Ella.

"Yes"

Athena's heart breaks at the fear and dejection in her children's eyes. They lay down, side by side, and she pulls up grass to cover them with. She tries comforting them while she drops one mouthful of bitter stalks after another over their shivering bodies, "Lie still, this will camouflage you as well as help keep you warm." She walks away feeling like a traitor, "A mother's place is protecting her children. It's one of the few lessons mother had a chance to teach me before the humans killed her. What would she say if she were here now? Dammit, I thought motherhood was supposed to be filled with love, fun, and laughter. Why has mine turned into guilt laden weariness?" She squeezes her eyes shut; willing away the dark thoughts. She must be alert and effective, no distractions. She takes her place beside Thor, once again completely focused on the task at hand.

Thor picks up the tell-tale, dead meat scent of coyotes. He hears his rivals bring down their prey then sing a blood curdling, hair raising, victory song. The celebration stops as if chopped off with an ax; tomb like silence blankets the night. Smacking sounds and low growls ring in Thor's keen ears as if they are being projected through a loudspeaker. The wolves trail their leader in silence while he follows his nose and ears toward their next meal. A hundred yards away, they find dry land hidden under a cedar thicket. Sweet smelling trees dull the black scent of mud. Short bushes grow so close together, the pack can't pass through without sounding like a bull moose ripping up the woods. Using head signals, Thor instructs the young members to stay put. Athena knows her mate's thoughts and breaks east while he moves west. They pick their way over unstable hummocks, keeping an eye out for some sort of trail that will gain them silent access to the coyote's position. They return in less than ten minutes.

Athena whispers, "I found a path large enough for me to easily fit through and the ground lies frozen almost solid. We can sneak right up on them."

"O.K., we'll go that way. All I discovered was an opening barely big enough for Nikita. Lead the way, My Love."

Athena retraces her route. Thor jerks his head in her direction, signaling the rest to follow. At the trailhead, Athena steps aside and lets Thor resume lead. Interlaced branches and snow make her path resemble a cave carved into a green and white mottled cliff face. The pack enters with the stealth of spring mist. Odors from cedar and frozen mud are no match for the reeking scent of coyote. The wolves also smell fresh deer blood spilling into the muck surrounding and their mouths water. Step by careful step, Thor leads his family through the thicket. They use all their willpower to keep their stomachs from grumbling. At this distance, any sound will alert the coyotes' acute hearing.

Thor stops at the clearing's edge to take in the scene and figure out his best approach. Several coyotes mill around on a rolling mat of swamp grass. Its roots grow in a thick tangle in rich, black peat. Flattened grass and its interwoven anchors form a platform strong enough to hold their weight; the deer wasn't so lucky. One leap from dry land sealed her fate. Her narrow hooves broke through the fragile covering, dropping her into the soup below. The more she thrashed, the more she sank. Once she was belly deep in mire, she made an easy kill. The now coyotes focus totally on indulging themselves.

They don't notice Thor until he speaks, "Greetings, Cousins."

The rival pack jumps and settles into a defensive stance around their prize. Their ears lay back, and their hackles rise. An electric, adrenaline tingle charges the air. Hearts race, muscles tense, smells of fear and courage float on a light breeze. The light brown group's largest member is about ¾ Thor's size. Thor's pack remains hidden. The coyote leader smiles, puffs out his chest, and raises his nose at an insolent angle.

Believing he has the upper hand due to superior numbers, an arrogant note saturates his words, "What do you want, Wolf?"

"I've come to take your kill."

"You must be insane, thinking you can take our kill alone."

"But he is not alone." answers Athena as she steps from the thicket and stands beside Thor. One by one, the rest of her family appears, flanking their parents on both sides. Each member's arrival sends a wave through the grass mat. The coyote leader crouches, ready to spring.

His lip curls and he snarls, "You don't scare me, Wolf. You may be bigger, but you only have six, I have ten. You don't stand a chance."

"Are you willing to risk the lives of your family on that belief?" Thor's tone carries a bone chilling quality.

The coyote leader leaps without warning, catching Thor by surprise and knocking him down. Athena charges, head down like a raging bull, and bowls over three opponents. Shiloh grabs an oncoming young female by the scruff of her neck, swings her in a high, rising arc, and slams her onto the deer carcass. The impact stuns the young coyote. She slides, limp as a lily pad, into the smelly mud. Shiloh spins in time to sidestep a rushing attack from behind. Momentum sends her adversary headlong into one of his pack mates. Demon and Avalanche circle, back to back, holding off a matching pair of reddish brown enemies. Nikita strikes with quick, vicious precision. She grabs a coyote half again her size by the throat and bites down until he stops kicking.

Thor recovers in an instant; rolling with the blow, he lands on his feet. The leaders circle, sizing each other up; murder dances in their eyes. One of Athena's victims jumps up and blindsides her in the shoulder. The coyote bounces off Thor's mate as if she hit a maple tree. Athena rears up on her hind legs as her attacker hits the ground. Focusing all her weight into huge front feet, she comes down with the force of a bear and drives her rival into the muck. She doesn't see the dark shape sneaking in behind her. The assassain's hind leg muscles coil as he prepares a lethal strike. Nikita slips, silent as a snowflake, in beside the would be assailant and clamps powerful jaws onto his hind leg, shattering the bone. White hot pain races along his nerves and slams into his brain. His ear piercing scream rips through the night. Athena turns toward the uproar in time to see him limping away, yipping like a puppy.

"Thanks, Nikita."

"No problem, Mom. Look out!"

Athena dodges a gray blur bearing down on her and bats it in the head with her left paw. The coyote does three somersaults and splashes into the water. Close to their left, Shiloh backs away from two advancing opponents, waiting for a chance to attack. Tandem foes study her severe intensity. Athena and Nikita run into her enemies from either side, slamming them together. The coyotes' heads connect, sounding like a large branch breaking, and slump into a heap.

Anger flames in Shiloh's eyes, "I had things under control." She charges off toward Demon and Avalanche. She knocks down their first opponent, picks it up by the scruff, shakes it senseless, and throws it into the thicket. Now Shiloh leaps onto the coyote facing Demon, locks her jaws onto his throat, and repeatedly slams him into the ground. After the fourth impact, her foe stops fighting; unconsciousness carries him into its dark depths. She spits him out and spins, hoping for more combatants. Releasing some fury over losing Bandit exhilarates her like nothing she has ever experienced. Shiloh casts murderous red eyes from one side to another. Demon and Avalanche back up in fear; the smell of crazed hatred rolls off Shiloh so sharply it burns their noses. Their sister-mate stands quivering; a sizzling battle rush hums through her muscles.

Athena braves a cautious approach into Shiloh's line of sight, "Okay, Shiloh, it's over. Settle down, nice and easy."

For a moment, Shiloh looks as if she doesn't recognize Athena. Then her vision clears and she realizes the extent of her fury. Shock and shame overrun her, "Oh, Mother, I didn't want to stop. I could've killed somebody." Tears glide down her cheeks, glistening in the moonlight like icicles on a sunny winter day.

Athena snuggles her, "But you didn't, that's the important thing."

Thor and the rival leader lock in a rolling battle. Thor clamps onto his foe's foot and tastes blood in his mouth. He releases and jumps back, ready to strike again. He looks his enemy in the eye and warns him off, "Give it up, Cousin, you can't win. Don't force me to kill you."

"You arrogant flea ridden rodent, you think just because you're bigger, you'll win? I'll not surrender to you."

He leaps at Thor who ducks. When the coyote sails overhead, Thor drives his head into the leader's stomach. The coyote doubles over, rolls a few feet, then comes to rest on his right side, coughing and gasping. Before he can recuperate, Thor grabs his throat. The wolf's voice sounds muffled as he once again warns the coyote, "Look around you, Cousin, you are the only one left fighting. Gather what remains of your pack and leave. Don't force me to kill you."

Thor lifts his opponent and turns, first one way then the other, giving him a first-hand view of his fallen comrades and the wolves standing over them, Thor drops him and allows him a minute to decide.

"What's it going to be, life or death?"

Spite churns inside the coyote like the surface of a wind chopped lake "You've won this time, but watch your back. As soon as I get the chance, I'll seek revenge."

"I wouldn't expect anything less. For what it's worth, I'm only stealing your kill because I must in order to feed my family. I promise we won't take more than we need."

"I don't want your scraps or your pity."

The coyote leader gathers his family. Some stumble along semi-conscious, some limp, many bleed, but none have any life threatening injuries. They disappear into the thicket. Demon and Avalanche tip their heads back and start a victory song.

Thor cuts them off short, "Hey! We do not take pride in a meal stolen from cousins smaller than us. I only allowed this raid because we need it." His words hold an almost defeated undertone, "There this act carries neither pride nor honor. Now eat your fill so we can leave here."

CHAPTER 4

Harley and Ella huddle under their grass cover shivering more out of fear than cold. They hear their family fighting for their much needed meal. Suddenly, the night becomes deathly still; even the wind stops whispering in the trees. Such an abrupt end of the fighting peaks their anxiety. Soon, their untrained noses pick up an unfamiliar scent. Wet fur of some sort creeps ever closer. Could it be a harmless beaver? Or a fisher cat looking to dine on young wolf pups? Their muscles stay lock in terror until the strange smell moves out of range. Minutes stretch on like hours. The pups lie frozen in worry's stone cold fist.

Dreadful thoughts tumble around Ella's mind, "What if our family lost? Will there be anyone left to take care of us?" Her nerves are twist to the point of cracking, "Harley, do you think they're o.k.?"

"They're fine. There aren't any coyotes anywhere that can beat wolves, especially Mama and Daddy, they're the toughest wolves ever." Harley hopes her hammering heart doesn't give away her doubts. A knot tightens in her belly.

Ella looks like she wants to believe her sister, but just can't, "Yeah, you're probably right."

"Of course I am"

Anxiety saps Harley and Ella's strength. They soon lose their battle with sleep and drop into a fitful slumber sprinkled with soft whimpers and gentle kicks. Nearby, ears prick, yellow eyes narrow, a black nose lifts and pulls scents from the air. A furry, gray-brown shape rises off the ground and winces as it takes two painful steps forward. The head cocks and a snarl full of sharp teeth spreads across a set of black lips.

The coyote leader whispers, "Get up, everyone, we may have our chance at revenge. I smell wolf pups and can hear their lonesome whimpers."

The coyotes drag themselves to their feet. They've licked their wounds, but anger can't overcome their physical pain. A skinny female hobbles in front of the alpha and cowers down to speak with him.

He looks at her as if something vile just slithered before him, "What do you want?"

Her soft voice quivers, full of fear, "Backbite, please, we're all sore as hell. There's no way we can make a stealthy approach. Besides, what if those wolves catch us? We couldn't beat them when we were fresh, they'd kill us now."

Backbite snaps at her leg. She jumps sideways, avoiding a nasty cut by mere inches.

"How dare you question my orders, Mouse? You think that just because you're my mate, you can say whatever you like? You will do as I say, without hesitation, or I will kill you myself." Backbite stares into the eyes of each pack member, "That goes for the rest of you as well." They drop their heads in acquiescence. "That's more like it. Now, let's destroy some wolf pups.

Venison comes as a welcome treat; the wolves relish it. Athena gobbled her share in record time. Now she paces, ready to rejoin her babies. She is so nervous she doesn't bother licking the blood off her face. Thor walks over and stands beside her, "What's wrong, Love?"

"Something bad's about to happen. I can't explain it, but I know Harley and Ella are in danger."

"They're safe. We camouflaged them and told them to stay quiet. No one could ever find them. You're being silly."

"No dammit! I'm not. You can't understand because you're not a mother. I'm telling you, our babies are in trouble and I'm going to check on them, with or without you."

"Athena, you can't go alone. Those coyotes are probably slinking around out there somewhere. They'll ambush you and I doubt they're as civilized as we are. They're apt to kill you."

"I'm going."

"Aright, alright. I can see by the look in your eye I'm not going to talk you out of it. At least let the others finish eating, so we can all go together."

"They'd better hurry."

———————

Backbite follows his nose and ears through the swamp. He's glad they're sneaking up on babies; his injured pack bumbles along, unable to stalk properly. He himself can't crouch well with a bleeding front foot. Still, his patience wears thin. They stumble, crash, and splash around like a herd of startled moose. He turns and faces his family. His eyes glow red in the moonlight, his words sting their ears like a sub-zero wind.

"If you clumsy fools don't smarten up and quiet the hell down, I'm going to kick all your asses. Try not to let your incompetence screw this up too."

His pack cowers and shakes in fear. They know this isn't an idle threat and by the look on his face, someone may not recover from **this** raging fit. They continue in shaky silence; the fact that a misplaced step could be their last, floats in the back of their minds.

"That's it, I'm leaving, right now." barks Athena, "Something's wrong and I'm not wasting anymore time waiting for the rest of you."

She turns to storm away, but Thor cuts her off, "Hold on, we're all going together."

"Then hurry the hell, up."

"Come on, everybody, we're leaving, now."

Their pack gathers and Athena leads them toward her puppies. She smashes through the woods in reckless abandon. Her heart hammers, sending electrified adrenaline racing through her body. Her sense of urgency rages uncontrollably. Worried thoughts blast across her brain. "Hang on, Babies, Mama's coming."

Harley opens one eye; her foggy mind tries to focus, "What was that noise? Was it a beaver splashing, or something else?"

The air smells wrong, rotten somehow. Ella lies beside Harley, lost in her own nightmares. She whimpers and kicks a few times. Harley doesn't know whether she should wake her sister or not.

There could be a nightmare in the dark that's worse than the one in Ella's head. Indecision plants a butterfly of worry in the pit of Harley's stomach; she chokes down a nauseous lump rising inside her. That wrong smell grows thicker, the ground begins to buck and bob. Someone has entered their floating haven; someone unfriendly and dangerous.

Backbite grits his teeth against the pain in his foot. He puts as little weight on it as possible, trying not to limp anymore than he has to. His heart races, anticipating the bloody taste of revenge. No one makes a fool out of Backbite and gets away with it. Each agonizing step fuels his bloodlust, pushing him ever closer to the point of frenzy. He can smell young fear; the wolf pups are on this island somewhere. He catches a movement from the corner of his right eye, whips his head around and scans the flattened grass. Soft whimpers help him zero in on the pups' location. A malicious grin creases the coyote leader's lips as he prepares for the kill. Each step is a deliberate action, a savoring of this glorious moment. His focus narrows onto a small lump of shivering grass. He no longer cares whether the others still follow or not. Placing his sensitive nose against the unnatural pile, he drinks in the scent of innocence and terror.

An enormous gray streak hits him in the ribs, rolling him over. Devoid of all thought except the need to save her babies, Athena clamps down on the coyote's throat. His entire neck fits in her powerful jaws. He gurgles and kicks once before a crunching snap ends his fight. Athena tosses his dead body into the water as if it's no more than a stick. She braces, ready to fight the whole group if need be.

Her whole, looming figure exudes a determination to face any odds in defense of her children, "The rest of you have a choice, leave now or I'll Kill you all."

The menace in her deep, booming voice fills the coyotes with a fear they have never experienced. Its intensity makes some lose control of their bladders; the rest scramble for an exit, limping away as fast as their bruised bodies will allow.

Thor bounds from the bushes, followed by the family, "Are you o.k.? Are they safe?"

Harley and Ella squirm out from under their cover, "Mama, Daddy." They run to their parents who nuzzle and lick them.

Athena cries in relief. "Oh, My Babies, I was so worried about you."

As the last remnants of adrenaline wear off, all members assure themselves the little ones are safe. Each takes a turn nuzzling and licking both babies. Once everyone settles in for the night, Thor and Athena regurgitate part of their meal for the pups. Thor later checks the few minor injuries incurred by Shiloh and Nikita during their fight.

"Don't forget, Nikita," his soft tone holds a tenderness all fathers should have, "clean that mud off your feet before you go to sleep. You don't want to freeze to the ground if it turns cold."

"Yes, Father." Nikita takes one lick of a muddy paw and whispers, "Eeew, that tastes horrible. I'm not licking this shit off. I'll wait for it to dry then scrape it off."

Thor walks over to Shiloh, "How's the leg?"

"It's fine. I think I twisted it a little during a jump, no big deal."

"I heard you went a bit crazy back there. Anything you want to talk about?"

"No."

"As you wish, but bear in mind, I'll not stand for any reckless behavior that endangers my pack. Understood?"

"Perfectly"

"Good, now get some rest. We need it after our stressful night,"

Thor finishes his rounds then returns to Athena who lies with their sleeping pups. She sees him coming and takes him to one side, "How is everyone?"

"They're fine." he cocks his head to one side, a concerned look upon his face, "I'm guessing from your expression, you can't say the same. What's wrong?"

Athena hangs her head in shame, "I broke pack law. I killed one of our own kind. Murder is a horrible, human crime, almost unforgivable. Now you must decide whether or not I'm cast out. I will accept your decision, whatever it may be, just promise me that no matter what, you'll take care of our babies."

"Pack law be damned, you were protecting our young. Any mother would do the same. Besides, we no longer have a High Council to answer to. Humans killed or scattered the members long ago. Now, in the name of survival, we must give up some of our civilized behaviors." Thor's eyes narrow, "Anyone who intends to harm our family flirts with death."

Athena exhales a mighty sigh, "Thank you, Thor. I was so afraid I would never see my children again."

"I would never hurt you, my love, especially not like that. Not now, not ever."

Athena nuzzles Thor then returns to Harley and Ella, curling up around them. Thor stands watch for the remainder of the night; his family has earned a good, long rest. He paces, listens, and ponders, "Have I done the right thing? Is this move a good idea? I almost lost my pups tonight. Athena was forced into a heinous crime. I attacked a human, Bandit's dead, something dangerous brews inside Shiloh. Maybe we should've stayed home. But if we'd have done that, the humans would've killed us sooner of later. Damn them, damn them to the deepest reaches of The Dark Caves. All our problems circle back to those flea ridden vermin. So much pain, so much death, orchestrated by a puny bunch of furless, clawless monsters. If I didn't have responsibilities, I'd hunt down and kill every one of them. Will we ever get away from them? What if they've done the same thing to the buffalo as they did to us? What if I've made a horrible mistake? I will never forgive myself if I've led my family to their death. I'm not even sure I'm fit to lead anymore." Thor's doubts plague him deep into the night.

Late the next morning, Nikita awakens, stretches her hind legs, then she tries stretching her front legs, but realizes she can't lift her front feet. It turned cold last night and they froze to the ground.

"Uh-oh, now what do I do?" She looks toward Athena and whispers, "Mother, Mother, can I talk to you a minute?"

"What is it, Nikita?"

"Um . . . . well . . . . Father told me to lick the mud off my feet last night and I . . . uh . . . started to, but it tasted horrible. So, I decided I'd wait until it dried then scrape it off. Only problem is, it didn't dry." Nikita hangs her head, "My front feet froze to the ground. I can't move them, no matter how hard I try."

"Ni-ki-ta, why didn't you listen to your father? He doesn't tell you these things for the sole purpose of hearing himself talk."

"I know, I know, but it tasted so-o-o bad, and I didn't think it would get as cold as it did."

"Alright, well, let's get Father up and see what he thinks we should do."

"Oh no, Mother, please. Can we not wake Father? He'll be pissed at me for not listening and if we wake him, he'll be double pissed. You know how grouchy he is when he first gets up."

"O.K., we'll try something. Let me have a look."

Athena first tries pulling Nikita's right foot up. Grass beneath it gives a little and the skin stretches.

"Ow, ow, ow. Stop, stop."

"You've gotten yourself into a pretty good fix Daughter. Let's see if we can chew off the grass from around your feet."

Together, Nikita and Athena make short work of the greenery. As Nikita pulls the last few strands loose, Thor storms over, his eyes still bloodshot from lack of sleep, "What in hell is going on? I heard someone yelp."

Athena tries a soothing tone, "Nothing serious. Your daughter didn't clean her feet and they froze down."

"Dammit, Nikita, I told you to get the mud off your feet for that very reason. Don't you listen to anything I say?"

"I'm sorry, Father."

"You damn well better be. I'm busting my ass trying to keep everyone alive **and** find us a new home in the process. The least you could do is pay attention when I tell you something. I swear, sometimes you act like a human child."

Nikita start crying and Athena steps in, "Thor, enough. You're tired and upset. Maybe you should get some more rest then we'll discuss this."

"Very well, we'll rest for the remainder of today. Maybe things will be better tonight."

The wolves lounge in the sun. The twins wrestle and chase the pups around. Harley and Ella revel in the attention, playing until they can no longer stand. That evening, they all revisit their deer carcass and finish it off; the coyotes seem to have lost interest in it. Athena convinces Thor to talk calmly with Nikita. After some quiet discussion and mutual apologies, father and daughter nuzzle then lick each other's faces. Things return to some semblance of normalcy. With their bellies full and spirits high, they embark upon the next leg of their journey.

CHAPTER 5

Sunrise shoots purple and orange rays in a bursting display across the undersides of white puffy clouds. Swamp gives way to dry ground. Large hemlock trees grow interspersed with young spruce and fir. The black smell dissipates, replaced by the rank, skunk-like scent of hemlock. Mild storms over the last few days have deepened the snow. Today, it's cold and calm. The wolves stop to rest after a night spent running in sticks, mud, and water. Athena lies beside Shiloh, worry creases her face.

"Shiloh, are you o.k.?"

"I'm fine."

"Thor and I are concerned about you. Over the last few days, you seem different, quieter, short tempered."

"I-I miss Bandit."

"We all do. Losing him was a tragedy. Given time, we'll heal. Besides, we'll always have a piece of him in our hearts."

"I have more than that."

"What do you mean?"

Shiloh's voice goes quiet, "I'm pregnant."

"Shiloh, that's wonderful."

"I don't know. What if they look like Bandit? I don't think my heart can take that."

"When they come, they'll bring you more happiness than you thought possible, believe me. Even now, looking at my children makes all the pain of a bad day go away. Puppies are the greatest gift."

Thor slows their daily pace in response to Shiloh's news. There's no real reason to hurry anyway, the land they're traveling through now seems ideal. Game abounds, fresh snow lies atop a thick crust, making large animals easier to catch. No one has seen any human signs in days; this could be a good place to live. The pack's travel settles into a large hunting circle. They claim this territory as their own.

Uneventful weeks pass allowing the wolves to let their guard down. Harley and Ella can start learning how to hunt. Prey is easy enough to catch, so even when the over eager pups blow a stalk, the pack still eats. On a bright, sunny day, Thor watches Harley and Ella creep up on a small deer. Though young, they're learning fast; his chest swells with pride. The deer bolts. Being light, he runs atop the crusted snow. The pups aren't strong enough to chase him down and he soon bounds out of sight. They mope to Thor, heads down and tails sagging.

"Don't worry, Little Ones, soon you'll be big enough to run down an elk. I've been watching you grow stronger everyday. All you need is patience and persistence."

Harley and Ella brighten. With inflated egos and heads held high, they scamper off for more practice.

———————————

A cold, winter morning breaks clear and bitter; white vapor trails behind the wolves like steam from locomotives. Fluffy, powdery snow lays deep, cutting down the advantage of frozen crust. Thor runs hot on the trail of a bull elk. Athena lags back a few yards, ready to take over should he need a break. Nikita jogs along next in line for the relay. Harley and Ella help Demon and Avalanche flank the old bull preventing him from veering off either side. Shiloh heavy with pregnancy, blocks his retreat. They'll keep him running straight until he collapses. The elk struggles, drenched in sweat, thick chest heaving, aged graying chin drooping; great white puffs belch from his lathered mouth, and he slows. Soon the wolves will rush in and finish him off. It's late in the season and he's long since shed his horns, so they don't have to worry about huge antlers; however, they don't underestimate sharp hooves that can crush a skull like a rotten cantaloupe or slice open a shoulder as quick as any set of fangs.

Demon, Avalanche, Harley, and Ella tighten their circle as the elk crosses a small opening. Shiloh, though lagging behind, stays determined to do her part. Thor and Athena asked her to stay hidden and rest, but she refused. She waddles through the bull's path, ready to give birth any day now. Her swollen nipples drag in the snow, making her cold and uncomfortable. Halfway across the opening, she stops to catch her breath. Cold air sears her lungs as she pants and wheezes.

Hemlock trees surround the clearing. Fifty yards away, on Shiloh's left, a large pine supports an unnatural jumble of branches ¾ of the way up its trunk. She doesn't notice it or the peculiar scent emanating from that tangle. She takes two steps forward and hears a loud crack, followed by a high pitched whine. A deep burning numbness spreads across her chest; a cloud of snow explodes on her right.

The horrifying sound of a killing stick ricochets around the forest. The pack stops dead in its tracks. Thor and Athena do a quick head count then look at each other, "Shiloh," they gasp in unison. They turn and run for the clearing at top speed. Nightmarish visions of Bandit's death wrestle with Thor's judgment. He can think of nothing except getting to Shiloh and saving his grandchildren. He abandons caution completely. Athena, as wrapped in fear as Thor, charges through the woods by his side. The rest of their pack pushes themselves to keep up. More cracks and whines greet them when they burst into the open. Here and there, snow puffs up from the ground in little geysers. Wolves dash every which way, causing all the confusion they can. They kick snow high into the air while they run, creating a blinding blizzard. Random dark spots flit around the white out. The human sitting in the tree becomes so rattled by this sudden appearance and strange behavior of seven wolves, he can't hit anything. He slings bullets wantonly, hoping he'll get lucky and kill one. Athena rushes to Shiloh, who walks a drunken line across the clearing, dazed and confused.

Athena gives her a nudge, "Shiloh, you're bleeding."

Shiloh looks down and notices a red sheet on her white chest that reaches her knees.

Athena nudges her again, "Quick, we've got to get back into the brush. There's a sneaky human with a killing stick around here somewhere."

The realization makes sense of Shilo's pain and that rotten egg smell coming from gray clouds floating out of the pine tree. She hobbles into the bracken thinking, "Damn humans bring stink and pain wherever they go."

When Shiloh and Athena are out of the dell, their pack melts into the woods. They catch up to the girls resting by a small stream. Water gurgles over stones under the ice. A hemlock's branches, weighted down by snow, provide a blind on two sides of them. Thor places everyone on guard around the hideout while Athena licks blood off Shiloh's chest.

Shiloh squirms, "I'm fine, Athena, stop fussing over me."

"Hush, I want to determine that for myself."

A thorough cleaning satisfies Athena the wound isn't drastic. She finishes tending Shiloh then sits beside Thor in the protective circle. He can tell by her slumped shoulders she is tired and worried. He rests his head across her broad shoulders.

"She okay?"

"I think she'll be fine. The cut isn't as bad as it first looked. We shouldn't have to worry much about infection because it's winter. I'll still keep it clean, though. We should limit her travel for a few days, at least until the wound starts healing well. We shouldn't risk re-opening it. The pregnancy will weaken her and slow recovery. She says she's fine but I don't know how much stress this will put on the pups."

"We can't wait. I don't want us taking a chance on humans coming after us again. We were lucky last time, this one may be more cautious than the last. If he brings his whole pack with killing sticks, we won't get away. We'll start out slow, but we must leave." Thor growls, "I was foolish thinking we could make a home here. The only place we have any hope of being safe lies in The Land of the Buffalo."

"If we travel now, Shiloh could lose her puppies. I don't want to lose anymore children. Do you?"

Thor grits his teeth in frustration, "Alright, fine, we'll find some high ground where we can see and rest there until dark, but then we have to move."

"We'd better get a drink before we go."

Athena pads to the edge of the brook, scrapes the snow off, bounces up on her hind legs, and drives her front feet into the ice. After three tries, she bashes a hole down to the water. Thor explains his plan while everyone takes turns drinking.

"I was hoping we could settle here, but this human attack makes that impossible. Therefore, we'll find some high ground, rest for today, and head west tonight. It seems we won't have peace until we reach The Land of the Buffalo."

Shiloh shuffles forward, "Thor, please, I don't want to be the reason we leave this wonderful place. I'll be fine in a few days."

"We don't have a few days, Shiloh. Humans may come after us anytime now." Her crestfallen look tugs at a tender spot in his heart, "Don't blame yourself. You're not the reason we're leaving, those two legged parasites are."

Thor learned this area very well in the short time they've been here; he knows a great hiding place. A mile away, a hardwood ridge with steep ledges near its top rises out of the valley. On the peak of that outcroppings rests a small cave. From its entrance, they can look through bare treetops and see the forest on three sides of them. A well placed sentry can hide and watch the one blind spot above and behind. They take a long route, knocking snow off softwood boughs in the lowland, obliterating parts of their trail. Higher up the ridge, they stay on slippery, black stones and windswept, frozen crust to avoid leaving tracks. Shiloh pants hard as she approaches the cave, blood trickles down her chest. The climb proves hard on her, but worthwhile for it will be even harder on humans.

Thor stands on the pinnacle over their hide-out, searching a spectacular view. Hardwoods marching down the ridge slowly give way to softwoods on the valley floor. Virgin snow lies fresh and unblemished; a frosted filigree of branches reflects the sun into thousands of sparkling diamonds and miniature rainbows. The sky stretches overhead in a perfect ocean of blue; no clouds mar its face. Five miles straight ahead, he can make out a human society. Grayish, white haze, spewn from chimneys scattered like sown seeds throughout the town, hangs over it in a suffocating blanket. He can detect the acidic burn of wood smoke from here. Trees encircling the settlement look less healthy than ones in the valley.

"Why do humans bring sickness and death wherever they go?" he wonders.

Thor makes his way down a narrow trail to the cavity. Its roof rises just tall enough for him to stand upright. It's six feet to the rear and the ceiling tapers down until it meets the floor in back. In front lies a shelf with a few, short spruce trees growing on the edge. The wolves can crowd together and stay out of sight; yet, be able to see any enemies sneaking up on them.

Thor looks at his gathered family, "I need a volunteer to go up and watch our backs."

"I will," Demon offers.

"I'll go too," Avalanche adds.

"There's only room enough for one of you up there," Thor explains, "Demon, you take first watch. Avalanche, in a couple of hours, go relieve him. I want us switching often so we stay sharp. Be careful climbing up, that trail is slick. Once on top, you'll see a boulder with a depression under one side of it. If you squeeze in there you can be out of the wind and still see the entire area. I'll take first shift down here and trade with Mother in a few hours."

Early that afternoon, while the pack sleeps peacefully behind her, Athena hears a twig snap and a squirrel's high pitched chatter. A blue jay sends his warning call through the crisp, clear air. Athena crouches behind the spruces and peers between snow laden branches. A light wind blows off the top of their cave and away from her. She can't smell it yet, but something approaches.

Avalanche lies curled in a ball and tucked as far under the boulder as he can get. Bitter cold leeches from the ground, past his thick fur, and settles into his bones. Wind blows straight on him; the snowdrift building in front of him offers little comfort. Frigid air drains his energy and he starts nodding off. He comes full awake in an instant when a frightening scent floats into his nostrils, faint and dangerous. He opens one eye, not daring to move until he can determine its location. The scratchy scrape of a hemlock branch rubbing against something foreign followed by snow thudding to the ground sounds very close. That scent comes again, strong and sickening. Avalanche raises his hackles and although it disgusts him, pulls a large dose of the stench into his nose. It's coming from straight ahead, ready to break into the clearing.

Athena catches movement in the mature softwoods below and hears snow crunch under large flat feet. Her suspicions prove true when three men creep into the hardwoods. They walk four yards apart, scanning the ground in close scrutiny. She trembles in anger and fear. If the humans get too close to them on this pinnacle, they'll be trapped. If the wolves run too soon, they'll make easy targets on the wide open scree.

She takes a deep breath calming her fluttering nerves and lets it out in a slow, quiet sigh, "What are we going to do?"

Avalanche tries stilling his shivering muscles as two humans push through the bracken. They separate and study their surroundings with the intensity of seasoned hunters. Haunting yellow eyes watch them from behind a low snowdrift, Avalanche's mind rolls in a similar turmoil as Athena's. If he moves to warn the others, he'll be killed. If he waits too long, they'll be killed.

Athena slides back toward Thor an inch at a time; a sharp whistle pierces the air. She freezes and her heart stops. She hears men above her for the first time. Thor's eyes snap open. Athena makes a shushing gesture with her lips and looks toward the ceiling then across the valley.

On the ridge top, a fat man cocks an ear, catching the faint whistle. He waves an arm catching his buddy's attention, "That's the signal, they're givin' it up. Must be John figures if we ain't found 'em by now, we ain't gonna. Let's git off this cold ass rock and find a warm fire somewhere."

"Hold on, I need a break"

The humans lean against the boulder Avalanche hides under. "I told him this was a waste of time." the fat man complains.

"Yeah, but ya know John, he hates to give up once he's shot at somethin'."

"Well maybe he'll start takin' better aim if we stop helpin' him chase after every critter he grazes."

Avalanche quivers from the tension. His heart hammers so loud, he's afraid the hunters will hear it. He wills his body to be still.

"He is a nervy fella, ain't he?"

"You ain't kiddin'. Once he sees a critter he gets so wound up he can't hit the broad side of a barn from the inside." The big man shivers, "C'mon, let's get outta here 'fore I freeze."

They push themselves upright and clamber off one side of the point. Snow cascades onto the trail to Athena's right; still not quite inside, a few frozen pieces bounce off her foot. Using the ruckus as a cover, she scrambles into the cave.

She whispers in Thor's ear, "What do we do? If they find us, we're dead. I don't want to wake everyone and give away our position, but I don't want to get caught unprepared either."

"We sit tight. If they find us, we fight. It's too late to get away anyway.

The men stumble past. One turns his ankle on Thor's narrow path and rolls several feet down the slope before grabbing a hemlock sapling, thus halting his descent. His bearded companion roars laughter until he slips, falls on his back, and slides to the bottom. The humans below gather around their snow covered friends, help them up, then joke about their misfortune as they disappear into the softwoods. Athena follows their progress by the snapping branches and chattering squirrels while Thor noses the air searching for stragglers. She creeps onto the balcony and slowly stands. A pea sized pellet of snow bounces off her snout. She spins, drops to a defensive crouch, and looks up growling into Avalanche's sheepish expression.

"Sorry, Mother, sorry. I wanted to let you know it's clear up here."

"Dammit, Avalanche, don't scare me like that. I almost choked on my heart. Come down and trade watch with Nikita."

Thor releases a long, pent up breath.

The pups sit up yawning, "What's going on?"

Athena forces her voice to be calm, "Just some humans passing by."

"Humans?" They sit and quake.

"Don't worry, they're long gone. We weren't in any real danger anyway, just some strays."

The two look doubtful, "If you say so."

"I do. Now go back to bed."

The half moon rises, clear and bright, in a cloudless sky bedazzled by millions of sparkling stars. Night air turns so cold, it freezes sap inside the trees, causing it to expand until exploding from the branches. Popping limbs sound like killing sticks. Every breath burns the wolves' lungs and pours out their mouths like smoke from a chimney. Athena cleans and checks Shiloh's wound. When she's finished, she joins Thor on the balcony.

"Thor, I don't think we should go yet. Shiloh's wound is still too fresh. A lot of movement will cause it to re-open. Those humans aren't coming back, let's stay a few days and let her heal."

"I don't want us taking any chances. You know how mankind acts. Now they know we're around, they'll band together and force us out. They hate us, Athena, and I will not lose any more children to them."

"Shiloh shouldn't over exert herself, hard travel stresses unborn pups. You have good intentions, My Love, but in trying to save your children, you may lose your grandchildren. Please don't make me give up my last link with Bandit."

Athena looks at Thor with so much pain in her eyes that he drops his head, heaves a frustrated sigh, and concedes, "I'll compromise with you. Two days, no more, and if we see any human activity beforehand, we leave. O.K?"

Athena's face brightens. In this moment, she reminds him of the young wolf she once was, and his heart swells.

"Thank you, Thor. You've made the right choice, you won't regret it. We'll be fine, you'll see."

Thor extends his compromise for several days. The group stays close by their shelter and he limits hunting to only small animals. He won't chance running into humans while going on long jaunts, chasing large prey. The youngsters get bored and unruly. Thor takes them out daily so they can hone their skills on rabbits, partridges, mice, and one early born white tailed fawn while he keeps a sharp watch.

Today, Demon and Avalanche stand guard at the foot of their ridge while Harley and Ella dive headfirst into the snow after mice. Thor sits on the ledge, watching. A smile illuminates his face; he chuckles as Harley and Ella first stand on their hind legs then drop forward (throwing their hind feet high into the air) and drive their heads into the frozen crust. Ella emerges holding a mouse in her teeth. Harley snatches it and Ella chases her in circles. Thor enjoys seeing them burn off some pent up energy; they'll be less apt to irritate everyone if they're tired.

The sun shines bright and warm; Thor basks in this reprieve from winter's cold. Yesterday's warmth and last night's cold caused the snow to settle then freeze into a decent crust. If they can get away from humans before the snow gets deep again, they'll be very successful hunting. A disturbing thought scampers around in his head, "If everyday were this perfect, life would be easy, but that's not going to happen as long as humans hang around. We'll always suffer." He turns around and sees Shiloh licking blood from the rabbit Demon brought her, off her snout, "How are you feeling?"

"Fine"

"Will you be able to travel tonight?"

"If you need me to travel, I'll be ready."

"Good, get plenty of rest today, we'll leave at moonrise."

A heavy curtain of clouds obscures the moon. Night breaks dark and warm; the wolves must take care not to overheat themselves in their thick, winter coats. Sweet smelling maple sap overpowers the hemlock's pungent odor. Moisture from wet snow hangs in the air like a blanket. Water drips from every branch and an occasional whoomp of snow falling off softwood boughs interrupts the silence. Thor's pack leaves behind the best home they've found since beginning their forced voyage.

CHAPTER 6

Spring struggles against winter's icy grip, working in vain to finally burst free in a torrent of color and new life. Shiloh tries not to let the pain from her burning chest wound show on her face. She pants and wheezes as she waddles along behind the pack. She's so tired; she always feels tired. Athena told her she could have the pups at any time.

It should be a time of hope and joy, but Shiloh's thoughts stay troubled, "What if I lose my babies because it turns cold? What if I have more than our pack can carry? Will I have to decide which ones to leave behind? Will Thor break pack law and kill them quickly or just leave them to starve? No, Athena won't allow her grandchildren to die. Will she?"

"Hello-o-o, Shiloh, you in there?"

Shiloh snaps back and sees Athena's concerned face in front of her, "I'm sorry, Athena. I guess I wandered off in thought. What do you need?"

"I asked if you're o.k., you're falling behind. I came back to get you."

"Oh, I'm fine. I slowed when I drifted into thought is all."

"Happy thoughts I hope."

"Yeah"

"Well let's catch up, Thor said we'd stop at daybreak."

Athena and Shiloh hustle to overtake their pack as red fingers start reaching across the sky, painting the underbellies of clouds deep purple. Cold moisture in the air forewarns snow before day's end. Thor stops and sends everyone out looking for a suitable resting place. He watches Athena and Shiloh jog through the wide open, snow spotted field toward him. They add beauty to the now orange sunrise behind them.

Athena reaches her mate and nuzzles him in unmasked affection, "We made it."

"I was beginning to wonder."

"No worries, Love, We're big girls." Athena gives Shiloh a conspiratorial wink, "Besides, we know better than to leave you boys to think for yourselves. Nikita would have more than she could handle rescuing all of you."

"Very funny."

Demon and Avalanche find an enormous brush pile in the middle of a cleared acre. Its human scent lies there, old, wispy, close to death. Since the brush was cut late last season, it still holds most of its leaves and needles which should keep melt-water from reaching the ground, unless temperatures spike. Their pack burrows in, rearranges a few annoying branches, curls up together, then drifts into blissful slumber. Despite Thor and Athena's objection, Shiloh volunteers for first watch. She lies just inside the brush pile.

A cramp knots her side, she winces and whispers, "Not yet, Little Ones, wait until we're safe."

Thor rouses his family at moonrise. The sun's brother grows bold again. He shows ¾ of his face in an inky, clear sky. The air regains its bite. Frost sparkles on everything in sight; the landscape seems made of crystals. Beyond the clearing lies an old sugar bush dotted with small softwoods. Half grown fir trees, covered in six inches of fresh snow, make excellent cover; the wolves can travel in secrecy tonight. They restart their journey, as silent as ever.

Around moon peak, on top of a steep rise, the pack surprises an aged white tailed deer in his bed. They eat their fill on the easy prey and move on. Thor hates leaving uneaten food, but he can't shake a haunting feeling of being pursued. He senses humans lurk behind every tree and boulder. His nerves twist so tight they vibrate. His eyes never stop moving; his nose searches for man's scent. He ignores burning leg muscles and travels throughout the night. His family reaches the base of a mountain as a yellow-orange sun begins painting the sky in dawn hues. Thor decides they should push on; few men venture into this kind of wild terrain.

Temperatures rise with the sun. Melting snow soaks the wolves in no time. Travel becomes very hard. It's tougher plowing through deep, wet snow than fluffy powder; it's like wading through quicksand. Nikita has trouble keeping her head above the suffocating, white mire. Everyone's spirits rise when they reach a windswept face pocked with large holes from long since fallen rocks. They've traded wallowing in snow for walking on ice, but are equipped to handle such difficulties. They have rough, black pads on the bottom of their feet that give good traction on all types of terrain.

Thor's senses run on high alert. His gut twists in a worried knot. Just ahead, two boulders lie in a wide vee. Athena expends the last of her energy catching Thor.

"Thor . . . . pant, pant, wait . . . let's stop, here . . . . gasp . . . the boulders . . . . will . . . pant, gasp . . . give us protection . . . pant, whew . . . from wind . . . huff, puff . . . we need . . . rest . . . it's sun peak . . . and we've . . . . whew . . . traveled all . . . night."

Thor stops, scanning the trees around them, "For awhile, I want to move again by nightfall. I feel like we're being watched. I don't like this place. Something is very wrong here."

"What's the scent?"

"That's the worst part. I can find no scent, just a feeling."

"We should stay alert, you're feelings are usually right."

Their family joins them and they all nestle into the ell. Athena lies in back, Shiloh curls up next to her, then everyone else surrounds Shiloh for protection and warmth. Thor can't rest, his senses vibrate. He stands guard over his loved ones, watching, waiting.

The day gets warmer; moisture holds scents tight against the ground. Wet wood, stone, tree sap, squirrels, and something unfamiliar press together in a strange concoction so thick he can taste the danger in it. The forest lies quiet, nothing moves. Even dripping melt water sounds muted. Thor moves up from their haven to just below the ridge crest, allowing a better view without making him a detectable target. Blending into his rocky background, he scans the mixed hardwoods below. A light wind ruffles his fur. Silence and tense energy coil around him like a nervous snake. A high pitched, pain filled howl splits the air.

"Oh no, that came from the pack." Thor dives down the slope and races toward his family, slipping and sliding at breakneck speed. His heart pounds against his ribs as the ear shattering scream renders his mind senseless, "Damn, I never should've left. I should've stood guard." He feels like he's running in swamp mud; his feet won't move fast enough. He forces his legs onward until he charges upon the scene. The wolves stand in a half circle outside their lair. Another wail rips intoThor's brain. He pushes past Demon and Avalanche to find Shiloh lying on her side panting as if she's run down a deer. Athena and Nikita hover on either side of her, talking in soothing tones.

"Athena, what's happening?" Thor asks.

"Shiloh is having her pups."

"But, isn't it early?"

Shush. Yes, but she'll be fine." Athena gives him an angry look. "There's no sense in upsetting her."

"Oh—uh—yes, of course. Is there anything I can do to help?"

"You and the boys can stop gawking at her. Go hunting or something, Nikita and I can handle a simple birth."

Thor faces his sons, "Come, you heard your mother, let's go hunting."

Athena can't help but chuckle and shake her head, "Even after all the births he's seen, he still gets nervous as a chased rabbit."

The males make a poor attempt at finding food. Shiloh's cries echo through the trees; each outburst draws their attention toward the boulders guarding their females. Deep concern shows on every face.

"Don't worry," Thor assures them, "your mother knows what to do. All of you came into this world healthy." His posture exudes a confidence he doesn't feel. He doesn't recall Athena sounding as if she were in this much pain."

The hunters do catch a few partridge and a couple of mice; agreeing they'll give all their meat to the new mother. The forest has been quiet for some time now.

Thor can't stand the anticipation any longer, "Come on, Boys, let's get back and check on the girls." He leads them through the brush, trying to keep his paws from shaking.

They walk in on a happy scene. Shiloh's labor melted her into a bowl inside of which squirm five newborns, clean, hungry, and healthy. Their mewling cries, mixed with the sight of puppies fighting for a nipple, bring Thor back to when his own children were born. Pride builds a lump inside his throat and a tear in his eye. Athena can see strong emotions on her mate's face and comes to his side.

She nuzzles him while staring into his eyes, "Congratulations, Grandfather, you old softie, you have five grandchildren."

His voice carries an awed tone, "I'm a grandfather. Athena, how did we get so old?"

"Speak for yourself, I am far from old. I'll be in by prime for many years to come."

"And you'll always be the most beautiful female in the world."

"Keep talking like that and you'll have to take a romp in the moss with me."

"But there's no moss."

"We'll pretend."

A lascivious smile crosses his face, "I love you, Athena. I always will."

"I love you too, Thor. You are my protector. You have all my faith and trust. Now come meet your grandchildren before you put me 'in season' out of season."

They step inside the vee. Thor's eyes meet Shiloh's, tenderness settles into his every word, "Bandit would be very proud. You have given him wonderful children who will be as strong and brave as he was."

The mention of Bandit's name pulls hard on everyone's heart. Shiloh smiles through mixed emotions conjured from past death and present birth, "Thank you, Thor. Your approval means a lot."

"Get some rest, you've worked hard today, you must be exhausted." Thor swallows the unease welling up inside him from this order. He masks frightful thoughts floating in his mind, "I hope she doesn't need too much time. We have got to get out of here."

The pack sleeps, exhausted from hard travel and unexpected excitement. Thor paces in silence, watching, listening. His senses still tell him something dangerous creeps through the brush, just out of sight, but he can't figure out what. The forest sits soundless once again. If not for the game they found earlier, Thor would swear this place was dead. Snow sparkles in light cast by an almost full moon. Temperatures turn cold, an out of place odor laces sharp, night air; a scent he can't identify. He freezes, straining his ears. "Is that a crunch of footsteps or my imagination?" Thor shakes his head, untangling his thoughts, "Maybe a short walk will calm my nerves. Shiloh's delivery made me as jittery as Athena's always did."

Thor takes four steps forward and stops. A pack of pure white wolves materializes before him. He bites down shock and anger at himself for not detecting them. Their leader moves closer as another nine members form a half circle in front of Thor. He stands almost as large as Athena and has long, straight hair that stands on end, giving him the appearance of a star seen through a haze. Thor's mind struggles with whether he should be friendly or brace for a fight.

Demon glides up beside him, "Don't worry, Father, we are here."

Thor peers out the corner of one eye then the other. His pack flanks him on both sides. He's impressed; his young ones now use expert stealth. The rival elder walks toward Thor carrying the dignity and self assurance of a mountain lion. Thor senses no fear or malice from him.

The white wolf's voice patters light and soft as a spring rain, "Hello, Brother. What are you doing in my forest?"

"We are passing through, we mean no harm nor do we wish to fight."

"Neither do we, but we can't have strangers in our territory. I'll appreciate your moving on now."

"We can't."

"Why's that?"

"One of my family members gave birth today. She and her pups won't be able to move on for at least a couple of weeks."

"So that's what those terrible noises were. We've been watching you since you arrived, but couldn't get close enough to ascertain a cause for the disturbance. I hope the mother is okay. She sounded as if she were in more pain than any female I have ever heard give birth."

"She is well and the pups seem strong. Her first litter came early after much hard travel and high stress. We are lucky we didn't lose any."

"I am glad to hear that. Now, before I allow you to stay, we must discuss the terms. First, it must be brief and it must be quiet. Second, you can hunt on our mountain, but don't go in the valley, humans live there. We've taken great pains ensuring they leave us alone. I will not stand for you leading mankind onto my mountain. Third, we will share large kills with you and you will do the same for us. If you waste any food, you will be banished instantly. Finally, I wish you no ill, but want you out of my territory as soon as possible."

Thor bows his head, "We shall abide by your rules, thank you for your patience and generosity."

"Good. Now that we are in agreement, I would love to meet the little ones."

Thor leads him to their shelter, "Shiloh, this is . . . ." He looks at his new friend, "I never got your name."

"Comet"

"Shiloh, this is Comet. Comet, Shiloh and my grandchildren,"

"They are a fine looking bunch, Shiloh, you must be very proud."

"I am. This is my first litter. I never realized how much pain and pleasure come with puppies."

"There will be much more of both, I assure you. Watching them grow makes it all worthwhile. May I meet the happy father?"

Shiloh hangs her head, her face washed in sadness, "He was killed saving Thor from a human."

"I am so sorry for your loss. If it's any comfort, your mate died a hero. There is no greater sacrifice than giving your life saving another. I am sure his children will be as strong and brave as he was."

"Thank you, you're very kind."

"Now that we've met and I've determined your intentions, we will leave so you can rest."

Comet's pack melts into the background. He stops at the edge of sight and faces Thor, "One more thing, we're going on a moose hunt tonight. Would you join us?"

"We'd be honored."

"Good, we'll show you the right way to hunt moose."

The wolves turn an old cow moose up the ridge yet again. They've chased their quarry up and down this bank many times; she's grows weak. They must work hard at pointing her uphill for she stays determined to take the easier, downward route. Using cooperation and ingrained stubbornness, they force her to follow their plans. When they reach the top, they harry her toward the den. Hunters nip the cow's belly and ankles, being ever watchful for a powerful kick. They chase her onto a flattened boulder that juts off the ridge face like a pointing finger. The moose runs past its edge into thin air and cries out in shock. She plummets ten feet onto a pile of sharp, bone strewn rubble. The heavy impact breaks her ribs, driving one into her heart, and killing her in an instant.

Thor smiles, "Damn, Comet, that was the easiest kill I've ever seen."

Comet beams, "As you can tell by the bone pile, this is one of our favorite tactics. It prevents injury to us from cornered prey. Let's go down and take our share so our hungry pack mates may eat."

When they congregate around the carcass, their celebration song bursts forth, long and hearty. The wolves eat their fill then each brings a piece for the new mother. Both families lie together under a bright, icy moon. Frigid air gives the stars extra sparkle. Athena wraps around her grandchildren, protecting them from the cold while Shiloh gets some exercise with a young male from Comet's pack.

Shiloh limps until built up pins and needles leave her legs. After some stretches, she trots to the ridge top then runs full speed through the forest, dodging trees and expending pent up energy. Moonfire, a hopeful youth about her age who has spent all the time he could with Shiloh, races beside her. They run a five mile loop then walk for a while to cool down.

When they stop for a rest, Moonfire loses himself in the warm depths of Shiloh's eyes. His hammering heart has more to do with emotion than physical exertion. He braves a bold question, "Shall we take a bath in the snow?"

"Sounds like a great idea."

They dive and roll in clean, white crystals. Shiloh lies on her back, squirming in pleasure, when a gob of snow splats on the side of her face. Her astonished look meets Moonfire's impish one.

"Oh, so that's how you want it, Huh?"

She pops to her feet and heaves snow at him as if she's digging for a bone. He laughs and tries getting in front of her. She follows his circular progress, drenching him the whole way. He realizes he can't get around her, so dashes in and tackles her. They roll and wrestle until both are spent. Lying side by side, they rest in the forest's tranquility.

"Moonfire, how'd you get your name?"

There was a full moon when I first opened my white eyes. The light reflected a red glow in them. It spooked my father at first, He said it looked like fire and Mother put the two together."

"Let me see. Turn your head toward the moon." A bright red light shines in his eyes, lending his face a sinister look. Shiloh's heart skips a beat, "Wow, you're right, it is spooky. It's cool too though."

Moonfire's chest fills with love and courage. After many days of following her from a distance, hoping he could get closer to her, he bares his feelings for her, "Shiloh," he drops his head shyly, "I know we just met, and this will probably seem sudden, but will you stay with us? I want to be your mate. I want to care for you and your pups."

Shiloh's eyes show conflicting emotions flooding her heart, "I'm sorry, Moonfire, I can't. You would be a perfect mate, but I still love Bandit. If I became your mate, I would feel like a traitor to him."

Moonfire bites his quivering lip and blinks away tears of rejection, "I understand. I don't like your decision and hope you will change it, but I respect your wishes." He swallows a crushing pain in his chest.

"Thank you. You are very kind and I know we can be great friends." A tear of regret slips down her cheek.

"I feel as though we have grown very close in the time we've spent together and I've come to love you more than I could ever tell you. Enough so that if I can't have your love in return, I shall gladly accept your friendship." He breathes a heavy sigh, "Come, let's get back before the others think we've gotten lost."

CHAPTER 7

Thor and comet sit atop the mountain, looking out across the forest and wide open fields abutting man dens. Sheep mill around beside a long, unpainted barn. Temperatures drop at the crack of dawn; therefore, scents and sounds pass through the air with ease. The canine friends' sharp ears detect horses inside. Barnyard stench, buried in the smell of evergreens, travels on a stiff breeze blowing in their faces. Pink smears on the horizon give way to orange, then the sun herself. The peace and tranquility surrounding this place help Thor understand why it's called "Thinking Rock". He turns to his companion, who sits, snout up, eyes closed and wind flattening his unruly hair.

"Comet"

"Yes"

"I've wanted to ask you a question for a few days now, but I didn't want to sound rude."

"By all means, My Friend, ask me anything you like."

Thor grins and relaxes a little, "Alright, here goes. How do you keep your pack pure white?"

"Fair question. We are an elite group, best of our kind, and we have a strict selection process. When a female has pups, only white ones are kept for training. The others we bring to packs on either side of our mountain for adoption. If the white pups fail their education, they are given up as well."

"Sounds harsh"

"Our very survival depends on it. We live on skill and the fear we instill in humans. We've developed unsurpassed stealth; able to cover our scent so well we can sneak up on their food before it has a chance to warn its keepers."

"How do you cover your scent? I've never heard of wolves doing such a thing."

"That is one of many secrets sacred to my pack. Secrets we will never share for if used carelessly, mankind will figure out a way to thwart them. Our mystique has earned us the name, "The Ghost Pack" among those vile creatures. In five generations, none of our line has been killed or captured by them. We get around their killing sticks, death meat, and can steal bait from their leg catchers. Any human that wanders onto my mountain never returns. We will live forever, and perhaps, if we generate enough numbers, drive man out of all wolf forests."

Thor's face drops, "My father thought he could defeat humans. He died in a lot of pain. His cries still echo in my memory."

"I am sorry for your loss. I mean no disrespect, but we have bred and trained for the end of humans for a long time. We are better prepared than any lupine has ever been."

"I hope for all your sakes, Comet, that you are right. If you attack and fail, man will hunt down and kill every wolf he can find."

Thor sits alone on Thinking Rock. Dark clouds obscure the afternoon sun, threatening rain. Heat and moisture on the snow cause a thick mist to rise and hang in the evergreen branches. Fog thickens through tears building in his eyes. His heart crumbles and knots twist in his stomach. The harshness of warm, damp days and bitter cold nights proves too much for the newborns; two of them died last night. Athena-strongest female he has ever known-is devastated. Shiloh slowly drowns in guilt and spends all her time guarding her babies. This leaves Thor with the task of setting up a singing. Comet offered to take the responsibility, but Thor declined, saying it was his duty.

"My duty," Thor thinks, "my damned sense of duty got us into this mess in the first place. I should've planned more, like Comet. I was blinded by my need to get away from humans. I didn't assess all the risks."

Comet approaches the rock. His fur glistens with water droplets from a recent snow bath. He takes a tentative step; the snow collapses under his foot. He stumbles forward then looks up, ashamed of his clumsiness, "Forgive me, Thor, I don't mean to intrude. I've come to offer whatever help I can give."

"Thank you, but there isn't much you can do."

Comet settles in beside his friend, "I can listen. You look worried."

"I am. Shiloh won't let anyone near her pups, including the dead ones. She shoulders so much blame for their death that I'm afraid she'll lose control when, and if, we have a singing. Athena won't talk to me, she just sits and cries. I think she holds me responsible. I had no choice you know. I had to move us, the humans would have killed us all. Damn them. I've lost my parents, my son, and now my grandchildren because of those flea infested rodents. Why won't they let us live in peace?"

"Because havoc and destruction are their nature. They want to control their environment and we won't be controlled. We are forever bound to clash with them."

"I suppose you're right. They don't leave us many alternatives. Live unhappy under human control or die running. What's the right thing to do?"

"Each of us must decide that for ourselves."

"I feel like I'm leading my family to inevitable doom. What if I get them all killed?"

"Your family follows you because they believe in you, not because you force them. Any one of them can strike off on their own any time they want, but they choose to stay by your side. I think they want freedom from humans as much as you do. If your family dies on this trip, it will be because they follow their own dreams. Lead as best you can and let guilt be damned."

"You're probably right. Thank you, Comet. Perhaps now I can find the courage to organize a singing."

"My pack will hunt for yours over the next few days so yours may grieve."

"Thank you again, Comet. If I can ever do anything to repay you, just ask."

———

Thor spends many hours coaxing Shiloh's pups away from her. He decides to leave his dead grandchildren on Comet's mountain, for it stays free of scavengers. Innocent puppies cannot be left for the bone pickers; they deserve Mother Earth's welcoming embrace. He finds a quiet hollow under a fallen log, halfway down the south side. Spruce saplings grow around it, turning it into a mausoleum. Light reflects off a thin layer of ice on the log's surface, making it look like a crystal tombstone. The pack gathers under a full moon. Somewhat warm air shifts over spotty remnants of snow. Starshine, a pregnant wolf from Comet's family, offers to care for Shiloh's pups during the funeral. Shiloh flat out refuses, unable to let them out of sight. Her absence crushes the family's souls. Their sense of loss overwhelms them. Athena sits beside Thor, holding her head down. She has cried all her tears; her silent sorrow worries him more than her sobbing.

Thor lifts his head toward the moon and begins a long, chilling howl. One by one, the others join in. Their different pitches and tones combine, creating a sad, pain filled melody that hangs in the heavy air as it drifts across the valley. Thor gets some relief when he hears Athena's deep, baritone wail. The death song helps one let go. Stars twinkle in response; the puppies' souls rest with their father now. The pack sings and cries throughout the night.

––––––––––––––––––––

Thor's clan stays on Comet's mountain for two months; their hearts heal slowly. Shiloh slowly lets her children wander from the haven to play. Many were afraid she would stifle their growth by smothering them in worry. They're old enough for traveling. In response to their growing freedom, Athena watches them more diligently than ever. Wherever the puppies are, she hovers close by, growling at anyone who comes near. She even lashed out at Thor once for making one of them yip while he wrestled with them. Athena bowled Thor over, bit down on his ear, and told him if he couldn't use more care around the little ones, then he had better leave them alone. Broken hearted, he limped off. She later apologized, but he hasn't wrestled with the puppies since.

Today, Thor teaches Harley and Ella more hunting skills. He starts with some pointers on picking up and sorting scents. He moves on to stalking and a lecture about the importance of patience. They are fast learners and as soon as they overcome their youthful hyperness, they'll make excellent hunters. The sky becomes dark and a cold, gentle rain falls from lazy, black clouds. Between rain and icy ground, scents don't carry very far. The young wolves will have to be right on top of their prey before they can detect it. Thor leaves Harley and Ella practicing track and corner methods.

Harley soon picks up a strange, woody, musky smell. Curious, she talks Ella into helping her track this strange animal. They nose around, struggling with keeping on its trail. The scent leads them to an evergreen thicket. Mist lifts off the bracken like a stage curtain. Rustling and grunting sounds come from its center.

Harley finds an entry point then turns toward Ella. "Sneak around the back, I'll come through and flush it to you."

Ella looks at her sister like she's crazy, "We don't know what's in there. I didn't even leave any tracks on this frozen ground to indicate the size of that animal. It could be a catamount for all we know."

"It's not a catamount."

"How do you know?"

"Cause there's only one hemlock moving at a time in there. If it was a catamount, there'd be more. Now will you please go around back so we can find out what's in there?"

"I still don't think it's a good idea."

"Stop being a coward."

"I am not a coward."

"Then prove it, go around back"

Ella gives the thicket a wide, cautious berth. She stands on her hind legs, signaling Harley she's ready. Harley crouches low and follows the strange scent into its evergreen jungle. Her chosen path runs narrow; limbs grow tight against the ground and upper branches bend to the breaking point from piles of wet snow clinging on them. Picking her way through, she bumps a spruce tree; a large snowball tumbles onto her head. She freezes, afraid she may have scared off her target. Snow melts from inside her ears and drips down both sides of her face. Low grunting noises sound closer. Step by slow step, Harley creeps forward.

A small hemlock, about eight feet tall, rustles and shakes. A plump, black creature climbs down it. Branches pinned to the ground by ice, block Harley's view. Frustrated curiosity overrides her sense of caution; she simply must get closer. The distant tree moves again and a fine snow spray cascades into a blinding white out. The grunting, black mass reaches the ground; Harley hears its claws ticking on ice. Its woody, musky smell grows very strong; it almost covers the pungent scent of hemlock. This strange creature sniffs at the tree's base. Harley wants a look at it before it disappears. Her heart pounds in excitement as she slides her head between snow laden boughs. Once her snout gets halfway into the hideout, a sharp, piercing pain blazes in her face. She yelps, howls, and backs out of the bushes as fast as possible, causing several avalanches in the process. Ella charges around the thicket and finds Harley running in circles, covered in snow and pawing at her face.

"Harley, Harley, what's wrong?"

"Ow, ow, my face, it's on fire. Holy shit, it hurts like hell."

"Hold still, let me take a look." Harley sits quivering while Ella surveys the damage, "Your face looks like it's been stung by a whole nest full of giant wasps and they all left their stingers in you. What kind of animal did you run into?"

"I don't know. I never saw it."

"We'd better go find Father, he'll know what to do."

The youngsters head for their pack. They don't get far before they see Thor thundering toward them. He stops short, takes one look at Harley's face, shakes his head, and chuckles.

Harley whimpers, "It's not funny, Father, it really hurts." Needlelike spines stick out of her nose, lips and gums. Her snout starts swelling.

"I'm sorry Harley, it's just you look a little silly. I guess I should've included a warning about porcupines in your lessons."

"What's a pork-pine?"

"You've got his quills in you, you must've seen him."

"It was in a thicket. I poked my nose in then felt unbelievable pain. When I got out, I had these . . . quills stuck in my snout."

"A porcupine is a short, fat animal, about the size of a raccoon, with sharp stickers called quills all over its body. If it feels threatened, it lashes out with its tail and embeds those quills in its attacker. As you have learned, it's quite painful."

"Am I gonna die?"

"No, but by the time I get the quills out, you may wish you had."

The trio returns to their den and the moment Athena sees her babies, she jumps down Thor's throat, "What the hell happened?"

"Harley found a porcupine in a thicket."

"Where the hell were you?"

"Doing a scout, watching for enemies. That is part of my job you know."

"Your job is to keep my babies safe, not wander off and leave them alone."

The uproar eventually settles with mutual apologies and Thor sets about removing quills from Harley's nose. Ensuing howls and squeals bring wolves from both groups running ; a large crowd gathers and watches the operation. At its conclusion, Harley stands crying, blood dripping from her snout. The sight breaks Thor's heart.

He clears his throat to prevent his voice from cracking, "I'm sorry I had to do that, Harley, but the quills would've caused infection if

I hadn't. I couldn't get them all, some embedded themselves pretty deep, so I snipped their ends off. They should work their way out in a few days. I hope you two learned something from this."

"Stay away from pork-pines," Harley answers around her swollen and sore mouth.

"Be more careful when following a strange scent," Ella snickers.

Athena and Shiloh sit in warm, afternoon sunshine watching the pups roll and tumble in playful bliss. Athena winces at every yelp or squeal from Harley. She knows it's necessary, but can't stand to watch. In an attempt at keeping her mind off the torturous deed, she strikes a conversation with Shiloh.

"Have you decided what to name the little ones?"

"Yes, I thought about it for a very long time. I wanted it right. The all black one I'm calling Outlaw, in memory of Bandit. I considered using Bandit's name, but that would be too painful for me. I believe Outlaw is close enough to still be a tribute. The black and grey one I'm calling Phantom because he always disappears on me. I swear that boy will give me a heart attack. And last, but not least, my pure white daughter. Since I can tell she will grow up beautiful, I named her Goddess. What do you think?"

"Those are fine names, Bandit would be proud." Athena drops her head, a sad note invades her speech, "I wish he were here to enjoy his children."

Shiloh leans against her, "So do I. So do I."

CHAPTER 8

Rain bloated clouds obscure Brother Moon. Night waits in silent expectation for the coming storm. Whether it hits as rain or snow will depend on the temperature. Wolves gather around their respective leaders. The Ghost Pack stands out against its brown surroundings. They have begun adopting their spring and summer hiding techniques. Harley's face continues swelling from porcupine poison. Athena stands beside Thor, a sad look on her face. Shiloh's puppies romp and wrestle around many legs. The rest of their clan waits behind their parents.

Thor and Comet face each other, "Comet, I thank you for all you've done. We would've been hard pressed without you."

"Thor my friend, if wolves are to survive the human scourge, we must look out for one another. Now, when you get off our mountain, hurry to the river. It's wide and deep, so your crossing will be easier while it's still frozen. Don't dally. All this warm weather we're having has no doubt weakened the ice."

Moonfire takes a few tentative steps toward Shiloh, "I wish you would stay. You'll be most welcome here."

"Perhaps, but my dark colored sons would not. I can't leave them. I'm not over Bandit either, my heart still aches for him. Although we can't be mates, I will forever be your friend, Moonfire, and I will miss you."

"And I you, sweet Shiloh."

Moonfire nuzzles her-his heart caught in powerful jaws of longing-hangs his head, then vanishes into the brush. He can't watch her leave; fearing he may never recover from this intense pain. Thor's pack finishes saying goodbye and continues their journey. Shiloh, carrying Goddess by her scruff, looks back when a lone, sad howl emanates from the bushes.

Goddess pricks her ears, "What was that, Mama?"

"A broken hearted wolf"

"He sounds sad."

"You'll seldom hear a sadder sound."

Filled with conflicting feelings of regret for leaving and loyalty to Bandit, Shiloh trots across frozen duff to catch the others.

Nikita joins her, holding a puppy in her mouth and carrying a happy spring in her step. Her words come out muffled and hard to understand, "Thank you for letting me carry Phantom. Caring for babies helps ease my pain of being barren."

"No need to thank me, Nikita. You did a wonderful job with Harley and Ella. You're a natural when it comes to children"

Nikita senses sorrow in her pack sister and decides to stay close in case she's needed.

———————

Rain starts as a drizzle, progresses into a downpour, switches to freezing rain, and then snow; falling in heavy flakes, half the size of a wolf paw. The pack first gets soaked then plagued by chills when their coats begin freezing. The puppies cry in uncomfortable protest. Shiloh gives Goddess to Avalanche then slips and slides her way down a steep slope catching Thor's attention at the bottom.

"Thor, can we please stop? My babies are cold and hungry. I'm afraid if they get any colder, I'll lose them."

"Yes, we can. Athena has been asking me to stop for the last two miles. I've had a hard time finding a suitable place to get out of the weather in these hardwoods. We need thick cover so we can keep our body heat close. There's an old human den down on that flat. I'm going to sneak over and see if it's abandoned. It should be. Comet said there haven't been humans on his mountain in a long time."

Athena, standing beside him, can't keep the fear off her face or out of her voice, "I'm going with you."

"It's too risky. One wolf can stay less visible than two. Besides, if you're up here, I won't worry about you, I can concentrate on what I'm doing."

"Very well, but promise me you'll be careful."

"Careful as I can be."

Thor nuzzles Athena then slinks over the hill. Athena gathers her pack in a depression just big enough to conceal themon top of the rise. She rests her mighty chin on the divit's edge and watches her mate.

Thor slips from tree to tree, using all the stealth and wile thousands of years of evolution have given him. His nerves tingle with excitement. Brother moon still hides behind a layer of obese clouds. Fat snowflakes dull visibility to a few feet for humans, a few yards for wolves. Snow piles up, ensuring silent steps and heavy air holds scents in submission. The old hunting camp sits on a shelf partway down a steep ridge. This 10'x12' shack stands covered in wide, gray boards hung horizontally on the walls; its human scents faded into thin existence.

Thor uses a thick blackberry patch for cover, sliding between thorny brambles without a sound. He closes within a few feet of the den's back side. No noise from inside yet. He strains his senses for danger; heart pounding in his ears. Strange odors mingle in and overlap fresh forest scents. Musty rot and wet leaves wrestle for control of the air. One slow step at a time, Thor works his way to the front. A solid, outward swinging, antique door covered in chipped, red paint stands, hitched closed on the inside by baling wire stretched to its limit, leaving it ajar. Thor sets one foot on a crumbling cinder block stair; ears pricked, senses on high alert. Trace odors of human lie buried under smells of must, mice, and chipmunks. He inches his nose in while scanning the area with acute eyes and ears. No movement, no noise; he slips inside.

An ancient braided rug in the room's center decomposes under a deep layer of leaves. A wooden table over the rug sags in the middle. Both plastic coated chairs rest overturned upon the floor. A few ashes remain scattered around where a woodstove once stood. A hole in the wall shows the home of a missing, makeshift chimney. Gnawed 2x4's and piles of scat mark this as a favorite porcupine hangout. Thor creeps out, makes a couple of wide, slow circles around the den, then runs up the hill.

A relieved Athena greets him, "What's it like down there?"

"It's safe, there haven't been humans around in a long time. Let's get out of this nasty weather."

The wolves move downhill then file into their shack. Thor stands at one corner, keeping watch during his family's entrance. Harley reaches the door and stops dead. A woody, musky scent finds her nose.

Her heart races as she backs away, "Oh no. I'm not going in there. I smell pork pine." Her swollen lips and gums ache in fright.

"Don't worry," her father reassures her, "there haven't been any pork pines here in a long while."

Harley sums up his grin, a doubtful look on her face, unsure whether or not she should believe him.

"Come, Harley, I'll go in with you."

Harley follows Thor into complete darkness. He stops, letting his eyes adjust. She keeps walking, nerves twisted tight. She whips her head back and forth, trying to see everything at once. Nikita steps on some dried bird bones; they crackle like dead leaves. Harley spins toward the sound and takes a few backward steps. She bumps the old decrepit table, knocking a mold covered leg out from under it. She jumps forward with a yelp and the table crashes to the floor, sending up a cloud of stale smelling dust. Harley barrels for the door, screaming, "Ahhh, pork pine." She runs full speed into the door, popping its baling wire. It bounces off an ash tree growing beside the shack and slams shut behind her. Harley crashes through the brush, heedless of distance or direction. The pack falls down from laughing so hard.

Athens regains control first, "Thor, you'd better go find our daughter before she hurts herself."

"I'll go too, Father." Ella chimes in, wiping away a tear and fighting off resurging giggles.

Thor pushes the door open and they walk into blinding snow. A light wind picks up forcing the large flakes into a steady, diagonal descent.

Thor looks around, a tinge of concern in his voice, "We'd better find your sister soon. We could lose her trail in a hurry."

Thor and Ella follow Harley's tracks into the brush.

Ella calls out, "Harley, Harley, where are you?" Soft whimpers catch her attention, "Father, I think she's over here."

A few more minutes of searching reveal Harley, huddled under a fallen log. Short spruce trees growing all around it catch falling snow and form a screen in front of the hiding place. If not for Harley's frightened whines, they would have missed her.

Ella sticks her nose in the brush, "Harley, it's o.k., there's no danger, you have nothing to be afraid of."

"Says you. I was the one attacked by pork pines."

"No you weren't. You bumped into some kind of human thing and it fell over."

"Are you sure?"

"Father and I both saw it. Right, Father?"

"It's true, Harley. If you would've given your eyes a few seconds to adjust, you would've seen it."

"I was afraid pork pines were sneaking up behind me."

"Now would I lead you into danger?"

Harley hangs her head, "No, but I don't ever want to get attacked by pork pines again. It hurts like crazy."

"There's something else you should know about porcupines. They don't attack unless startled or cornered. They don't leap out of the darkness like a catamount, they hide from trouble. Now, let's get back to the den and out of this miserable storm."

"You're sure it's safe?"

"Positive"

Harley creeps out of her haven looking anxious and scared. Shivering, she casts her eyes in all directions at once.

Ella stands in front of her and lays a soft comforting chin on Harley's shoulder, "Don't worry, Harley, Father and I will protect you. You're safe with us. We'll go into that human den together. I'll stand beside you until your eyes focus then we'll find a cozy spot and rest together, o.k.?"

"O.K. but only if you stay beside me until morning."

"Deal"

The trio trots back and re-enters their shack. Harley's steps shake with trepidation. Demon and Avalanche snicker; Thor throws them a silencing glance. Harley and Ella make a slow trek toward a back corner where remnants of a mouse chewed blanket lie then settle in for the night. Thor's group sleeps in relative comfort, despite ghostly creaks and groans from their dilapidated cabin.

Snow lets up by morning as temperatures drop well below freezinf. A fresh white blanket sparkles in the bright sunshine like colorful crystal dust. A stiff breeze makes ice coated trees snap and pop like firecrackers. Nikita wakes first and picks her way outside. On the way back from relieving herself, she notices their haven listing to its left at an alarming angle.

She charges inside, "Everyone, wake up, we must get outside, now. Our den is no longer safe."

"Aw c'mon, Nikita, we just got to sleep." complains Demon.

"I'm going to feed my puppies before I go anywhere." adds Shiloh.

The walls voice strained creaks and groans; much different than the ones they've heard all night.

Thor jumps up, fear racing through his veins, "Everybody out, now. Nikita, Athena, help Shiloh grab the pups. Go, go, go."

Demon's sleepy eyes go wide when he sees one whole wall move. He kicks Avalanche awake then half drags him out the door. An urgent feeling electrifies the air.

Thor stands by the door screaming, "Move it, faster, faster, get the hell out of here."

The wolves scurry out into chest deep snow. A loud crack and an ear piercing screech split the forest's silence. They look back in awe as the shack tumbles into a billowing cloud of white powder.

Standing on quaking knees, Thor nuzzles Nikita and licks her face. "I'm proud of you, Daughter. You saved our lives." He faces the pack and breathes a long sigh, "As long as we're already keyed up, let's find some breakfast, shall we? Athena, you can stay and keep watch while Shiloh feeds her babies. We should be able to make an easy kill in this deep snow."

Athena finds Shiloh a sheltered spot under a ledge outcrop, near the hilltop. She digs out snow until she makes an opening big enough for them to fit through, one at a time. Once inside, she lies out of sight where she can watch the landscape. Soon, soft suckling sounds from content puppies lull her to the verge of sleep.

The pack finds an old moose frozen in a mud hole. He fell asleep standing in knee deep muck; the sudden drop in temperature left him immobile. His horns haven't started growing in yet, leaving him defenseless. Thor tears into his prey's jugular vein, making his kill as quick and painless as possible. The canines gorge themselves then bring plenty back for Shiloh and Athena. When they finish eating, Nikita, Athena, and Shiloh each pick up a dozing puppy and they're on their way once more.

Steep mountain slopes quickly give way to a barren looking alder swamp. The wolves hurry in hopes of getting through while it's still frozen. Ella travels beside Harley at the line's center, "Harley"

"What?"

"Do you think we'll run into any coyotes?"

"I don't know. If we do, Mother and Father will make short work of them. Just like last time."

"I suppose, but I sure do hate swamps."

———————————————

The sun arcs high and temperatures rise. Alder swamp fades into an old growth, spruce forest. Melting snow tumbles out of softwood branches and lands on the ground in muffled whumps. Scattered "skunk" spruces release their namesake odor into the fresh Spring air. Few animals live in these woods. Large trees steal light and moisture needed for growing grass. As a result, deer, elk, and moose have no reason to come here. A smattering of stray squirrels scolds the lupines from safe distances.

Thor's pack travels hard throughout the day. When Father Sun begins settling into dusk, they hear running water. Warm, heavy air distorts sound distance and direction. Thor, unsure where the river lies, almost stumbles off its sheer bank. He jumps back and watches a snowball tumble onto the frozen river. This six foot drop worries him; jumping on ice after heat rots away its strength could plunge a wolf into bitter, cold water. They follow the river downstream for a couple hundred yards. Trees back off from the waterway, leaving a stony beach. The river widens to a half mile. Boulders stick up like highway markers. Water rumbles an angry protest at being covered.

Thor studies their situation, "We must cross here. We can't waste any more time searching for a better spot. Comet said this river becomes very angry once it thaws."

Athena sets Phantom at her feet, "Stay here, Little One." She looks across the expanse and crinkles a worried brow, "I don't know,

Thor, the river sounds awfully loud. That usually means thin ice. I think we should find a safer place."

"If we waste time, considering temperatures continue rising, the ice will get too thin to walk on anywhere. We've got some snow to help distribute our weigh. We must cross here."

"Alright, but I don't like it."

Athena looks down and finds Phantom gone. Fear shoots through her heart like a frozen spike, "Phantom, where are you?" She turns one way then the other; he's nowhere in sight. Sickening Panic builds in her gut. She looks behind her and sees him sitting close with a goofy grin and tongue hanging out. Relief warms Athena's soul like a summer day, "I swear, Grandson, you're going to make me old before my time." She picks him up and starts toward the river behind Thor.

Wind whistles down this wide open channel, driving moisture laden air past their heavy coats, settling a chill in their bones. Athena, Nikita, and Shiloh walk with the puppies turned away from it in an attempt to keep them warm. Noise from stiff breezes dampens the sound of rumbling water. It also masks cracking ice. Thor avoids protruding rocks like they're death meat; ice doesn't freeze very deep around stones. In scattered, snow free patches-ranging in size from a fox bed to a bear's den-water shows through its frozen coating.

Thor calls a warning, "Watch your step. Stay away from bald spots, the ice is thin there."

Hairline cracks go unnoticed as they creep across clear areas then hide under the snow. On the river's far side stands a short, undercut bank. Roots from a large birch tree stick out into thin air like arthritic fingers reaching for a hold on life. Atop the bank, an open, hardwood forest starts. This stretch of wilderness looks younger than the softwoods they just left and should be teeming with game.

Bellies grumble at the thought of food, anticipation lifts spirits. Evergreen shadows end in sun-bathed brilliance. Temperatures rise dramatically out here. They make slow, cautious progress; pops and snaps set Thor on edge. He doesn't dare run for fear of punching through an unseen weak spot. A loud crack and dull splash stop Thor's heart. He whirls around to see Athena over half submerged in frigid water. Her front feet cling on the slippery surface while she holds a crying, sopping wet Phantom as high as she can. Demon and Avalanche rush to rescue their mother.

They barely hear Thor's shouts, "Wait, wait, you have to approach with caution or you'll end up in the water beside her.

Thor catches them as they slow to a soft walk. Athena struggles against the strong current, frigid water sapping her strength; She can't hold on much longer. Athena turns her head left and in a quick motion, uses her remaining energy to toss Phantom as far as possible. He flies through the air, legs splayed, tail tucked, and screaming at the top of his lungs. He hits the wet snow at Avalanche's feet with a whoomp. Avalanche digs out the sputtering, whimpering puppy then rushes him ashore.

Thor and Demon creep closer to Athena; ice creaks and groans beneath their feet. They can see fatigue in her eyes. She slowly slips further into the freezing water. Athena turns to Thor, a look of resignation on her face, and in a weak voice says, "I love you" then slides under the ice.

CHAPTER 9

A horrifying scream erupts from Thor's lungs. "Athena, no-o-o-o."

Demon blocks Thor's path before he can make a blind charge into his own demise, "Father, no. We must use caution if we are to save her."

"Help her, we have to help her. By The Great Forest Spirits, I can't lose her. What are we going to do?" Thor babbles as he fights to get past his son.

"Let's go downstream, perhaps we can find another opening where she'll surface."

Father and son hurry carefully downstream. Thor sees Athena through the ice as she floats past a bald spot. Fear constricts his throat, "There she is. Demon, she just went by. We have to hurry, she's not moving. Damn it, Demon, she's drowning." Thor's heart pounds against his ribs; he can't think straight, His legs wobble like saplings in a windstorm. Blinded by tears, he looks at Demon for help.

Demon's heart crushes under the weight of desperation in his father's eyes, "We'll save her, Father, don't worry. I think she'll land against that big rock." Demon points his nose toward a boulder about twenty yards away, "We'll get there first and pull her out." He speaks with a confidence he doesn't feel. The pain contorting Thor's face pulls at the seams of Demon's soul. He doesn't know what else to do. Fear clouds his mind, keeping him from being sure of anything.

They hurry to within ten feet from a large hunk of blue ledge then lie on their bellies, thus distributing their weight, and inch forward. Jackhammering hearts threaten to shatter the ice beneath them. Every inch seems like a mile; they spend forever reaching the opening around that boulder. The thinning ice groans a protest against its unexpected load. Water splashes on the rock, giving it a glassy sheen that reflects sunlight in blinding rays. Thor and Demon reach the edge atop a clear, lightly frozen coating; they can see water swirling underneath them.

Time mires in eternity, convincing Demon he's made a mistake. A change in current must have sent his mother elsewhere. Jagged teeth of grief and guilt chew on his heart. Thor searches the black water, senses strung to the breaking point. His nerve endings vibrate with anxious energy. He doesn't feel cold back-spray soaking his heavy coat. Every ounce of his being focuses its concentration on finding his mate.

Athena raises a gray-brown paw out of the water and hooks the ice just below them, Thor dives in. Frigid water steals his breath and clamps a deadly hand on his heart. Athena loses her grip and slips away. Thor swims under the ice; muscles tightening and cramping, his body screams for warmth. He feels his way along until bumping into her shoulder. Fumbling for her neck, he grabs her scruff and tugs; she doesn't move. Thor's tortured lungs force him to retreat.

An anxious Demon greets him, "Father, should I come in and help?"

The cold dip clears Thor's mind. He rests his front paws on the snow and pants, "No . . . I may . . . . need you . . . . to . . . help pull . . . her out . . . wait for me."

Thor inhales all the moisture-laden air he can hold then dives again. Very little light pierces the river. He can see nothing more than shadows in this shallow abyss. He finds Athena's limp form and traces his paw down her rump. One of her hind legs stretches toward the bottom. He finds where it snagged between two rocks; a thin taste of blood floats in the water. He latches his jaws on to her ankle and tugs; it doesn't budge. Thor's lungs scream for oxygen. Black spots begin floating through his vision. Panic tugs on every corner of his mind. He changes direction and pulls upstream. In slow motion, Athena's foot inches loose and the rushing water grabs her. Thor holds fast, trying not to lose her in the swift current. Pushing his strained body past its very limits, he swims back to the hole, then breaks the surface, gasping and disoriented. A sideways jerk grabs his attention. Avalanche heaves on Athena's tail, Demon takes her scruff as it rolls above the froth and pulls her head onto the ice. Thor puts a shoulder under her rump. Using the last of his strength, he pushes his mate free of the frigid water. Demon and Avalanche skid her to safety and scramble back. They yank Thor clear of the icy cauldron just as he loses his grip on the ice, drag him away from the weak edge, then drop him beside Athena. Thor shivers violently; Athena doesn't move at all. Horror burrows into Thor's soul. He scrambles to stand, but his worn out legs won't hold him and he collapses.

"Demon," Thor croaks, "she's not breathing. Please do something. Don't let her die."

"Oh shit." Demon cries out in shock, "Avalanche, help me. We need to get the water out of her lungs."

Athena lays on her side, Demon stands by her back. Avalanche, at her chest, asks, "What do I do?"

"I don't know, I don't know, I don't know." Thoughts scramble around his mind like a flushed covey of quail, "Wait, I have an idea. I don't know if it'll work, but it's worth a try. Do the same thing I do."

Demon raises his front half into the air then drops both feet onto Athena's chest. Avalanche follows suit and they soon have a rhythm going; offsetting each other's blows. Tears roll down Thor's cheeks as he lies helpless in the snow. Dread tightens its stranglehold on everyone's souls with each passing second. Time and time again, the boys hammer Athena's chest. Her body jerks with every impact. Thor reaches the verge of losing hope when Athena coughs, chokes, vomits what seems like a gallon of water, and gasps for air.

Thor babbles around half buried sobs, "Oh thank you, Great Forest Spirits. Athena, my love, I thought I'd lost you."

Athena sucks in a labored breath and heaves up more water. "Phantom, is Phantom o.k.? Where's Phantom?", she hacks.

Avalanche nuzzles his mother. "Phantom is fine thanks to you. You saved his life."

Athena relaxes; Thor crawls tight to her and lays his head on her shoulder. No one sees or hears Demon standing off to one side, crying in relief. When he regains control, he sees his parents shivering like leaves in a hurricane and realizes they aren't safe yet.

"Avalanche, help me. We must get Mother and Father ashore, dry them off, and get them warm. Otherwise, they'll catch a killing cold."

Thor forces his rusty joints to work, grunting to a painful stand, "I'm fine, get Mother somewhere warm. I can make it on my own."

Demon and Avalanche help Athena upright then sandwich her between them while they struggle toward shore; they soon lose Thor. Every step sends torturous prickles up Thor's legs and into his shoulders. He grits his teeth and limps on all four feet. Chilled muscles fight commands from his brain; they hurt, they want rest. He falls steadily behind, dark spots dance across his vision, the world goes gray then black. He crumples into the snow, unable to rise.

Athena looks around, lost and confused. Her cold, befuddled mind can no longer make sense of what's happening. A presence on either side holds her up. For some reason, she travels over a wide open expanse toward some trees. Knotted muscles send pain weaving into her broken thoughts. She hangs her head and starts sliding to the ground. A strained voice in her ear rouses her, "Mother, please, you have to help us. We can't carry you on our own. We'll be there soon, then you can rest and get warm." Forcing feeble power into her exhausted limbs, Athena pushes onward.

Darkness covers Thor like a blanket. Sleep, his long lost friend, closes in for a visit. Voices call from far away, trying to scare off his friend. He fights the annoying vermin, but they poke, prod and lick his face, bringing him back to reality. Thor opens his eyes then puzzles over Ella's worried face.

"Father? Father, are you o.k.? C'mon, Father, Harley and I will help you. We must get you off the ice and out of the wind. We need your assistance though, you're too heavy for us. Father, can you hear me?"

"Yes, I can hear you." Thor sounds as if he's talking through a mouthful of mud. His eyes droop closed.

"No, Father, don't fall asleep, not yet. Harley, help me get him up."

The youngsters push together and roll Thor onto his stomach. They lick his face until he wakes up. Working as a team, the three struggle getting Thor upright. He weaves and staggers in a light-headed swoon.

Frustration wriggles into Ella's words, "No, no, no. Father, come on, help out a little." With Harley holding his left shoulder, Ella the right, they start a slow trek toward the far side.

Shiloh finds a narrow feeder stream with short banks then leads Demon, Avalanche, and Athena to it. They climb into a hardwood forest, taking silent steps on wet leaves scattered in a thick mat across the ground. Crows circle and caw in a clear sky right overhead.

Shiloh leads on, "This way, Nikita and I found a cozy den that some foxes thoughtfully lined with grass and moss for us."

Athena mumbles in confused fatigue, "Where are the babies?"

"They're fine, Nikita's watching them."

They enter an excavated hole beneath a partially uprooted tree. The walls are packed dirt arcing roofward. An intricate white root tangle swirls about the ceiling, adding a bit of artwork. Their mansion of a den should hold the entire pack. It'll be a tight fit, but tonight they'll need all the closeness and warmth they can get.

Athena's surprise shows in her tired voice, "How did you talk foxes into leaving such a nice den?"

Shiloh grins, "Nikita can be very persuasive when pressed. She filled Mother and Father Fox with more fear than they have ever felt. Those two ran away as fast as they could when they heard the snarls that came out of her mouth."

The puppies, overjoyed at seeing Shiloh, jump up and stumble over one another getting to her.

"Mama, Mama, we missed you. We're hungry, when do we eat?"

"Hush now, go back with Aunt Nikita. I must tend to Grandmother before I can feed you."

"What's wrong?"

"Is she o.k.?"

"Can we help?"

"She's fine, just tired, and you three can help by getting out from underfoot."

Nikita has the den's lining scraped into one thick bed. Shiloh helps Demon and Avalanche lead Athena to it then gently lay her down.

Demon once again assumes the role of leader, "Shiloh, stay and feed your pups. Nikita and Avalanche, snuggle Mother. Warm her up as quick as possible. I'll see if Harley and Ella need help with Father."

Demon steps into blinding sunshine. Squinting so he can scan around while his eyes adjust, he spots the rest of his family nearing the riverbank. He hustles down so he can help them lead Thor to safety, "Harley, Ella, over here. Shiloh found an easy path and a good den. We already have Mother settled in."

Thor staggers through the rocky brook, flounders up its bank, and mumbles the whole way. They squeeze him into the den and he blinks at the confusing darkness. His entire face brightens once he sees Athena nestled between Avalanche and Nikita. Harley and Ella lead him to his mate's side. Thor drops beside Athena like a felled tree. They smile, drape a paw on each other's shoulder and slip into a deep, shivering slumber. Demon crowds the pack in a tight ball around their benefactors. Outlaw, Goddess, and Phantom whine in defiance, for the interruption of their feeding. They tumble and roll to Shiloh's new location beside Thor then settle back down and finish their meal sprawled over one another in a fuzzy entanglement.

Cold radiates from Thor and Athena as if they're frozen blocks of meat.

Shiloh looks at the others, worry standing out in all her features, "Maybe we should lick excess water off their coats."

Demon agrees and everyone takes part in the task, drying their parents in no time. The adults both shiver hard; their youngsters exchange frightened glances then squeeze together again.

Day fades into clear, cold night. Stars twinkle in bright exuberance. New frost glints off dead leaves like moon struck crystal. Air outside their den carries a sharp bite. The inside stays quite comfortable; yet, Thor and Athena shiver as if their blood runs laced with ice. Demon snuggles closer against his mother, worry embedded in his head like a jagged stick.

"What if something happens? What if they don't warm up? I'm not ready for the responsibility of being leader. I don't think Avalanche wants it either. We'll be lost without their guidance. Mother, Father, please pull through this. Don't leave us on our own."

Brother moon hovers at his peak, owls hoot in the distance, howling coyotes make Harley and Ella stir in fear. High and out of sight, a whippoorwill calls from the midnight sky. Thor and Athena stop shivering, the puppies whimper until they find a teat, and Demon tries closing his mind in an attempt at sleep. Night animals go about their lives, oblivious of the strange wolf pack in their midst, except the evicted foxes.

Mother and Father Fox spent weeks last fall preparing that new den. They can't start a family without a home. Mother Fox bubbles in a vengeful stew, "Those filthy wolves will pay. No one kicks me out of my own den."

"Why not wait and see if they move on, Firestorm? They are not from this area and I'm sure Stone Eyes won't allow another wolf pack to stay in his territory for long."

Firestorm bears down on him with a disgusted stare, "Fern, you're a coward. Your mother coddled you too much. Don't you want a place to raise your family?"

"Of course I do, but I don't think its worth getting killed over."

"No one's going to get killed, stupid. I've been watching them and have it all figured out. They're worn out from fighting the river, so they'll sleep soundly. While they snooze, we sneak in and steal those precious pups of theirs. They'll be so distraught when they find their babies gone, they'll do anything to get them back. I'll demand our den and enough food to keep us full for weeks, that way you can spend all your time and energy on starting a family for me."

"I don't know, Firestorm. Some would call sneaking into a den full of wolves suicide."

"And I still say you're a coward. C'mon, let's get started."

The foxes creep through busy woods until they approach their home. The thick musty smell of wet wolves hangs heavy in the air. Sleepy snorts and grunts float across night's darkness. Someone whimpers from a nightmare, someone's foot scratches the den floor in a dream run. Firestorm and Fern slink inside, stop, then let their eyes adjust.

Shiloh weeps in her slumber; her mind plays the same scene over and over. Cold air and deep snow envelop her. Athena asks to talk in private. Shiloh begins worrying, "I haven't seen Bandit. That's strange, he's faster than I am, he should be back by now. I'll look for him when I'm done talking with Athena. Maybe he's bragging to Demon and Avalanche about tonight's exploits. He does love stretching a story." Athena says something that doesn't quite register in Shiloh's mind, "What do you mean 'Bandit's dead'? He can't be dead, I just saw him a few minutes ago." Athena looks at her with sad Basset Hound eyes. The truth hits Shiloh like a mid winter gale.

Her knees go weak, her stomach drops to her feet, and her heart crushes as a cruel wave of despair smashes her spirit. Shiloh's salty tears mix with the dry moss under her head. She starts swimming out of pain flooded dreams when an ominous scent trickles into her nose. It's a sharp, biting odor, similar to the lingering stench in their den, only stronger. Her eyes pop open when the connection slams into her brain. The foxes are here.

Something brushes Shiloh's leg; Goddess squeaks a surprised yip. Shiloh strikes as fast as a rattlesnake, catching Firestorm by the middle of her back. Firestorm drops Goddess and fights; her snapping jaws strain toward Shiloh's ear. Shiloh crushes her spine like a dry twig. Fern backs toward the door, but Demon materializes behind him. He snatches the fox by his neck and shakes him until it breaks.

Shiloh frantically checks her children for injuries, "Filthy, sneaking foxes. I knew we should've killed them outright. We only wanted to borrow their damn den, not keep it. What thanks do we get for letting them live? They come in the night and try stealing my baby."

Demon and Avalanche carry the bodies out then drop them behind a downed tree. Athena and Thor still shiver when they return. The weight of the whole world sits on Demon's shoulders, "I'm worried about Mother and Father, Avalanche. They should've warmed up by now. If we can't warm them, I'm afraid we'll lose them. Then what do we do?"

"For now, we try not to worry. Let's take things one step at a time."

"Easier said than done."

"I know, but if we don't try we'll go crazy from stress."

The adolescents crawl back in beside their parents and sleep in short, worried bouts. The sun begins its daily trek in a brilliant display of orange and red coating the fat underbellies of massive rain clouds. Temperatures find a comfortable place and rest there. Animals buzz about actively this morning. Deer wander around, digging old acorns from the leaf litter; mice scurry through duff, looking for leftover seed caches. Demon watches from his dark hole, uneasy about the developing day.

Avalanche creeps up alongside him, being careful not to wake anyone, "You look troubled, Demon. What's wrong?"

"There's a storm building." he casts a concerned look skyward, "Forest activity predicts it'll be a big one. We sit pretty low here, I'm afraid too much rain will flood us out."

"Should we find higher ground?"

"I don't think we have time. Mother and Father shouldn't be out in a thunderstorm until they are warm. This is probably the warmest, driest place we'll find before the storm hits. I think we should continue warming them and hope for the best."

———————————————

Thunder rumbles a warning; lightning flashes and explodes a distant tree. A million pieces fly in all directions, leaving a black shattered stump bearing witness to Mother Nature's power. The wind picks up, the sky darkens, and paw-sized raindrops pound the forest floor in atomic fury. Trees whip around in a swirling turbulence. Leaves and twigs race by, hurrying to reach their new destination.

Demon gazes into the tempest from the outer edge of his family circle. Thor and Athena have stopped shivering, but Demon's mind still twists in rhythm with the storm. Escape plans and regrets scurry around his conscience. The crying puppies crowd close to Shiloh who sings a soothing melody. She can smell danger in the air, yet buries her concerns under a song. Demon lays a worried head on antsy paws, closes gritty eyes, and sighs.

The storm worsens each hour. Rain beats down in a steady sheet; a small rivulet starts running into their den. It soon soaks the once dry moss and their floor turns into a puddle. Demon crowds his parents toward the only dry corner left in their shelter then crams everyone together in hopes they'll stay somewhat warm. Smells of saturated moss and mud fill the confined space. Lightning flashes, streaks, and strikes the river; sparks dance across it in a dazzling, pyrotechnic display. An ear shattering thunderclap shakes the ground. Hail mixes with horizontal sheets of rain. An angry wind shrieks; a cracking, whooshing sound snaps Demon's head up. A large birch tree crashes across their entrance, sending a spray of dirty water into the den. Demon decides it's too dangerous for a venture out to inspect damage and waits out the tempest in anxious agitation.

The storm blows until nightfall. Finally, rain eases to a drizzle then stops altogether. Winds calm and push a few remaining clouds out of Brother Moon's face. The wolves squeeze through tangled branches, shake water off their coats, and breathe in fresh, spring air. Thor stands between Demon and Avalanche, air rattles in and out of his lungs like a cold breeze through dry blackberry bushes. Phlegm makes every breath a chore.

"You've done well, my sons. You kept our pack safe and dry while Mother and I recuperated."

"No credit goes to me, Father." Avalanche interjects, "Demon was the one making decisions."

"I couldn't have done it without your calm head and sound advice, Avalanche. You deserve as much credit as I do."

"Regardless," Thor wheezes, "it puts my mind at ease knowing you two can handle the responsibility of caring for the pack."

"I'm in no hurry to do it on a regular basis." Demon gives Thor a humble smile, "I'm glad you're up and about again."

Thor nods, "Let's find a dry, resting spot and take it easy until tomorrow night. We need to get traveling again."

"Are you sure you and Mother are up for it?" Avalanche carries a concerned look, "You may get sicker if you try journeying too soon."

"First, we find a dry place in this dreaded landscape," Thor coughs and sneezes several times. Panting, he continues, "Then we'll relax until tomorrow night and go from there. I want to keep moving so the humans can't catch us. Sitting in one place for long always proves dangerous."

"Perhaps you should rest here with Mother," Demon offers, "Avalanche and I will take Harley, Ella, and Nikita hunting for a decent place to sleep."

Thor sits watching, pride swelling his chest, as Demon gathers the family and forms an organized search party, "My son will soon succeed me. How did I get old so fast?" He shakes a weary head, struggles upright and limps on tingly legs to Athena's side. He curls his body partway around her, trading heat and comfort, then drifts into a fevered sleep.

———————————————

Avalanche and Nikita go north, Harley and Ella west, and Demon moves east. The young wolves worry about their parents while searching in earnest, hoping they'll find a suitable place for their convalescence. Both pairs voice shared fears to each other and their confidence in Demon, should the worst happen. Demon spends the night searching the land and his heart, second guessing his abilities. He rejoins his siblings at false dawn.

White fingers of clouds streak the sky, lending a haunted feel to the damp morning. Winded and wet, Harley and Ella arrive last. Harley takes a moment, catches her breath, then blurts out, "We found something."

The news rolls a boulder of worry off Demon's shoulders, "Thank The Great Forest Spirits. Let's move Mother and Father then we can finally get some sleep."

Full sunrise brings a warm eastern zephyr. Purple clouds, their bottoms smeared red, zip across the sky in a vigorous sprint. Rainwater, blown from softwood boughs beside the river, sounds like a soft shower. Demon and Avalanche stand on either side of Athena, Nikita and Shiloh support a protesting Thor; Shiloh holds Phantom by his scruff. He squirms, wanting to get down and run around.

Shiloh scolds him through gently clenched teeth, "Be still, Phantom. You can run and play when we get settled in the cave Harley and Ella found, but if you keep fidgeting, you'll take a nap."

Phantom sighs and goes limp. Even though he doesn't like the situation, he has almost learned obedience. Harley and Ella lead their group toward higher ground and yet another temporary home.

CHAPTER 10

Passing clouds obscure Brother Moon, a warm breeze whispers through happy trees, and Mother Nature conducts a gentle symphony of spring sounds. Inside their spacious cavity cut deep into red stone, Thor and Athena surface from fever inflamed sleep. Their noses feel dry, eyes swell to mere slits, lungs rattle with loose phlegm, sneezes run amok, and coughs sound fatal. Demon watches his parents struggle to their feet. Steam rolling off their bodies distorts the white striations throughout the ceiling.

Concern lies deep on Demon's face, "Father, I think we should stay here until you and Mother are well."

"I won't endanger the pack by staying in one place for long. We don't know how close the humans may be. Once we start seeing large buffalo herds, we'll know we've escaped them. Then, and only then, can we settle down. Let's press on."

A coughing fit consumes Athena; her lungs sound like they're full of gravel, and she spits up some blood. Her voice comes out barely audible, "Please, Thor, the children have found us a nice dry cave. Let's stay here a few days. I don't think I can travel far, I'm having trouble breathing."

Thor licks her nose, "You're running a high fever. I don't want you getting sicker. If you think we're safe here, we'll stay."

"Thank you, Love." Athena flops down and plummets into dreamless sleep.

"Father," Demon ventures, "perhaps you should get some rest as well. Shiloh can watch over you while I take the others on a scout and do some hunting."

"Are you sure you don't need me?"

"We always need you, but we can get by on our own for a few days. What we need most, is you healthy again."

"You've grown wise, My Son. I'm proud of you."

Thor curls himself around Athena and lays his head across the back of her neck. Her rough breathing becomes more relaxed.

Demon stands at the cave mouth scanning the area. Their sanctuary sits high on a red slate ridge. A sheer cliff rises twenty feet off its top, leafless hardwoods spread a half mile below, all the way to the river. He can hear ice cracking and grating over itself, longing to break free and run downstream. The gentle slope offers an easy climb, but their shelter's position allows quick detection of intruders. A tiny feeder brook trickles downhill thirty yards to his left; a short drop in temperature will turn it into an icicle.

Demon takes a deep draught of rain scented air. A long exhale clears both his mind and lungs, "Alright, Everyone, I want scouting parties. Harley and Ella, go southeast, Avalanche and Nikita, southwest. I'll look for a trail to the top of this cliff and get a bird's eye view. Stay sharp, we don't know if, or how many humans may be creeping around. If you do find some, avoid them then give me their location when we meet here at moon-peak. Shiloh, will you keep a close watch over Mother and Father?"

"Of course."

The scouting parties embark on their appointed searches. Demon starts west along a narrowing ridge that dead ends against more cliffs then turns back east, checking on his parents when he passes their cave. They rest in relative comfort; Shiloh feeds her pups in hopes they'll take a nap once they're full. Demon continues his trek, only to find more vertical rises. He almost abandons his search when he notices an old dry streambed carved along the slate wall. This deep crevasse resembles a roofless hallway winding at a steep incline to the cliff top.

Demon picks his way over loose rocks and slick ice patches. The surrounding walls steadily shorten until they disappear at the base of an oversized beech tree. Its roots stick out like gnarled fingers exploring the barren rock. Demon wriggles through the roots and walks to the cliff's edge. A cloudy blanket peels itself off Brother Moon and his spotlight illuminates the landscape, presenting a spectacular view. Mature forest marches for miles in either direction. The wide blue snake of river divides hardwoods on this side from softwoods on the other. This wild tract lives unscarred by trails, roads, or human dens. No smoke rises from the forest to indicate any kind of man's presence; a very good sign. On the other hand, this wilderness sits almost silent. A blue jay calls and squirrels chatter at each other in the distance; however, no large animal scents reach his nose.

Demon exhales, hanging his head in frustration, "Is there no place where we can live? We finally discover a forest without humans and it lacks food. I hope Mother and Father recover soon. We'll be hard pressed finding enough to eat."

A last ditch effort at scouting the cliff top in all directions produces no sign of significant game. A couple of mice sneak between fallen leaves; a few squirrels and chipmunks sleep in lofty beds. Demon eats the mice then files away the tree dwellers' locations in his memory for later. He pads down the steep trail toward their cave where Athena and Thor doze fitfully. Shiloh keeps a watchful position near the entry while her pups play inside.

"How are Mother and Father?" Demon asks.

"I think they're getting worse. Father got up several times, asked where everybody was, paced a little, then went back to sleep. Mother raised her head once, looked around through squinted, bloodshot eyes, flopped down, and has slept ever since."

"Has anyone been back yet?"

"No, but they should be soon, moon-peak is almost here."

Demon tiptoes in to check on his parents. Heat rolls off them like a forest fire. He slips out shaking his head, worried eyes cast on the ground. He lies down opposite Shiloh to await his family's return.

Everyone gets back right at moon-peak. No happy expressions raise any hope in the forlorn atmosphere. Harley and Ella found nothing; no humans, no food. Avalanche and Nikita found an old collapsed human den, but no food other than mice and squirrels. If Thor and Athena don't get well soon, their pack could starve.

Demon struggles to keep his voice calm, "Well, your reports sound bleak. However, we've gotten through rough times before. Get some sleep, maybe things will look better tomorrow."

Shiloh scrambles around the den in a panic, "Phantom, Phantom, has anyone seen Phantom? He was just here playing a minute ago. Neither Goddess nor Outlaw saw him leave. Everyone look, we have to find him. Phantom? Phantom, where are you?"

The family fans out into the night, calling his name.

Shiloh's heart races, worry bunches her stomach muscles in a hard knot, "Oh no, oh no, oh no. Ple-e-e-ase, Great Forest Spirits, I've lost Bandit and two of my babies, don't make me lose Phantom too." Tears roll down her cheeks as she paces back and forth, straining her senses for some sign of her child.

Nikita moves back and forth in methodical precision, scanning the forest floor with her nose, trying to differentiate Phantom's scent from everyone else's. Adrenaline sharpens her olfactory abilities to new heights. A smorgasbord of smells filters through her brain; she has spent many hours tending them, so she knows the puppies' scents better than anyone, except Shiloh. As Nikita gets further from their den, her pack's odors slowly thin out. Demon's overlaps Avalanche's, Harley's layers on Ella's, and buried under these lingers the smell of one small pup. She follows it downhill; its ever increasing potency gives her hope. The scent leads to a blackberry patch, about a hundred yards from their den. Through leafless stalks bristling with sharp thorns, she sees a flat stone covering a shallow hole. One tiny whimper sneaks out of the hide away. These brambles grow entwined so tight even Nikita can't fit between them.

"Phantom, it's Aunt Nikita. Come on out and we'll get you back to your mom."

A little black nose—not much bigger than the berries that will soon grow on these hibernating bushes—pokes out into the open and sniffs the air.

Phantom catches Nikita's scent, squirms free from his hole, bounds toward her, and sits shaking at her feet, "Aunt Nikita, I was so scared. I went exploring and got lost. I tried and tried, but couldn't find my way home. I was all alone. I thought a hawk or an owl would swoop down and eat me."

Nikita lays her head over Phantom's front shoulders in a protective, comforting gesture while he cries; she can smell his immense fear, "There, there, Phantom, you're safe now. I won't let anything hurt you. C'mon, let's get you home, your mother is worried sick about you."

Nikita carries Phantom back to the cave.

As soon as Shiloh sees him, she rushes to her son, "Phantom! Oh Great Forest Spirits, I thought I'd lost you. What happened? Where did you go? Thank you, Nikita. Thank you, thank you, I am forever in your debt."

Nikita sets Phantom down. Shiloh scoops him up and brings him into their den. When they reach the back wall, Goddess and Outlaw waddle over, curious about his adventure. Shiloh covers Phantom in kisses and checks him for injuries. Once she determines he's not hurt, she lies nose to nose with him, trying to keep her voice calm, "What happened?"

Phantom bows his head, "I—uh—went—ah—exploring and—got—um—lost."

Shiloh holds her frightened temper at bay, "What have I told you about wandering off?"

"Don't do it cause it's dangerous."

"Then why did you?"

"I dunno. I guess I just wanted a look around."

Shiloh's eyes darken, she grumbles through gritted teeth, "I ought to nip you good. You know better and yet you wandered off anyway. Do you have any idea how scared and worried I was? I though I'd lost you too."

"Sorry, Mom."

"You are not to leave the den for three days. You can relieve yourself outside, within eyeshot, and come right back in, that's it. If you disobey once, and I mean just once, I'll give you a nipping that will be told of for generations. Do you understand?"

""Yes, Mom"

"Eat some supper and go to bed." Shiloh lies down, curls around her suckling pups and lets the comfort of their safety lull her to sleep.

During Phantom's scolding, Nikita steps to the cave's lip, tips her head up and looses a long, deep, gathering howl. The others come running then Nikita fills them in on her discovery of Phantom and his subsequent grounding. Phantom looks over his mother's side and catches Demon's eye. The older wolf shakes his head in disappointment. The pup's heart breaks and he drops back, forgetting his supper.

By morning, Thor and Athena awaken so weak and delirious they can't rise from their beds. The cool spring breeze blowing across their bodies does nothing against their fevered temperatures. Athena lays, eyes half open, talking with Bandit. Thor pants, drool dripping from his tongue, yet shivers like a cornered rabbit.

Demon, on the verge of tears, watches his parents, "Avalanche, what're we going to do? They're dehydrated, but too weak to reach the brook. There's no snow or ice we can carry to them. If we don't do something soon, they'll die."

"Perhaps the human den Nikita found holds something useful. Humans use things to carry water. There could be something like that there."

"Good idea, I'll bring Nikita and check it out. You take Harley and Ella hunting, they need all the practice they can get. They're getting better, but are still a little clumsy. Stress how important it is for them to pay attention, we can't afford to miss any game. I can't concentrate on anything right now, so I won't be any help."

Demon finds Nikita and together they set off down the ridge. Avalanche watches as his brother embarks on what may well be the most important mission of his life. He gathers Harley and Ella then sets about burying his concern in their lessons.

The human den lies crumbled into its stone cellar, eaves resting on the ground. Several rotten boards stick out between the shingles like unruly hair. Saplings push skyward through the roof. An eerie haunted presence hangs about the whole place.

Demon smells around, "I don't like this one bit. There's no trace of human scent, but just being around anything of theirs really creeps me out. Let's get on with it. The sooner we start, the sooner we finish."

Demon searches the ruins' left side, Nikita takes the right. In no time, they each gain entry. Rubble piled tight together makes progress slow. Saplings sway in a light breeze that scrapes them against decayed rafters, torturing their trunks and making them shriek in pain. Demon's eyes dart in every direction while he paws through all sorts of human waste, hoping to find a water carrier as fast as possible. His heart races, blood pounds in his ears he stays ready to spring into flight at any moment. He squeezes between two timbers and flops over some shingles on the floor. A loud high pitched yelp drives his heart into his throat.

Avalanche, Harley, and Ella make the best of what slim pickings the forest offers. They travel a great distance from their den and collect a decent cache of squirrels, mice, and voles.

Harley stares at the pile, a pondering look on her face. "Avalanche, how do we get all this back? It's not a very big pile, but it'll still take a couple of trips."

"We'll eat it, run back, then regurgitate our meal. Mother and Father may be weakened beyond eating whole meat anyway."

They gobble their catch and start trekking home, keeping an eye open for more tidbits along the way. They travel a zigzag pattern to cover more ground. In their path stands a huge oak, spreading its branches like a blooming flower. Avalanche noses around in the leaves, eating acorns.

"C'mon, you two, dig in. It's not meat, but it's better than nothing."

Harley moves under the tree then her nose picks up a musky, woody scent. Her heart rate surges. She looks left, right, and her eyes go wide when she gazes up to see a big gray shape slowly emerge from a hole in the tree trunk.

"Oh no-oh no-oh no." she whispers while retreating on her belly.

Avalanche notices Harley's reaction, crouches, and asks in a hushed voice, "What's wrong?"

"Porcupine. We gotta leave. I don't wanna get stabbed by thousands of quills, again."

Avalanche glances up; the gray shape stumbles across a broad branch. "Don't move, Harley. That's not a porcupine, it's a raccoon. He's just coming out of hibernation and will be an easy catch."

"Are you sure it's not a porcupine?"

"I'm positive. Stay still, I'll sneak over. Maybe he'll come close enough so I can grab him."

Avalanche creeps toward the raccoon's hideout and lies down, blending into the leaves. The coon stumbles about, slow and senseless; he acts as if he's been batted in the head. He reaches a fork in his branch, decides he's going the wrong way, and returns to its bole. He blinks, yawns, stretches, then starts down the tree. On his drunken descent, he missteps and tumbles to the ground. Avalanche pounces, snatches him in powerful jaws, and shakes him violently, snapping his neck in an instant.

He drops the coon and grins, "We'll save this delicacy for Shiloh, it'll help her produce milk. Thank The Great Forest Spirits, I don't smell rabies on him. Raccoons are a great treat, but they're prone to the disease. If we eat a rabid coon, we become infected ourselves. Here, smell this. It's what a healthy one smells like. Rabies carries a sharp acidic scent. Give a wide berth to **ANY** animal exuding that type of odor. One bite will transfer the sickness and even small animals who are rabid will attack anything in their path. They're made ferocious by pain and fever."

Harley and Ella take turns sniffing the carcass. Satisfied his young hunters have the scent of safe coon meat embedded in their instincts, Avalanche lifts his prize and they travel homeward. Shiloh lavishes gratitude on the mighty hunters for bringing such a treat. Her stomach has rumbled for hours. Thor and Athena eat their regurgitated meal using small, slow bites. In the rear corner of their den, Avalanche settles in beside Shiloh.

His worried tone hitches his words, "Mother and Father are hotter now than when we left. Have you seen or heard anything from Demon or Nikita?"

Concern clouds her eyes, "No"

"Damn. I hope nothing has happened."

"Nikita, Nikita, where are you?"

Demon hears pained whimpers and cries coming from the other side of the human den. Fear grasps his heart in an icy grip, "Oh dear, Great Forest Spirits, please let her be okay. I can't stand to lose anymore family."

He works his way through a tangled mess of wood and garbage; adrenaline courses down his veins like floodwater in a spring brook. Frustration builds in his mind as he runs headlong into one dead end after another.

"Nikita, can you hear me?"

"Yes Demon, over here."

He looks over a fallen beam and sees her beyond a small pile of rubble, "I've found you. Thank The Great Forest Spirits. Are you okay?" He flips aside a punky piece of plywood with his nose to get to her.

"Yeah, I just stepped on one of these pointy metal things sticking out of that flat wooden square. It burns like hell."

"Let me see."

Nikita lifts her right front paw, revealing a hole the size of a hefty clover stem. Blood drips and spatters a tiny rhythm off a pane of glass lying on the floor. "I've licked it clean, but can't stop the bleeding."

"Let's get out of this filthy trap and I'll see what I can do."

Demon and Nikita work their way toward the warm sunshine and fresh air of open forest. Unable to put any weight on her injured foot, Nikita hobbles on three legs. She crowds out and limps to where Demon digs a patch of leaves down to bare earth. He urinates on the dirt and mixes it into mud.

"Dab your foot in the muck, maybe it'll seal the hole and stop the bleeding."

Nikita sticks her wound into the concoction. She screws her face into a painful mask, "Demon, that stings. Are you sure you know what you're doing?'

"No, but it's the best I can come up with on short notice. There is one bonus though, look what I found in the leaves." Demon points out two thick plastic cups nestled in the overturned duff.

Nikita checks her foot, "I think there are two bonuses. It seems your imitation mud has clotted my cut."

"That's great. Are you able to carry one of these things?"

"Of course I can. I hurt my foot, not my mouth."

After one last check to make sure Nikita won't start bleeding again, they each grab a water carrier and slowly hurry toward their den.

Thor and Athena lick water from the cups with weak greed. The mineral water's stony taste works like an elixir for body and soul. Their spirits rise as their fevers drop. After a day of sleep, Thor regains some strength.

In morning's quiet warmth, he toddles to Demon's side, "That was very clever of you, Demon. Getting water carriers for Mother and I. Did you run into any trouble?"

"Again, Father, I can't take all the credit. It was Avalanche's idea I just followed through with it. We had a little trouble. Nikita stepped on a metal splinter in the old human den where we found those water carriers. Poked a hole in her foot, it's nothing serious though."

"How's the hunting?"

"Terrible, there's mature forest for miles around. Squirrels and blue jays are all we can find. Avalanche, Harley, and Ella were lucky enough to find a raccoon. They let Shiloh have it."

"Good decision, she needs all the meat she can get. We will leave here tonight and look for a better place."

"I don't think you should push yourself, or Mother, just yet. Spend a couple more days resting. Moving too soon may bring your fever back." Seeing the irritated look on Thor's face, Demon quickly adds. "I mean no disrespect, Father. I fear for your health is all."

Thor relaxes, "Of course. You are a good son and give good advice, which I will take, so long as you don't get too used to giving it. I am still leader."

"A position I do not wish for.", Demon replies solemnly.

CHAPTER 11

Thor and Athena spend three days regaining their strength. Thor insists on traveling as soon as possible. He's not happy until they're moving again, even though their first few days go slow. They spend a week going up and over the mountain. The delay works in their favor, though. Warm weather follows them to the peak, saving them extra strain from fighting through deep snow. Their days run short, Demon and Avalanche persuade Thor to move slow and stop often, for Athena's sake. Athena never argues this point; she knows her boys worry about their father and are working around his stubborn streak. Nikita's foot poses another concern; her wound won't heal. Pus oozes out of her sore and swollen pad.

Father sun creeps across the landscape, dimming himself behind the horizon. The wolves camp in a cozy, pine grove. Its sandy soil thawed and drained early, so they have a somewhat dry place to lie down. Damp, fresh, spring air stirs the pine scent. Happy chickadees call goodnight to each other. A defiant squirrel gnaws a pinecone high above the wolves; pieces of cone rain down on the slumbering predators. They neither notice nor stir. They're enveloped in complete peace. There's no need to huddle together for warmth, but they stay close for protection.

In the process of shedding their heavy winter fur, their coats look ragged. Thor's pack lays snug in a deep bed of pine needles, comfortable and content. Even Nikita gets some sound sleep despite the constant burning throb in her foot. Thor and Athena stand watching dusk turn to night, before rousing everyone for another night's travel.

Athena leans on Thor; her heart swells with love for her mate and family, "You know, Thor, even though we've had some hard times, I wouldn't trade it for any other life. We have each other, a perfect bunch of children, and now a beautiful batch of grandchildren. All in all, we are very lucky."

Thor licks Athena's snout, "And I am the luckiest of all, for I have found my one true love with whom I plan on spending the rest of my life."

Athena smiles, happy tears sparkle in the corners of her eyes like twinkling stars, "We have so few of these moments. Let's go for a walk and let the others sleep awhile. Please, Thor, spend some time alone with me. I miss you a great deal."

"I miss you too, but I don't dare stop any longer than necessary. It seems as though every time we find a happy place, humans show their ugly faces and destroy it. We won't be safe until we reach The Land of the Buffalo"

"The Land of the Buffalo, The Land of the Buffalo, I'm so damn sick of hearing about The Land of the Buffalo. You push so damn hard for it, yet we don't know if it's safe or if it even exists. Your pipe dream is driving a wedge between us, Thor. You need to think about what's more important, this Land of the Buffalo or me."

"Athena, please, you know I love you more than anything, that's why I push so hard. I want to keep you and our family safe and happy."

"Then prove it. Let the children sleep and spend a night with me."

"I can't"

"Damn you" Athena storms off, tears streaming down her face.

"Athena, wait, don't go." She doesn't look back. Thor drops his head, fighting tears of his own, "Why doesn't she understand me?" Guilt rips open his heart, "I wish I could take a night off and run like we were yearlings, but I have responsibilities. I must care for my family. Granted, Demon has become very responsible, but I can't give him leadership. He's too young, I must do my duty."

He sighs in frustration then, heavy hearted, Thor moves from wolf to wolf, taking his time waking them. He hopes Athena will calm down soon. If she doesn't, they could be stuck here awhile. Even though he's leader and carries more foolish pride than most, he still knows when not to push her.

Shiloh stands, drops her front half downward with her forelegs straight out, then her rear, stretching cramped muscles. She yawns and looks down at her pups. Shock snaps her awake; Phantom is gone. Her heart and mind race in panic, "Oh Great Forest Spirits, please help me find him. Everyone, get up, Phantom's missing again. Come on, quick, help me find my baby."

Athena walks through the grove, mind reeling and vision blurring behind a wall of tears. She finds a boulder with a dead tree leaning against it, walks up the trunk, and jumps atop the rock. She stands, a heartbroken creature, staring through the forest, but not seeing it.

Painful thoughts course through her mind like snake venom in blood, "Damn Thor and his Land of the Buffalo. He doesn't understand. I need some attention once in a while. He loves his leadership more than me. I'm tired of coming in second. How can that boy say he loves me then ignore me? He's never there for me. Maybe a younger, prettier wolf could keep his attention. I'm big and ugly. If I was smaller, he might love me more. Should I move out of the pack? No, I can't. I wouldn't get to see my grandchildren. Maybe I should just stop whining and accept what I have. No one else will want me anyway."

Athena's attention jumps back to reality when a sad howling sound reaches her. She blinks away tears, cocks her head, and listens. Her eyes grow big and round when dreadful words echo back from the trees, "Phantom is missing". Maternal instincts push all self worry from her mind, finding her grandson dominates every thought. Adrenaline dumps a boost of energy into her veins. She leaps off her rock and hits the ground running.

Shiloh can't get her brain and body working together. She takes off looking for Phantom, remembers Outlaw and Goddess, runs back, thinks better of it, then strikes off after Phantom again.

Thor steps in front of her, interrupting her mad pacing, "Shiloh, stop a minute. You'll ruin the trail running back and forth like this. Take a few deep breaths, calm down. Nikita, watch Outlaw and Goddess. Demon, Avalanche, sniff around and find Phantom's scent"

Harley and Ella come forward, "What can we do, Father?"

"Sit with Shiloh. Try to keep her calm until we find a track."

Demon and Avalanche work in ever broadening, concentric circles. They search the immediate area in no time then bring Thor bad news, "Dampness has deadened the trail. We can't get so much as a faint whiff of it."

"Alright, we'll split up and search by sight and sound. Shiloh, are you calm enough to search in an organized manner?"

"I think so"

Athena thunders into the conference, panting hard, "Have you—found him—yet?"

Thor's surprise shows on his face, "How did you know?"

"A mother's—senses never—dull when it—comes to—protecting—children."

"You never cease to amaze me."

"Have—you—found—Phantom?"

"No"

"Then stop trying to get on my good side and mobilize a search. You can flatter me later."

"Sorry. Everyone, form a circle around where Shiloh and the pups were sleeping. We'll fan out from there, keep each other in sight. He couldn't have gotten far."

The pack spreads out, sniffing the air and ground. Eyes and ears strain for any helpful information. Thor's nose detects an unwelcome odor. Something buried deep in his memory, something painful. He follows it, blocking everything else out, putting all his concentration on the scent. He pushes through a pine thicket. Thick, sweet smells from dense undergrowth work at covering the nightmare odor. He bulls past interwoven branches into a small clearing dotted with large poplar trees. In the center lies a calf carcass. Beside the small bovine stands Phantom, nosing the meat, and about to take a bite.

Thor roars with the force of thunder, "Phantom, no! Don't touch it."

Startled, Phantom leaps and spins, peeing himself on the way down, "Holy smokes, Grandfather, you scared the wits out of me."

"That's not very hard, since you're witless in the first place. What the hell do you think you're doing?"

Phantom hangs his head; shame flattens his heart. He looks up at Thor, choking on sadness, "I was exploring"

"Damn it, Phantom, how many times do we have to tell you not to wander off alone? Do you have any idea what you almost bit into? It's death meat. You never ever taste something before you identify it. Lucky for you, the humans didn't put much effort into hiding the stench of their poison. I followed it and found you. You could've died. Great Forest Spirits, will you never listen? It's high time you learned to mind your elders. Get over here."

Phantom looks tiny and frail crawling toward Thor. Thor nips the boy's hindquarters repeatedly. Phantom screeches sharp high-pitched yelps.

Nearby, Shiloh hears his pained cries, "That's Phantom. No, no, no, don't let him be hurt."

A band of fear clamps her heart; she drowns it in anger. Whatever hurt her child will pay a high price. She makes a mad, blind charge through the forest. She bursts onto the scene, ready to destroy any threat. The sight of Thor nipping Phantom shocks her.

She takes a menacing step toward him, "What are you doing to my baby? Get away from him."

Thor spins and slams his head into her shoulder. Shiloh crashes onto her side, air rushes from her lungs. He stands snarling over her. The fallen wolf rolls on her back and tucks her tail between her legs, showing submission.

Thor stares into her face, anger burns in his eyes like a forest fire, "Number one, you don't tell me what to do, **ever**. Number two, if **you** can't train this child to mind, **I** will. Number three, he nearly ate death meat. I'd say a good sound nipping is far better than a long slow death."

"I'm sorry, Thor, I didn't realize how much danger he was in. I heard my baby crying and rushed to save him. Is he okay? May I check on him?"

"Yes, he is well and you may tend him."

Shiloh rolls over and slinks toward a bawling Phantom. She looks him over, checking every inch of his body, then covers him in kisses. No matter how hard she tries, she can't soothe his incessant crying.

When he can finally speak, he asks, "Why does Grandfather hate me? I didn't mean to make him hate me. I just got bored and went exploring."

"Oh my poor Phantom. Grandfather doesn't hate you. He loves you very much. He scolded and nipped you because he wants you to remember the dangers of wandering off. Telling you doesn't do any good. I hope now you'll listen."

"I'm sorry, Mother. I promise I'll never make you or Grandfather angry at me ever again."

"That's a tall order, Son. I hope you take your promise seriously."

"I do, Mother, I do."

The deflated tone in his voice tugs at her soul, "All the same, I'm keeping a close eye on you from now on. You're standing on shaky ground, so watch your step."

Thor's pack regroups at the campsite and settles their rattled nerves. Shiloh keeps Phantom within nipping distance. He sits, head down, moping. Athena separates herself, brooding over their endless travel.

Thor approaches with great caution, "Can we talk?"

Athena sighs, "No need, I already know what it's about. We must move on. That death meat means humans are nearby. You know, sometimes I hate it when you're right,"

"Athena, I want you to know, I love you very much. Once this trip ends, I'll spend all the time you need together. I must continue pushing so I can keep our family safe. I want to find a place where Phantom can explore without being killed by human infection, where Outlaw and Goddess can find suitable mates, maybe start packs of their own. Where we can live in peace."

"I know. It's just damn hard sometimes. I feel so alone, like you don't have time for me."

"I'm sorry, Love. I don't mean to make you feel sad and lonely. You are my soul-mate, my everything."

Athena nuzzles Thor then licks his snout, "And you are mine, 'til our teeth fallout and we can no longer hunt. I want us always together. Now, as much as I hate the idea, we'd better move on."

Together, they rejoin the group, make sure all are accounted for, and leave. Thor leads, ever watchful for potential danger. Soon, they find a large field with a human den and his cache of live food in its center. Thor is glad wet spring air holds scents down; he doesn't want to deal with the sickening stench of people right now.

The wolves skirt this field, staying just inside the woods. Thor keeps an eye trained on the farm. The others, sensing his agitation, stay vigilant as well. Thor spies a fenced-in barnyard. Memories flutter through his mind like evil butterflies: Bandit warning him to avoid humans, Bandit challenging his authority, Bandit saving his life, and Bandit lying in a puddle of his own blood, a large smoking hole in his back. Thor shivers at the monstrosity of his waking nightmare. Tears push against his eyes, threatening to spill over at any moment. His heart tightens and cramps in an agonizing sense of loss.

"Oh, My Son." he whispers, "if only I had listened, not let my pride and arrogance get in the way."

Athena's tender voice floats into his pain, "Thor, are you okay?"

Thor bounces out of his sad reverie and gazes into Athena's eyes as she stands beside him, "Yes"

"Are you sure? You've been stopped, staring at that human place for a long time. You have a far off, thoughtful look about you. What's wrong?"

"Nothing, I said I'm fine. I'm simply being careful. I don't want us running into any unexpected killing sticks or leg catchers. Is it alright with you if I keep us safe?"

Athena knows he's hiding something. She can feel sadness rolling off him even through his anger. She suspects it has something to do with Bandit. This settlement resembles the one where they lost their son. Her heart tears in two; half going to her mate, half twisting and writhing in the agony of their loss. She becomes wrought with a sense of helplessness, "How I wish you would share your pain, My Beloved. If I could ease some of your guilt, perhaps you could let the rest go."

Thor resumes his former pace, Athena follows; Harley, Ella and Shiloh each carry a puppy. Their trek through the night runs fairly easy. Spring prances in the air. Night birds chirp, peepers sing their chorus at ear piercing levels. Warm, wet air hangs low and heavy. A new scent reaches Thor's sensitive nose. A strange smell, something he can't place. He stops short. New odors always mean danger on this adventure. It's like a bear, but not quite. Something sharp, acrid; it resembles a skunk, only bigger, stronger. He looks back, a question on his face. Nods tell him everyone has caught the scent. They follow the trail in a slow and careful fashion. The stinging aroma grows ever stronger; it's coming from beyond a scrub pine ahead.

Thor stops and prepares a scout, "Shiloh, Nikita, stay with the babies."

Phantom squirms to be released, "Grandfather, let me help. I can sneak in and out before any creature knows I'm there."

"I admire your courage, Phantom, but this could be a life threatening situation. I'd feel better if you had some training before participating in a reconnaissance maneuver."

"But I can help."

"No, and that's final. I love you, Grandson, but I will not stand for you challenging my authority."

Shiloh sets him down and cuts off her son's argument, "Phantom, hush before you get a serious nipping from **BOTH,** Grandfather and I."

"Yes, Mother" Phantom sits and hangs his head, ears drooped, eyes on the ground, shoulders slumped in utter dejection.

Thor's tone softens, "Your time will come, Grandson, be patient, give yourself time to grow and learn. Now, Demon, Avalanche, and Harley, sweep the right flank. Mother, Ella, and I will go left. No one approaches until I signal. Understood?"

"Understood" The others whisper in unison.

The dark forest holds its breath; heavy air crushes that overpowering stench to the ground. Thick and rank, it can almost be seen floating between the branches of the screen ahead. Thor's group splits to follow their instructions. Their eyes begin watering as they close in. Thor crouches and peers under the evergreens. In the thicket's middle lies what looks like an elk carcass. Demon scans this scene from the other side. When he catches his father's attention, he shakes his head. Thor gives a nod and the wolves close their circle upon the carrion.

Demon drapes a forepaw over his nostrils. His sensitive nose burns as if he has inhaled a hornet, "Father, what could leave such a terrible scent?"

"I have no idea. This smells far worse than any skunk I've ever encountered. Whatever it was, it ruined the meat."

"Ahem, excuse me."

The lupines whirl about, looking for the strange voice. Avalanche spots a large barred owl tucked in one of the taller pines, "There, in the tree."

When everyone faces him, the owl continues speaking, "I apologize for my interruption, but if you will indulge me, I can answer your question,"

"Please do," Thor responds, "one can never have too much information. We appreciate anything you can tell us."

"Very good. That nasty aroma, which I'm sure burns your acute olfactory sensors, comes from a wolverine."

"What is a wolverine?"

"A huge member of the weasel family. A vicious, gluttonous carnivore, rather than share its meal, whether his own or a stolen one, he'll spray the leftovers with urine, so no one else an eat it."

"What a selfish, wasteful act."

"I quite agree"

"Is he still around?"

"I haven't seen him in a couple of days, but I suggest caution on your travels. The wolverine won't hesitate to take on a wolf pack. He carries an arrogance that keeps him sneaky and cocky enough to try stealing one of your pups."

Thor's eyes narrow, "I will destroy anyone who even thinks of harming my family."

"Very valiant, brave leader. However, don't underestimate a wolverine. They are strong, quick, cunning, and unwavering in their attacks. You will likely lose members of your pack in a direct confrontation. I mean no slight against your fighting skills when I implore you to avoid this nasty animal."

"I will take your advice, you know this creature better than I. We hope to be out of this territory soon anyway."

"I am honored by your decision. Now if you will excuse me, I must hunt before night ends." Owl lifts off in shocking silence. His perch sits almost motionless as he becomes a mere shadow in the starlight.

Thor barks a quick, decisive order, "Let's regroup and gain some distance on this place."

Unsure of wolverine's stealth, the wolves form a protective bunch; their rear guards walk backward. Travel slows, buy nothing can sneak up on them. They focus eyes and ears in all directions. Thor keeps this formation until he's sure they clear the stinking creature's hunting grounds.

CHAPTER 12

Temperatures rise, snow leaves, and game runs abundant. Nikita's foot finally heals, so the pack can make some real progress. They spend more time moving and less hunting. They do much of their hunting on the run, snatching small game as they go. Warm spring days lead into summer and the land becomes less mountainous. Fields grow larger and avoiding mankind becomes harder. By moving at night, they prevent most encounters. Humans pepper the scattered forests with their horrible poison. This gives the adolescent members ample opportunity for learning the smell of death meat. The pups discover many different human related scents (cattle, sheep, pigs). When the sound of killing sticks rings across the countryside, hunting becomes next to impossible. Dodging man makes the wolves go days without eating. They bypass easy penned up kills and stick with skittish game in the woods.

Today, the wild canines make a rare push into daylight. Mankind hasn't been present for a couple of days, so Thor decides they should take advantage of their good luck. A hot Father Sun erases the paintings of an early dawn sky. Brightness and heat blanket the flattening countryside. Things change every day. Most of the leafy trees around them are unidentifiable. Boulders stick out of the ground here and there.

It's in this stone strewn wood that a low rumbling growl finds its way inside Thor's ears. He stops dead; Athena almost runs into him. She starts to speak, but he holds up a paw for silence. Again, a deep throated warning sound. Thor creeps forward, tips his head back and inhales deeply while casting his nose side to side. On the first pass, he picks an odd scent from a cacophony of smells dancing in the air. Amidst the duff, wood, and leafy odors hides something different. He would guess woodchuck, but they belong in fields and don't growl, they hide.

Athena takes a dozen soft treads to Thor's side and whispers in his ear, "I'll be **So** glad when we reach a place where we can recognize scents and sounds. These guessing games we've been playing for the last several months are getting old. Once again, the question is, 'What do you think it is?'"

"I think it's a ground digger of some sort. They're not dangerous back home, but after all the strange things we've seen on this trip, I'm not taking any chances."

"Shall we set up our usual half circle approach?"

"It's worked well so far. I see no reason to abandon it now."

The lupines fall back out of the unknown animal's probable hearing distance. They gather behind a sweet, gummy smelling bush with broad leaves and white flowers. This dense plant makes perfect cover. Mosquitoes buzz in thick, black swarms around perfumey buds.

Thor lays out his plan, "We'll use a simple half circle approach, Demon, Avalanche, and Harley, cover the right. Mother, Ella, and I have the left. Shiloh and Nikita, take center. Outlaw, Goddess, and Phantom, stay behind this bush. Don't move. We don't know what this creature is or what its capabilities are. I want you safe."

At five months old, the puppies have been traveling on their own for some time. Their freedom makes them indignant and cocky. Phantom protests first, "But, Grandfather, we're not babies anymore. We can help."

"No, you are too inexperienced for this."

Outlaw joins the argument, "How are we supposed to gain experience hiding behind a bush?"

"Unknown animals are not the ones to practice on."

Goddess decides to add her opinion, "We are fast and silent. We can close the circle so this creature can't get away. It might be food."

"I'll not risk your safety or the safety of anyone else. If this situation becomes dangerous, someone could get hurt or killed watching out for you. **And,** there's the possibility of you getting in the way. How do you think you'd feel if you caused a death?" Phantom looks ready to rebut; Thor cuts him off, a deep glare settles in his eye and menace in his voice, "Use extreme caution, Grandson. You've tested my patience and authority as far as you're gong to. This debate is over."

Phantom's jaw snaps shut and his head droops. Thor's fiery stare lands on the other two who drop in submission.

Thor stands tall, his voice fills with half quelled anger, "Good, now that the insubordination has ended, let's continue our mission. If not for needing silence, I would nip some sense into you stubborn zealots."

Thor closes his eyes and takes three deep breaths, calming his agitation; he needs his wits at peak performance. He opens his eyes and leads the woodland soldiers on their inquisitive venture. They fan out and take their positions. Light, quiet footfalls propel them toward something scratching the earth. They ignore gnats and mosquitoes bent on entering ears, eyes, and noses. A sneeze or scratch could alert attentive quarry of their exact location. It's possible this creature already knows they're around; giving it a target to home in on could be disastrous. The digging sounds stop. A low grumbling noise takes their place. The wolves freeze; they have been sensed. Everyone holds their breath. Tension hums in the air, drowning out the mosquitoes.

Shiloh's quarter-grown pups sit in a circle pouting. Childish sullenness hangs about them as thick as the black flies. Teeth snap and heads twitch in retaliation of insect invasion. Gnats pepper Goddess' white coat. This smelly shrub attracts every tiny invader imaginable.

She scratches her neck and growls, "Damn it, Phantom, if you hadn't opened your mouth, Grandfather would've found us a more suitable place to wait."

"You didn't hesitate chiming in, so don't try dumping this all on me."

"I wouldn't have said anything on my own. You got me going."

"Oh, that's just typical. Don't take responsibility for your own decision. Blame someone else whenever possible and someone else always means me. I'm sick of it."

"You're a bad influence on me. I'd be much better off if you'd never been born, you're nothing but trouble. Either you're off exploring alone, even after all the adults told you not to, or you drag me and Outlaw into some predicament that gets us nipped."

"Don't go bringing me into your argument. I don't want any part of it. As a matter of fact, you two may wanna knock it off. You're getting loud, and if Grandfather has to give up his search, he'll nip the holy hell out of us, no matter who's involved."

Phantom and Goddess sit across from each other; angry daggers shoot from narrowed eyes. Rustling leaves on the opposite side of their screen catch Outlaw's attention. He cocks his head and intensifies his concentration. Scuffing noises from a short-legged animal put the youngsters on anxious alert.

Outlaw shivers, "Did you guys hear that?" He turns toward the others; he can't keep fear out of his voice or off his face. Phantom and Goddess both nod. Quick jerks in their chest hair betray hammering pulses.

Rattling shuffles, coming from their right, turn and move in the direction their family went. Worry washes into the pups' blood like a mighty spring flood. They must act now or it will cripple them, but none can make their brain work. An earthy smell underlaid with a hint of danger, very much like the one they overheard Thor describe, wafts past the bush's perfume.

Goddess sits shaking, "What do we do?"

Outlaw shrugs. Phantom buries his fear in bravado, "Aw c'mon, you two," he whispers in a confident tone, "for a couple of big brave wolves, you act like scaredy-cats. I'll tell you what we do. We sweep in behind that noise maker and stop it before it reaches Mother and Aunt Nikita. We'll be heroes. Grandfather will have to include us in every search from now on. He'll be so proud of our bravery and cunning, we won't be considered babies anymore."

Outlaw beams like Father Sun, "I don't know about you, Goddess, but I like that idea. We're not children any longer. We deserve a chance to prove ourselves. It's the best shot we've got. If we wait for the adults, we'll never get a chance. We must not waste this golden opportunity."

Goddess looks doubtful, "I don't know. Grandfather told us to wait here. We should obey him. He gets very angry when we don't. I do not look forward to a hard nipping and that's just what we'll get."

"Do you believe this crap, Outlaw? A little while ago, our brave sister was arguing with Grandfather for a chance at excitement, then she had courage enough to start an argument with me, now she's afraid of a little nipping. If you're too scared, Sister, you can stay here shaking like a leaf. We males will seize the honor and glory due us."

Phantom smiles at Outlaw and each slips out from opposite sides of the bush. Before they get very far, Goddess grumbles, "Wait for me, damn you. You guys need somebody to think for you. Otherwise, you'll charge headlong into a bear or something."

She breezes past Phantom and takes a position in their flanking line's center. The three swallow indecisive lumps. None wants to appear afraid in front of the others, so they don confident masks and steal off toward an unrecognized target.

Thor listens, looks, and sniffs. Definite menace laces growls coming from behind the boulder they're facing. This is no herbivore feigning ferocity; something truly dangerous awaits them. He hears high pitched squeaks and grunts between snarls. A mother and her children? Extra care must be taken. Mothers are vicious when it comes to protecting their young. The forest becomes silent as death. Using head and paw signals, Thor motions his pack forward.

Nerves charge with adrenaline, peaking their already sharp senses. Thor hears pine borers chewing into trees on his left. Demon sees an inchworm crawling over leaves fifty yards away. Avalanche tastes the stranger's anger. Athena smells its determination. Shiloh and Nikita feel vibrations from the mother's beleaguered tread in and out of her den. Harley and Ella can't sort the overwhelming rushes of sensory input; such a flood of stimuli makes them very nervous. Tension from impending confrontation builds so thick around them, they can chew on it.

Goddess spots a black rump waddling across the forest floor. Anger radiates off this short beast; it smells foul and scary. The stranger looks about the size of a woodchuck and shares the earthy smell of ground diggers, but that's where its similarities end. It is gray instead of brown and has wide black stripes down its sides. Streaks of white flash in the sun. They create a sharp contrast with its black head. The creature breathes hard; it has run a long way.

Goddess wonders, "Did it hear the pack? Will it try an attack from behind? This little thing has no hope going against a mighty wolf pack. Why doesn't it just run away?"

Phantom and Outlaw are wound tight. They quiver in anticipation of a fight. Blood pounds in their ears so hard, they can't hear their shaky steps crunching leaves and snapping twigs. Goddess makes shushing motions at them, to no avail. The males use every ounce of self control they have preventing themselves from rushing in before they come within striking distance. Their quarry stops, takes in a long draught of air, and whirls. The wolf pups freeze, their foe's narrow head looks mean. A deep, frightening snarl tears a jagged hole in the silence. Gleaming white teeth flash as the creature snaps its fangs. Fear squeezes the youngsters' hearts. A collective thought runs through their minds, "Oh Great Forest Spirits, what have we gotten ourselves into?"

––––––––––––

The adult wolves circle, then converge on the boulder's face. A very irate ground digger meets them. She stands in front of a burrow built with a mound of dirt at its entrance to help protect it from predators. Fear and anger dance on a light breeze; twisting, turning, becoming one. The mother snarls, growls, and raises her hackles in warning. She faces each intruder in turn then spits a question at the group, "What do you wolves think you're doing in my territory?"

Thor steps forward from her right, "We mean you no harm. We were passing through and caught your scent. Being from the northeast, we didn't recognize it. Therefore, we came to investigate." He tilts his head and gives the stranger a quizzical look, "I mean no disrespect, but what type of ground digger are you? We've never seen your kind before."

The stranger swells with pride, "I am a badger, and don't try distracting me with your amiable talk. How do I know you're not attempting to lower my guard so you can steal my children?"

"I suppose you don't. I can only say that we wish to pass in peace. Whether or not you believe me is your decision."

High pitched, piercing screams and malicious snarls slice the tension charged air like fangs through fresh meat. Shiloh takes off running; her calls echo off distant hills, "Outlaw! Hang on, Mama's coming."

More screams and yips curdle Thor's blood. Athena sprints on Shiloh's heels and the pack follows suit. Their hearts pump terror chilled blood into their brains. Dread and fear induce them to disregard caution as they tear headlong toward the puppies' horrible cries. Shiloh's mind spins, her body pours adrenaline into her system until she becomes blinded of everything except saving her babies.

Athena passes Shiloh as they explode through the brush. The snarling enemy, who has a terrified Phantom backed up against a tree, doesn't know what hits him. Athena scoops it up in her mouth, raises it high overhead, and slams it onto the ground. The vicious creature bounces up and takes a swipe at her head. Her super charged reflexes barely save her from four sharp claws. Shiloh moves in from the left then jerks her face aside as lightning fast teeth snap at her. The ground digger backs himself into a large tree, "C'mon, ya dirty friggin' wolves, I'll show ya what happens ta big fat flea bags that sneak up on **my** family. I'll tear every one a ya gutless freaks ta pieces. I ain't afraid a nuttin'."

Athena and Shiloh are taken aback; they've never encountered such a small creature with an attitude this big. The family forms a semi-circle around their enemy, heads lowered and lips rolled back. Deep growls build like distant thunder.

"Wait," a sharp voice from behind them barks, "if you truly are just passing through, prove it by leaving my mate alone."

Thor turns and sees the winded female badger waddling across a leaf littered floor, "I can't very well leave him alone when he's attacked my grandchildren, they're babies."

The male badger responds in his most menacing tone, "Those 'babies' were gonna ambush me. I got every right ta protect maself from a moose shit attack. I'll kill any flea bag what sneaks up behind me like a damned coward. Ya need ta teach yer pups better. Teach 'em ta attack head-on, like a real predator, not slinkin' aroun' from behind like a scavenger."

"Rumbler, enough." his mate interjects, "there is no need to be that insulting. They are, after all, mere children. Children do foolish things, and your mouth getting us killed won't do ours any good. Wolf Leader, may I suggest you check on your little ones? I will keep my mate under control."

Rumbler puffs out his chest in indignation, "The hell you will, Female. I'll do whatever I friggin' well please."

The female badger totters past Thor and stands nose to nose with Rumbler, "If you don't shut your mouth, **RIGHT NOW**, I'll kick your tail myself."

Rumbler deflates like a punctured deer stomach, "Yes, Dear."

His mate faces Thor, "My apologies, Wolf Leader. He means well, he just doesn't know when to shut up. Will you let us take our leave so we may tend our children while you care for yours?"

"Why should I even allow you to live?"

"Because, Rumbler may be a hot head, but he is also honest. If he says your grandchildren were ambushing him, then that's what happened. Therefore, they were on the verge of carrying out an unwarranted, unprovoked attack. He was defending himself."

"I believe my grandchildren were trying to protect us from your mate's ambush."

"Now why would a mighty wolf pack need children for protection, and why put youngsters in that kind of danger in the first place? Are you so careless, Wolf Leader?"

Thor straightens to his tallest height, "No, I am not. They moved away from where I hid them. They were disobeying my orders. I'll let you go, for now. If my grandchildren tell me a different story than your mate's, I'll come for you."

"Thank you, Wolf Leader. Come, Rumbler, let's go home." Rumbler looks as if he wants to protest. "Not another word, Rumbler. I would rather snuggle my babies than fight wolves."

Rumbler swings his jaw shut and shuffles out of sight, his mate hot on his tail. Menace melts from the air like snow in a warm spring rain.

Thor joins his group circled around their fallen pups. Athena and Shiloh lick Outlaw and Goddess' wounds while they lie half conscious in the duff.

Thor brushes Athena's shoulder, a solemn note in his words, "How are they?"

"They're in rough shape, but they'll live. Judging from spatter on the ground, they've lost a lot of blood. Goddess may have a scar on her face. Other than that, there shouldn't be any life threatening damage. The rest of their scars will be under their coats."

Relief quenches worry kindled in Thor's heart.

Phantom slinks toward Thor on his belly. A portrait of dejection, he rolls wet eyes up at his leader, "Grandfather, it's all my fault. I talked them into stalking the stranger. Goddess said it was a bad idea, but I wouldn't listen. I wanted to prove we aren't babies anymore. I could've gotten us all killed. We were sneaking up behind him when he suddenly spun around and attacked us. I didn't realize such a small creature could be that fast and strong. He had us beaten before we knew what happened. I messed up bad, I am so sorry. I wouldn't blame you if you hate me, I sure do. Will I be banished? I know I deserve it, I disobeyed your orders, I was too cocky." Phantom's heart overflows with shame; sobs shake his entire body.

Thor gazes at his two immobile grandchildren, making visible effort at controlling his fury, "I should nip you until you bleed. However, you are obviously sorry for what you've done. You may even suffer nightmares because of it. I won't cause you any more suffering. Your punishment will be caring for your brother and sister without fail or complaint. If I hear a single whine out of you, I will nip your tail off. Do I make myself clear?"

"Yes, Grandfather"

"Good, now, let's find a safe place where we can care for these two."

CHAPTER 13

The late summer morning breaks clear and hot. Dry searing heat presses down, as oppressive as a small cage. It's all around, there's no escaping it. The forest lies silent, stifling temperatures, still air, and lack of rain overwhelm even the insects. Everything dries out; leaves crackle as they crumble underfoot, trees and bushes wither, and brooks dry up. Animals grow gaunt; intense heat drains their energy. What little shade that can be found offers slim comfort.

The wolves lie inside a den they excavated out of an old ground digger's burrow they found in a soft mound of earth. Working together, they enlarged it. Surrounding trees grow close enough to offer shade, yet far enough away so their roots caused little interference in constructing their shelter. The earth holds cooler air than outside, but the family lays as far apart as possible, lessening the effects of escaping body heat on one another. Everyone pants, precious moisture drips from their tongues in large drops.

Harley slides over beside Ella and whispers in her ear, "One good thing about Outlaw and Goddess getting beat up, we don't have to travel in this heat. Can you imagine moving around out there? Even nighttime hasn't brought much relief in the last few moon phases. I'd much rather be holed up here."

Ella gawks at her sister, mouth agape, "I can't believe you just said that. There is nothing good about their dilemma. Great Forest Spirits, Harley, they could've been killed. How can you be so cold?"

"I'm not trying to be cold hearted. I'm just sick of this miserable heat and I'm looking for any silver lining I can find."

"Don't let Mother or Father hear you talk like that, they'll nip your tail off for sure. If Shiloh hears you, she'll strangle you. Maybe you'd better get some sleep before you say something as stupid as you just did to the wrong wolf."

"If you're gonna be so damned persnicity, I won't bother talking to you either." Harley wriggles toward a darker corner and closes her eyes, but the heat makes sleep impossible.

Goddess and Outlaw heal well. The pack females keep their wounds clean; preventing infection and discouraging flies from laying eggs in the openings. When he's sure the pups can travel, Thor sets his pack moving once more. The summer dry spell impedes their travel. Blinding heat saps strength and dehydration always lingers close by. In a few days, Athena convinces Thor to stop and let the puppies recuperate again; they've taken a desperate turn for the worst in all this heat. They lie motionless and whimpering. If the weather doesn't break soon, they'll be lost.

Tonight the bright half moon blazes in unhampered brilliance. Stars sparkle against a black satin sky. Thor sits under a shriveled bush, snuggling Athena despite the heat; neither speaking the dark fears lurking within their minds.

"Athena, do you think this damn drought will ever end? This heat really wears on my temper. I wish at least the nights would cool down. I want us to make some miles. I'm sick of traveling and just want to reach The Land of the Buffalo so we can finally settle down."

"We'll get there, have patience."

"I don't have time for patience. I don't know how much further we have to go, and I don't want us caught in strange territory through the winter."

"Winter is a long way off. You worry too much."

"That's my job."

"Stop worrying about things so far in the future. You'll give yourself gray hair."

"Yeah, you're probably right. I know one thing, though. Once we get relocated, no more trips for this old wolf. I wasn't meant to be a wandering soul."

Late the next day, while everyone sleeps, Phantom sits alone crying, "Oh Great Forest Spirits, I am so sorry for being arrogant. If you could find it in your hearts to save my siblings, I will spend the rest of my life protecting them. Please, don't let them die."

A week later, the temperature drops a little. Outlaw and Goddess finally gain their feet; they play in short cautious doses. Phantom never joins them. He's swallowed by a guilt induced melancholy. He watches his brother and sister like a bodyguard, always alert.

Thor decides it's time for putting on some serious miles; the pack has lain idle for too long.

As he gathers his pack for their next leg, Shiloh steps forward, suppressed anger quavers in her voice, "You can't expect my babies to do any hard traveling, they're barely healed."

"We must make up for lost time, end of story."

"No, my babies are too weak."

"Don't challenge me, Shiloh. I don't want to put you in your place, but I will. Do you think I enjoy these decisions? I'm screwed no matter what I say. Sit still, humans come along and kill us all. Move too soon, the babies get sick. Any judgment I make is wrong, all I can do is make my best guess every day."

"But . . . ."

"We're leaving tonight, that's final."

Outlaw breaks in, "It's okay, Mama, we're fine."

Shiloh turns left; both her injured children stand, strong and brave. Her heart swells with pride and pain. They lean on each other, trying not to make it look obvious. Outlaw's appearance screams fatigue and soreness. Goddess's fares no better.

"Are you sure?"

When Goddess speaks, the puckered white scar running across her once beautiful snout jumps and quivers, "We can travel."

"You are growing into brave wolves. You honor your father's memory with your strength and resolve. I am very proud of you. Get all the rest you can, it'll be a long night.

Father Sun sets in an explosion of red and yellow while long lost night sounds return. Crickets chirr a languid melody; bullfrogs add a slow drumbeat to the evening song. Heat shimmers across Brother Moon's face. Shiloh and Athena talk quietly while the others rise, preparing for their journey.

"Athena, I'm worried about Phantom. He doesn't explore at all anymore. He constantly watched over Outlaw and Goddess during their entire convalescence. Brought them anything they needed. I was proud of his compassion, but now I'm concerned. When he was exploring, it always drove me crazy. I never thought I would come to miss it. At least while he was giving me gray hair, he was happy. He's grown so forlorn, it breaks my heart."

"He feels guilty. I'm sure knowing one is responsible for his sibling's near death can be trying. Give him time, once Goddess and Outlaw are back romping around, his guilt will subside."

"It's been so long already. I fear he may never get over it. Do you think he'll start hurting himself to lessen his internal pain? I've heard of other guilt ridden wolves doing that."

"I doubt it will get that serious."

"I'm still afraid for his well being."

"If you like, I can ask Harley, Ella, and Nikita to help us keep an eye on little Phantom. Should it get as serious as you fear, we can protect him from himself."

"Thank you, Athena, that would take a huge load off my mind."

Thor paces; he's ready to move on. He vibrates from pent up, nervous energy, "Come on everyone, let's go, I want us covering as much ground as possible while it's cool."

Avalanche leans toward Demon and whispers, "Did he just say 'while it's cool'? It's hot as hell."

Thor whirls, his face a rictus of anger, and strides back until he's nose to nose with Avalanche, "I didn't ask for your opinion. If you continue giving it, I'll stomp the shit out of you. Got it?"

Avalanche drops and rolls over into a submissive posture, "Yes, Father. I meant no disrespect, I was only joking."

"Keep your jokes to yourself." Thor storms westward, "Let's go, I'm not waiting around any longer."

Athena calls Harley and Ella over, "Can you two take turns carrying Phantom? I want a word with your father."

"Of course, Mother." Harley answers in exaggerated self importance, "We'd be happy to look after the youngster."

Athena catches Thor and trots beside him, "You were rather hard on Avalanche, My Love. What's wrong?"

Thor hesitates, considers lying, but knows she'll see through it. He sighs, "Everything's wrong. It's hot, I'm tired, our grandchildren have been through so much and I'm sick of avoiding those damn humans."

"We haven't seen any humans for some time now."

"I have. While I've been scouting the last little while, I've come across humans every day. They keep getting closer. They carry killing sticks too. I don't know if they're hunting us or just hunting. Either way, they'll stumble across our family sooner or later."

"Why didn't you say anything?"

"I didn't want to worry anyone. I was afraid someone would charge after the men and try decoying them away. I was most worried about Phantom, he carries such a heavy load of guilt over Goddess and Outlaw getting hurt. He's liable to do something foolish in atonement."

"Shiloh and I have been discussing that very thing. I'll speak with the girls and ask them to help me keep an extra close eye on him until he snaps out of it."

"Good, that's one less thing for me to worry about."

"Now for you, Dear. How can I make you less cranky?"

"Kill every last human."

"I would if I could, but I can't. Maybe we can come up with something more realistic?"

"I don't know. I suppose putting some distance between us and those blood sucking parasites will help."

"Then let's do that."

Athens suppresses the urge to break into a run; good sense wins over her desire to please Thor. An all night jog will gain them more separation than a short run. They'll also need some energy for hunting. Drought decreases game; the pack has circled farther and farther afield finding meals. Having the ability to go a week between meals helps, but her wolves are losing weight.

The lupine group travels all night, watching the forest turn into miles of wide open spaces. Golden brown grasses grow over head high. Athena's the only one who doesn't have to stand on tiptoe in order to see into the distance. Dry stalks crackle at every touch, making hunting in this environment impossible. The wolves snatch crickets and grasshoppers off disturbed stems; a light meal at best.

Thor settles the group in a nearly dry streambed. They attack its luke warm nectar as if it's the best they ever had. Eastern skies begin paling. Demon and Avalanche set up a watch. The western horizon still seems to be at the other end of the world; grass stretches as far as their sharp eyes can see. Small clumps of trees dot this ocean of wavy brown. It looks like there may be a forest in the distance.

Athena sets Phantom down beside the thin murky trickle of water. He flops down, puts his head on his paws, and stares into the dense grassy sea. Athena's heart twists in sorrow, "Phantom, you must drink some water. Take advantage of it now, we don't know when we'll find more. Going too long without it will make you sick."

Phantom shuffles sideways, laps up a little brown liquid, then sighs, rippling the lazy surface. His eyes reflect clouds of guilt and remorse.

"Grandson, perhaps it is time we talk about what is bothering you."

No response

"Phantom . . . .Phantom!"

He looks up. Pain and torment show in every fiber of his being. Athena makes a conscious effort at holding back a gasp of shock that bounds to her lips.

Her tone softens, "Grandson, please don't bury your sorrows. If you let them fester, they will eat away at your soul like an infection. You can tell me anything. I will keep all of your secrets that don't endanger the pack."

Phantom fights an emotional overload struggling to break free. He sniffles, chokes, then finally breaks down. A flood of misery and self loathing bursts forth. Tears gush from his eyes like water from a broken beaver dam. He spends a few minutes regaining some semblance of self control.

Every cracked word oozes heartbreak, "It's all my fault, Grandmother. Outlaw and Goddess suffer so much because of me. I could've gotten them killed. And for what? My own arrogance. I thought I was grown up enough to lead a stalk. I ruined Goddess' beauty. That ugly scar on her snout will prevent her from finding a mate and having children. I ruined her life. Outlaw is scared all the time now. He doesn't admit it, but I know. When I lay beside him, I can hear his heart race and feel his muscles twitch at every strange sound. He has horrible dreams, kicking and crying throughout the day." Phantom strangles on a bout of sobs.

"You three endured a terrible ordeal. Healing takes time."

"They shouldn't have suffered it. They wanted to obey, I talked them out of it. I have to make everything better, but I don't know how. Maybe I should just leave. Grandfather should've banished me anyway, I'm just a reminder of Goddess and Outlaw's brush with death. I don't deserve love or family."

"Don't talk like that. Goddess and Outlaw will blame themselves if you leave and your mother will be heartbroken. Is that what you want, to cause more pain?"

"No-o-o," Phantom wails, "I want to make things better. If I stay, I'm a bad reminder. If I leave, I break hearts. What am I supposed to do?"

"Be patient. Time heals all wounds, running away makes them worse. You made a mistake, we all know that. We will not keep brow beating you for it and it's about time you stopped doing it to yourself. Learn from your mistake and move on. Outlaw's nightmares will decrease, Goddess will learn to live with her scar."

"But Goddess will never have a mate."

"You don't know that. There are wolves in the world who look beyond appearances and see into one's heart. Those are the mates worth having. Perhaps, she will be better off in the long run. She may find a better mate."

"That doesn't make sense, Grandmother."

"Just remember what I've said and as you grow older, it will become clear."

"I'll try."

"Good, now get some sleep. Your grandfather may want to do some more hard traveling tonight."

Phantom lies down again, thoughts swirling around each other. He raises his head, a less sullen look on his face, "Grandmother"

"Yes?"

"Thank you, I feel a little better now."

"You are welcome, Grandson. One more thing, there is no shame in a puppy crying. No one will think any less of you if you choose to let out more pain."

"Not today, maybe later. All I want now is sleep."

"Then rest easy, Little One."

Athena smiles as Phantom slips into a sound slumber. It's the first time he's dropped off this fast in weeks. A heavy burden melts from her heart. Tears of relief hover at the corners of her eyes. Thor, who has been listening to their conversation, senses her sadness. He creeps up beside her and she leans on his comforting shoulder.

Concern laces his whisper, "Are you okay?"

"I am now. You know, Thor, nothing causes a grandmother more sorrow than her grandchildren's pain."

"I do know, for the same applies to grandfathers. Do you think he'll let himself heal?"

"I hope so."

"Whatever happens from here, you must know you've done your best. It's his choice to let go of the guilt."

"I'm not finished yet. I plan on being there when he needs me."

"As do I. Come, get some rest. We will need to hunt tonight. I have a feeling it'll take everyone to find anywhere near enough food."

"I'm staying here."

"Then I'll stay with you."

Thor and Athena lie on either side of Phantom. He sleeps in a secure cocoon of love and tenderness.

The hot sticky day passes in slow discomfort. Dry scorching heat crushes every animal into the dirt. Night brings some relief. The clear sky quivers with residual heat rising off the ground. By midnight, torturous temperatures release their stranglehold on the world. Animals begin stirring and looking for water. Thor decides now is the time for a hunt. The wolves allay their thirst in the muddy drizzle beside their camp then spread out and look for either scents or tracks to follow. This method soon proves fruitless. When they do find a trail, no matter how quiet they are, the tall dry grass rustles like frosted corn in an autumn breeze. Prey runs away long before the wolves have any hope of sneaking up on them.

Thor tries a new approach. He sends Harley, Ella, Nikita, and Demon to a point half a mile upstream. Thor, Athena, and Avalanche squeeze into the narrow cut and work toward them. Their first try produces a few rabbits and almost a wild boar, so they continue the process. Early in the morning, when the world starts graying and mountaintops glow orange, their persistence pays off.

A mule deer—normally strong fast animals—limps toward a muddy puddle in hopes of slaking her raging thirst. The water runs around the crest of a bend in the streambed. Her exhaustion makes her careless; she heads straight for water. She doesn't hear or smell the wolves until it's too late. They take her down with minimal fight. Their celebration song echoes off distant mountains. Men and sheep alike, cower from the eerie chorus. Avalanche and Demon run back to get Shiloh and her pups. They return, each carrying a youngster.

Goddess and Outlaw protest, "Uncles, we are not babies anymore. We can walk fine on our own."

When she sets a quiet solemn Phantom on the ground, Shiloh tries soothing their egos, "You are big enough to walk and you'll

155

get plenty of chances before our journey ends, but we wanted to run tonight and you're not big enough to keep up with us yet. In time, I am sure you will out run everyone in the pack."

Their pride appeased, the two prance toward supper, chests puffed out and heads held high. The lupines gorge themselves then settle in for a good day's rest. Full bellies make for deep sleep and happy hopeful dreams.

CHAPTER 14

Brother Moon seems as angry as Father Sun. Night burns hot and still; heat wafts up from the ground in a wavering transparent curtain. Water becomes scarce and a relentless searing orb smolders overhead during the day, making sleep impossible. One must wake often, following the shade in its race with Father Sun. Brother Moon's companion seems hateful as he withers life beneath him. The night sky's guardian shines a bright blinding white spotlight on the day's destruction. Trees lose their leaves, high grass dries and falls over, forming a noisy mat. Animals become lethargic; neither night birds nor bats flit through the sky. A deep dark quiet settles over the world and carries an unnerving sense of doom.

The wolf pack rests in this open ocean of dead grass. They haven't found any water in two days; dehydration slows their movements. If not for the blood of occasional small game, they would be incapacitated. After traveling only ten miles, the group lays panting, exhausted.

"Damn heat," Thor complains, "we can't get any distance. How far does this sea of grass go, anyway? I don't think we want to get caught in open country like this for the winter. I bet the wind blows hard enough to carry a wolf off."

"Well, it could be worse," Athena adds, "at least we haven't lost anyone."

"That's true, and the grass has fallen over, so we can see where we're going now. I just wish we could go faster."

"I know you do, Dear. Try not to worry about it so much. We'll find a way through, no matter what Mother Nature throws at us."

"Careful what you say. Mother Nature takes a challenge like that very seriously."

A change in wind peaks Thor's attention. He draws in a delicious scent and starts salivating, "Get everyone together, we're moving."

"But Thor, we haven't been resting very long."

Thor turns toward Athena, a twinkle in his eye, "This'll be worth it, I smell water."

Athena jumps up and gathers her family while Thor gets a fix on the water's location. He paces, his acute sense of smell homes in on that smooth, life sustaining elixir. By the time the wolves converge, he finds a definite heading. They move southwest, their spirits higher than they've been in days. A faint cool smell of moisture floating on the dry air puts a spring in their step. As Father Sun breaks the horizon—his mean burning eye peeking over distant mountains like an angry cyclops—a small brook shows itself at the bottom of a deep natural ditch.

The wolves dive in, splashing, rolling, and playing like pups. Thor issues a warning, "Don't drink too much at once. I don't want anybody getting sick. Weakness in weather like this can be deadly."

They drink in small intermittent sips. When their surge of joyous energy exhausts itself, they lie down. Sleep comes much easier in the cool damp shade.

———————————————

Father Sun works toward his apex; heat grinds the earth hard as ever. A strange roaring sound rolls across the plain, followed by a sharp stinging scent; the kind of smell that burns sensitive noses. Thor cocks an ear and opens his eyes. The thunderous sound races toward them faster than any animal can move. Thor rises in a swift fluid motion and peers over the bank; only his eyes and ears show above the lip. A cloud of dust races eastward, its tail end getting taller and wider before settling. A rattling metallic sound chases the thunderous roar. A strange apparition stops in an instant and an odd, "yee-haw" emanates from the dust cloud.

Demon appears at Thor's side, "What is it, Father?"

"Humans"

"How can you be sure?"

"I suspected when I smelled the nasty stench of their machine, the yell confirmed it."

"What do you think they're doing out here?"

"I don't know, but it can't be good. We'll set watches. I think we're safe for now, but I don't want anyone doing anything other than observing. Go get some sleep, I'll take first shift."

Throughout their long hot day, Thor's lupines take turns watching this human induced dust cloud race around the prairie. Avalanche stands peeking our of his hiding spot in the ditch through gritty, red eyes. Sudden random cracks from killing sticks bring all to their feet. Avalanche assures them the shots aren't aimed their way and his family slowly falls back into fitful slumber. The humans finally settle and build a fire as night extinguishes Father Sun's relentless glow. The temperature fades with his red streaks. Smoke's acrid chilling smell creeps into the ditch. Thor's yellow eyes flash hatred as they peer over the bank at these humans. A smile dresses his face when a devious idea pops up in his mind. He casts a glance toward his family then back.

He rouses the pack, "How would you like to get a little retribution on these humans for some of the pain and suffering they've caused us?"

"What do you have in mind, Father?" inquires Demon.

"Just follow my lead" He starts out of the ditch.

Athena blocks his path, "Are you sure messing with humans in strange country is a good idea?"

"Don't worry, I'm fine tuning a plan in my head right now and we'll scout the area before we do anything. It'll be full dark when we get there. Humans can't see well at night. When they expose their eyes to firelight, they get even worse."

"They have killing sticks."

"If they can't see, they can't use them."

"Humans are careless enough to shoot at anything, whether they can see it or not. One of them could get lucky. I won't lose any more family members."

"We'll be careful."

"I don't like it."

"We'll be fine, trust me.", Thor cajoles his mate.

"I do trust you, it's the humans I don't trust. We've seen enough of their destructive nature to know better than tempt fate."

"Don't worry, Love, they've been tearing around all day, they're tired and stupid. We won't stay long enough to push our luck, I promise."

"Alright, but I'm coming with you and when I think you're getting reckless, I'll call this nonsense off. And if you don't listen to me, I'll knock you down and **drag,** you back."

"I wouldn't have it any other way." Thor gives her a deviant grin.

"Oh no, if I have to drag you back, you definitely won't enjoy the outcome."

"Yes, Dear. Now let's go have some fun."

Millions of twinkling stars in a moonless sky bear witness to the wolves' approach on the camp. Smells of humans, smoke, and killing sticks grow the closer they get. Thor leads a slow noisy stalk; dry grass crackles at each step. A light wind helps cover some of the racket. They time their movements to coincide with the wind, moving only when it blows. Beside the camp sits a strange smelling box on round feet. Its two round eyes sparkle in the firelight, and it bares silvery teeth.

Demon creeps close to Thor, his eyes fixed on this strange creature, and whispers, "What is that thing?"

"I'm not sure what it's called. Man gets inside and it carries them around at great speeds. That's what made the dust clouds earlier. They can't hurt you unless there's a human inside. They command these creatures to run over anything in their path. When men aren't in them, they sleep." Thor leads his family a safe distance away, "Okay, everyone, as I was just telling Demon, that odd creature can't hurt you unless there's a human in it. I don't know why, I guess it's the beast's nature. It won't interfere with our reconnoiter. We'll split into two groups, circle their camp and meet on the other side. Spread out, cover as much ground as possible without losing sight of each other. Scan the area carefully, remember all the details you can. Demon, Avalanche, Harley, and Ella, take the south side. Mother, Nikita, and I will cover the north. Be quiet, stay out of sight. Humans are weak, but if we get careless, they'll use their killing sticks. Any questions?"

Thor checks every face and gets a nod until his eyes meet Athena's. She looks worried, "Thor, why are we doing this?"

"Because, it'll be fun to scare the crap out of these useless humans."

"I don't like this. I have a bad feeling about it."

"If you're so damn worried, then go back and watch the pups with Shiloh."

"No, I'll stay. Maybe I can keep you from doing something even stupider than this lunacy."

"Ha-ha, very funny. Let's get going."

The wolves spread out, memorizing every rock, dip, and blade of grass. The oblivious humans continue their loud talk and raucous laughter. They drink from metal cylinders exuding a deep yeasty odor; the strange liquid inside makes them dumber than normal. Thor's crew meets on the west end of their target. Terrain reports are the same from everyone, flat and wide open. The lack of hiding places increases their risks tenfold. He considers bailing out, then forges on.

"Okay, here's my plan. We'll encircle the camp from a short trot out, far enough so they'll have a hard time getting us with a killing sick. I want at least four jumps separating us. When we're in position, I'll let out a long howl then duck and run to one side. Next, Demon looses a yip and howl from the opposite side then dodges. We'll alternate, one end to another, and wolf to wolf. They'll be so terrified, they won't know what to do. Maybe we'll get lucky and one or both will die of fright."

Thor's evil grin sends a frightened flutter through Athena's stomach., "What are we supposed to do when they start shooting? You know as well as I do, the first thing they'll do is go for their killing sticks. This is too dangerous."

"No it's not. If they start shooting, we just go out more and further apart. They can't hit what they can't see. Come on, let's get started."

Emmitt lumbers from his yellow and white International Scout toward Donnie's campfire. He carries an open beer in his right hand and a family size bag of plain potato chips in the other. The pair have been friends since early childhood. Emmitt, a large man, sports curly brown hair. Donnie, whip thin and wiry, has straight blonde hair. Both men work mundane jobs in a factory on the outskirts of a city they call home. This weekend in the wild poses a chance for them to blow some steam. Their third twelve pack of Budweiser rides tucked under Emmitt's left arm. He hands Donnie the chips then settles onto the rear seat of his Scout that they pulled out earlier and set next to the fire. They have no tent and minimal food; their main preparation was securing an ample supply of beer before starting their safari.

"This is the way ta spend a weekend." Emmitt slurs, "Racin' aroun' the prairie, shootin' at anythin' thet moves, an' drinkin' beer. It don't git no better'n that. I tell you what."

Donnie cracks another beer; he lists heavily to the left, "Ya got thet right. I'm gonna git so blasted I can't see, then drown muh mornin' hangover wit more beer, an' start the whole thin' over again."

"Jes so long as ya don't git sa blasted ya end up shootin' me ir yer own damn self. Ya shoot me an' all be pissed, ya kill yersef an' all never talk ta ya agin."

They roar laughter and slap their knees at Emmitt's brilliant witticism until tears roll down their cheeks.

"Got damn, Emmitt, thet is quite possibly the funniest thing I ever did hear."

"Jes call me Emmitt Costello."

The wolves take their positions. Athena's sense of imminent disaster increases. The peaceful night air shatters when Thor's bone chilling territorial howl echoes through the darkness. Seconds later, Demon unleashes a mournful cry from The Death Song. Ella follows with a yipping distress call so convincing, Athena almost rushes to her rescue. The chaos begins.

A banshee cry slices through Emmitt and Donnie's light hearted mood. Screams of different pitches break out all around the camp. Emmitt's blood runs cold, he's immobilized by fear and his beer drops from weakened fingers. Donnie nearly chokes on a mouthful on chips; he starts quivering as he breaks out in goose pimples. Both feel more sober than they have all day.

"Donnie, what in the hell was thet?"

Donnie's ashen face adds severity to his somber tone, "Wolves"

"Wolves don't attack people, do they?"

"How the hell should I know? I ain't no wolf expert. I'll tell ya this though, I ain't takin' no chances. I'm gittin' muh gun."

"Me too"

The men trip all over each other in their fervor to reach their vehicle. Donnie gets there first, fumbles with the door handle, rips it open, and grabs both revolvers off the front seat. He hands Emmitt his .357 Magnum then snaps open the oversized glove-box. As he rifles though it, assorted items spill out everywhere. The box of bullets he's looking for bounces to the ground. Emmitt bends over and picks up the shells.

"Here, ya dumped 'em in the dirt. Now stop tearin' muh rig ta pieces."

Donnie snatches the box from Emmitt's hand and tries loading his pistol. He drops more shells than he gets in the cylinder. Emmitt sinks to one knee and loads his Smith& Wesson with bullets falling from his friend's shaking fingers; blowing the dirt off each one before dropping it into the cylinder. The meticulous chore helps him bury some of the raging fear inside. They fill their shirt pockets with spare ammunition and walk—back to back—toward their fire while scanning the darkness.

"Ya see anythin', Donnie?"

"I can't see nuthin'. It's darker'n the bottom of a well at midnight."

Howls, yips, and hair raising cries echo across the vast expanse of nothingness. It sounds like all the demons from every level of hell have been released. Fear overwhelms Emmitt; he can't hide it anymore. He doubles over and pukes.

Donnie stops and places a hand on his shoulder, "Ya all right, Buddy?"

Emmitt hacks and spits, "No I ain't alright dammit. I'm scared shitless. What're we gonna do?"

"We're gonna stay close ta the fire, keep a sharp lookout, and shoot any damn thing thet moves."

Thor rides on cloud nine. He smells fear, hears terror in the humans' cries, and sees the big one get sick. He laughs so hard he almost misses his turn to howl. The sound that comes out of his throat more closely resembles a hyena than a wolf. Childish screams from the camp send him into powerful gales of giddiness; his knees buckle and he rolls onto his back. When he regains control, he runs a circle delivering the others an order, "Close in several paces. Let's see if we can make them soil themselves."

The gleeful wolves love this idea, except Athena, "Thor, don't be foolish. You're pushing our luck too far, this won't end well. They'll start shooting at anytime."

"No they won't, these weak humans are so scared they can't function. Even if they do shoot, they're shaking uncontrollably. They can't hit the broad side of a cliff. We'll just get a little closer. C'mo-o-o-n, I can tell you like this."

"Well, I must admit, I do enjoy sending the fear of death into them for a change."

"That's my girl. Now, let's go have some fun."

The wolves close in, heaping snarls upon howls. The humans whimper and shudder. Thor barks an order and the entire pack breaks into a warning song."

"Shit-shit-shit. Donnie, they're getting' closer. We gotta do sumpthin', they're gonna git us. I don't wanna git chewed up by wolves."

"Head back ta the Scout, I got an idea. I don't know why I didn't think of it before."

They trip and scramble toward the International. Thor seizes this opportunity by charging into the campsite, barking and growling. Emmitt stumbles over the heathstones—sending them into disarray—screams, shoots into the air, and soils himself. Thor snatches a large Igloo cooler full of food by the handle. He runs off, shaking it until its contents scatter onto the dead grass. Donnie fumbles with the driver's side door latch, breaking two fingernails to the quick. He swears and jams the fingers in his mouth. Emmitt jumps in the passenger side, leans over the seat, and pops open the driver's door. Donnie hops in and slams it shut, gasping around his fingers. He lays the pistol in his lap, reaches for the dash, and pulls the light switch. A half circle in front of them bursts to life. At the light's edge, a pair of red eyes float a couple of feet off the ground. A row of sharp, gleaming white teeth appears out of a black silhouette. A pink tongue flicks over the teeth; a snarl grabs their ears and chills their blood.

"Holy shit—holy shit—holy shit. Donnie, whadda we do?"

"Shoot the damn thing"

Avalanche closes his part of the circle in front of the metal beast. He sees the humans swallowed by it and stops. He can see their heads through a transparent square over their beast's snout. They seem very lively for creatures who have just been eaten. A blinding light erupts from the beast's eyes. Avalanche snarls a challenge. The monster's sides swing open and the humans step out; the crack and whine of killing sticks streak through the air. Avalanche turns to run. A puff of dirt flies up beside him and a bee sting stabs his right front foot. He yelps and takes off as fast as his injured limb will allow, disappearing into the blackness.

Thor's pack snarls and howls a deafening ruckus. Bullets whiz everywhere. The wolves scatter as the humans blast away in all directions. Fear switches sides.

The stinging smell of spent gunpowder burns Donnie's nose. Tears run down his cheeks from bloodshot eyes. Blinking and wiping his face, he reloads the pistol with trembling hands, breathing as if he's run a marathon. He hears repeated clicks as Emmitt continues pulling the trigger on his empty gun.

"Emmitt . . . . Emmitt, quit it, you'll break yer firin' pin."

"Ya think we gut any of 'em?"

"I got no idea. I do know one thing, I ain't goin' out there ta find out. Not 'til mornin' anyhow."

"What're we gonna do in the meantime?"

"First off, yer gonna change yer britches, then we're gonna sleep in the Scout."

"I doubt I'll sleep much tonight. Why can't we go home?"

"Cause, we're both wasted. We'll end up drivin' inta an arroyo or sumthin'."

"I ain't wasted no more. I ain't been this sober in days."

"Don't matter, the prairie all looks the same at night. Ya won't see any ditches till yer in 'em. Don't worry, we're safe in here."

"I still wanna go home."

"Quit yer whinin' and git sum sleep."

High on adrenaline, the wolves regroup at the ditch where Shiloh and her pups hide. They whoop, howl, and wrestle in jubilation. Avalanche comes in late and hangs back, holding up his front paw.

Athena simmers and stews until she can no longer stand it, "What the hell is wrong with all of you? This shit isn't funny, we're damn lucky no one got killed. As it is, Avalanche has been standing over there, injured, for some time and not a damned one of you noticed."

"I'm fine, Mother, really. It's only a scratch."

"Shiloh, will you take care of Avalanche please?" Athena whirls on Thor, "And you. What in the hell did you think you were doing charging through a human camp like that? Are you trying to get yourself killed? Cause if you are, I'll help you get started by kicking your furry little ass."

"I'm sorry, Dear. I got caught up in the moment." he shrugs a shoulder, "I wasn't thinking. Scaring those humans just felt so good, I got carried away."

"You're damn right, you weren't thinking. You got more than carried away, you got stupid. You scared the living hell out of me. Damn it Thor, don't ever do that to me again."

Thor hangs his head in shame. He knows better than argue or try consoling her; any words from him right now will only fuel her wrath. Maybe, he can make an argument once she calms down, but not before.

Athena continues her tirade, "What's worse, I let you talk *me* into it. I should've known better, you always get carried away with these things. Your hatred of humans and your obsession with getting even for all the heartache they've caused drowns out your good sense. You turn into a reckless adolescent. Of all the stupid idiotic stunts to pull, you pick the one most likely to get you killed."

Athena jams her nose against Thor's. He winces and squeezes his eyes shut at her approach, expecting to endure the physical brunt of her anger as well as the verbal. She snarls, barks, and stomps off sputtering, "Stupid, stupid, stupid." on her way around the bend.

Thor opens first one eye then the other and looks around. The others have disappeared, both out of respect for him and to avoid

Athena's fury. He shakes his head and sighs, "Seems like the longer we're together, the better I get at pissing her off. I hope those damn humans leave before morning. I don't want any reminders that might set her off again. I wonder how many days I'll have to tiptoe around her this time."

CHAPTER 15

Morning breaks clear and hot, same as every other morning for what seems like forever. The steel gray horizon threatens a long miserable day. Father Sun blossoms over distant mountains in brilliant yellow fire. Birds chirp from shaded areas under scorched grass and bushes. Thor opens awakens when he hears metallic crashes from the human camp. He rises on stiff limbs—every muscle in his body screams—and peeks over the bank. The men work on a hasty retreat from their campsite. The sides and rear of their metal monster hang open and they heave their possessions into it as fast as they can. Neither bothers picking up trash or smothering their fire. When finished, they close up the beast, jump in and roar off in a dusty blizzard.

Thor chuckles, "I bet those two never come into this prairie again." He turns to lie down, his muscles tighten and protest. "Damn, I guess I did more running last night than I thought. One more reminder that I'm not a pup anymore." He scans his family and finds Athena still missing, "I wonder if I should go check on her. No, better not. She was angrier than I've seen her in a long time. Showing my face too soon will piss her off all over again. I'd rather face a dozen humans with killing sticks than my female on a tirade. She'll come back when she's ready." He lays in some sparse shade and slips under an exhausted, dreamless, blanket of sleep.

Around a bend in the brook, Athena paces, wide awake. Her mind tumbles in a maelstrom of thought, "Maybe I shouldn't have yelled at everyone so much. That whole business was reckless and stupid, but they only wanted to blow some steam. I wish they could've come up with a better way, especially Thor. Damn him, he knows better. He had no right endangering our family's lives. It was fun to hear humans squeal in fear, though. What if someone got seriously hurt? I don't even know how bad Avalanche's wound is. I dumped my duty on Shiloh. I shouldn't have done that she has her own pups to worry about." She stops, closes her eyes and heaves a giant sigh. "I guess I'd better try to sleep a little. Maybe Thor and I can talk when we're rested."

Athena turns in place three times and settles onto the dusty ground. She let's the grass' gentle shishing clear her mind. Chirring grasshoppers join scattered birdsong to round out Mother Nature's calming symphony. Her storm of emotions abates and Athena lets herself be lulled to sleep.

When Father Sun hits his peak and temperatures reach unbearable levels, the acrid singeing smell of smoke wafts into Thor's nose. At once his brain registers the danger represented by this olfactory information. Sore muscles forgotten, he leaps to his feet. A thick black cloud hangs above him. A roaring fire, punctuated by the screams of animals being roasted alive, assaults his ears; a deafening and frightening racket. He turns to run for Athena and sees her charging around the corner.

Everyone jumps up, ready for action; although, no one knows what that action should be. The puppies sense a dilemma they don't understand and cringe, whimpering, against Shiloh's legs. Suffocating heat, fear, and indecision hover around the group like a swarm of bees. Their small brook does nothing to cool the fire blasted air.

Athena reaches her family and Thor addresses them, "Everyone, pay close attention. It is imperative that we stick together. I know you want to bolt, I'm fighting the urge myself, but if we separate, we die. We'll follow the brook downhill. Perhaps, we'll either find a watering hole big enough to hold all of us or get below the fire and run away from it. Keep your heads low, you'll inhale less smoke. Are we ready?"

The group nods in affirmation. Athena crowds close beside Thor and whispers in his ear, "Thor my love, I am **so** sorry for last bight. If anything should happen to either one of us, please know that I love you with every ounce of my being. I always have and always will."

Thor looks deep into the brown pools of Athena's eyes, "I love you too. Don't speak of bad things, we'll get through this, then we'll talk about last night. I have many things to apologize for. I will list them once our family is safe."

They repeatedly lick each other with an affection known only by old mates. Demon steps forward, "Ahem, I'm sorry for interrupting, but I really think we should get out of here."

Thor and Athena step apart looking a little shame faced. Thor pries his gaze from her adoring stare, "You're right, let's go." He leads in the direction he hopes will save them from agonizing death.

They hustle on holding a bundle of optimism; that soon changes. Terrorized animals jump the ditch in a panic stricken mad dash to escape. Most short-legged survivors can't make the leap. Some become trapped because of limbs snapped in their fall. Others run in circles, delirious from fear snapped minds. Fire closes in, temperatures soar, the very air burns their noses. The ditch's sides continue shortening, bringing smoke closer to the wolves' already tortured lungs. Soon, the banks disappear altogether and the sheer immensity of their dilemma looms before them. Smoke, fire, and death linger everywhere. A veil of steam swallows their brook. Thor looks back, the stream banks burst into a tunnel of flame.

The pups cry, tears roll from their blood shot, smoke filled eyes; fear and confusion cripples them. A rush of coyotes explodes out of a choking black cloud and charges straight through the wolf pack. Members of both families get knocked and battered helter-skelter. Dozens of feet kick and roll Phantom out of sight. When he struggles free from the forest of furry legs, he has no idea where he is. A smoky shroud cloaks sights and smells from the others. Roaring fire drowns his voice and hearing.

The stampede clears and the lupines regroup. Thor and Athena do a head count. Shiloh paces around her group, her heart racing to the point of explosion, and cries out, "Phantom . . . . where's Phantom? Has anyone seen Phantom?"

Thor stands in front of her and places a gentle paw on her shoulder, "Don't worry, he couldn't have gotten far." He looks back over his shoulder, "Everybody spread out, keep each other in sight at all times. We'll walk one way a few paces, turn and go another. We should find him right off. He's smart enough to stay put until we arrive."

Phantom freezes in terror; he can't see, hear, or smell any member of his family. His mind runs through a painful possibility, "What if they left, gave up on me? The Great Forest Spirits know, I've caused enough trouble to make my value plummet." His heart stops and a crushing sense of loneliness smothers him, "I'm on my own." Smoke burns his eyes and fills his lungs. He wanders in a circle, unsure which direction to take. Scorching heat all around him sears his skin. The fine ends of his hair singe. He stops, gathers his courage, and walks into the smothering cloud.

Stretched into a line—Shiloh keeps her remaining puppies close by at the center—the family starts walking in a slow, precise search. Each wolf keeps watch over the one on either side of him. Driven by fierce loyalty and determination, the hunt continues despite unbearable heat. The roaring fire makes hearing difficult, smoke hinders breathing. Animals fleeing death, threaten to scatter the search party in their blind hunt for safety. Every passing minute feeds the wolves' doubts of success.

Nikita crouches, hoping to find fresher air, and attempts a look below the blinding cloud. Soot covers her face and ash runs from her eyes. A flash of gray, about five feet to their right, catches her attention.

"Was that real or has the smoke screwed up my vision?" she wonders. Her oxygen deprived mind darkens her consciousness. She calls out, "Phantom, is that you?" Nikita looks left and realizes she's lost sight of Athena, "Oh great. Now what am I supposed to do? Taking time finding Athena could cost us our chance at saving Phantom. On the other hand, this could be nothing more than wind blown cinders." A picture of her nephew's face floats through her mind. Nikita makes her decision; she creeps along, calling In vain, "Phantom, it's Aunt Nikita. Don't be afraid, I'm coming to get you."

A blast of wind drives smoke in her face, blinding her. Two more steps and her feet tangle in a soft furry lump; she tumbles to the ground. The impact forces the wind from her lungs. She inhales several gulps of acidic air recuperating enough strength to rise. Phantom lies at her feet in an unconscious ball.

"Oh no, Phantom, please be okay. C'mon, don't be dead, the pack can't stand another loss." An ear placed on his ribs detects a gentle heartbeat. She hears slow rattly breaths struggling in and out of tortured lungs, "Thank The Great Forest Spirits. You're gonna be okay, Little One." Nikita stands and looks in the direction she came from. Wind swirls smoke about. When it clears, she feels as if the ground drops out from under her. She hits her knees, wide eyed at the sight before them. A four foot high wall of flame surrounds the two strays.

"Nikita . . . . Nikita, where are you?" Athena bobs her head, looking for an opening in the black and white wall around her, "Damn it, Demon, pass the word to your father. Nikita is missing."

Athena's news hits Demon like a club to the head. Being pack nanny, Nikita holds a special place in everyone's heart. He sends the message down toward the far end of their search line.

Thor calls a halt and comes running, "Did I get the right message? Nikita is missing?"

Pain and worry show through Athena's ash encrusted face, "I'm afraid so."

"Where did you last see her?"

"About five body lengths off to my left. She was well within sight. I looked right, and when I glanced back, she was gone. I've called and called, but I think the fire keeps drowning out my voice."

Fear and anxiety tug at Thor's heart, threatening to tear it in two, "Everyone, form a line stretching from both sides of your mother. We'll walk slowly, call together, and listen."

The wolves fall into formation. Voices reach new, higher pitches, ears strain for a response, noses filter scents from smoke, and the family hopes. Fear-induced adrenaline rushes sharpen their senses to an acuteness they've never before experienced. Nikita's faint worried barks reach them. They need all their restraint to keep from charging in for a hasty rescue. The family knows something must be very wrong; she doesn't get any closer on her own.

Thor comes up short at the fire wall. He catches glimpses of his daughter through the flicking orange flames, "Nikita are you okay?"

"I'm fine. I found Phantom, but he's unconscious. I think the smoke got to him. Stand back, I'll bring him to you."

"Nikita, no. The flames are rising and falling with the wind, they're too unpredictable. With the extra weight, you may not make it over."

Nikita grabs Phantom by the scruff of his neck and gets a running start. Just as Thor finishes his sentence, she leaps harder than she ever has, holding her nephew as high as possible. Halfway over, a gust of wind thrusts fire up around Nikita. Her belly hair bursts into flames. Dropping Phantom the instant she hits the black, barren, ground, she rolls around, trying to extinguish the fire that spreads up her sides and starts cooking her flesh. Searing heat raises then pops enormous blisters on her underside. A sickening smell of burnt hair and flesh meshes with stinging smoke. Her pain soaked screams wither everyone's souls.

Athena's maternal instinct kicks in the instant she sees her daughter astride the deadly hurdle. She rushes Nikita without any thought for her own safety and throws her huge body onto Nikita's, smothering the flames. She doesn't notice her own hair burn off in patches or the blisters that take its place; she directs all care and concern on her daughter.

Thor and the others thunder in, a flood of questions and admonishments pour from his mouth like a spring torrent, "Athena, are you okay? Is Nikita alright? Are either of you badly burnt? What were you thinking? You both pulled a very dangerous stunt."

Athena rises on unsteady legs, ready to drop on the first spark. Nikita groans and grits her teeth. Her entire belly shows one big popped blister. Clear fluid oozes from the deep red meat. Athena notices her lips moving and puts an ear to Nikita's mouth.

"Is Phantom okay?" Nikita asks in a smoke roughened, pain twisted voice.

"Yes, Daughter, thanks to you, Phantom will be fine. You are a hero."

"No, I'm not. I was scared sensless. I just did what my instincts told me."

"That's all any hero does."

"Shouldn't we get out of here?" Avalanche asks. He swings his head side to side, scanning their ashy surroundings, expecting an inferno to attack out of the smoke at any second.

Thor detects Avalanche's subdued fear, "I think we're safe. The fire has no feed here. We have time for assessing injuries before we do anything. We can't take a chance on hurting them worse by moving them too soon."

Phantom, groggy, sooty, and staggering, works his way past the crowd; his wracking cough precedes him. He walks on shaky legs and his lungs feel like they're full of blackberry thorns. Nikita lies on the ground, half comatose. He watches Athena's singed coat hover

over Nikita's burnt and blackened flesh. A pain-filled, guilt strangled whimper escapes his lips. Athena watches Phantom's heart break; the look on his face stabs her deep inside.

Sobs convulse his body as tears hit the ground, sending up puffs of gray ash, "Grandmother, Aunt Nikita, I'm so sorry. I didn't mean to get lost. The coyotes rolled me away from the group and I couldn't find you. I wasn't smart enough to detect anyone's scent in the smoke. You shouldn't have come for me, I cause nothing but pain. I'm so sorry. Please, tell me what to do. Tell me how I can fix it. Take Aunt Nikita's pain and give it to me. Please, Grandmother, you must know how. I don't want her suffering because of me."

Athena lifts Phantom's chin off his chest with an immense paw. She gazes into his tortured soul, "Grandson, you stop apologizing. You've done nothing wrong and have caused no one pain. You got lost because a scared pack of coyotes separated you from us. You were trapped in a ring of fire caused by humans and Aunt Nikita came to help you. That's what families are for. I understand you pain. It breaks my heart seeing Aunt Nikita burned and you hurting inside. The best thing we can do now is put away our guilt, help her to the brook, and cool her burns in the water."

Phantom brightens a little at the prospect of being able to help. Athena carefully lifts Nikita by her scruff. Phantom braces his aunt's side, keeping her from swinging and they make a cautious trek across the scorched ground. She soon lies in cool, comforting water. After licking ash from Nikita's wounds, Athena scoops mud from the streambed with her snout and applies it to he daughter's burns.

Shiloh steps forward, "Mother, someone else do that so I can tend your wounds."

"No, not until Nikita is as comfortable as possible."

At twilight, Shiloh whispers in Athena's ear as she watches over her daughter, "Mother, you may want to ask yourself how much of the speech you gave Phantom applies to you."

Athena gives her a weak smile, "You're right, I should put my guilt aside. I can't help feeling like I failed her, though. She was right beside me before I lost sight of her."

I feel the same way about losing Phantom, again. But, if we wallow in guilt and don't take care of ourselves, that guilt will be transferred onto our children. Please, let me help soothe your burns."

Athena sighs, "Very well"

Small eyes peek out from behind a boulder and watch the females walk toward another muddy spot downriver. Phantom hobbles along the darkening stream. He stares at Nikita's wet body lying peacefully in the shallow water. Her chest rises and falls in an uneven rhythm.

Tears build in his eyes, "Don't worry, Aunt Nikita, I'm here for whatever you need. I'll help keep you safe."

He squints as a gust of wind whips ash around them in a swirling cloud. He begins his all night vigil by pacing the stream's edge, watching, listening for signs of danger. A band of remorse wrapped around his chest squeezes exhaustion into submission. He vibrates, wide awake, ready to fight. His burning pain becomes a dull annoyance.

Downstream, Shiloh gets Athena rolling in a small pool. Soot, ash, dirt, and burnt hair, peel off her like a snake shedding his old skin. Its cooling effect on her burns, coupled with the cleaning of her wounds feels magical. When she gets out, Shiloh checks her over and licks off a few last remnants of crud from her injuries.

"Your burns don't look too bad, Mother. Would you like some mud on them?"

"No, thank you, I feel much better. If we travel tomorrow, I'll coat my wounds to keep ash out of them. Otherwise, I'll be fine."

"Okay" Shiloh dips her head, "What's your opinion of Nikita's condition? From what I saw, it's grim."

"Honestly, I'm not sure. She is in bad shape. On the other hand, she's a fighter and can beat almost anything out of pure stubbornness."

Shiloh chuckles, "That's true. She's the toughest little wolf I know. I've seen wolves twice her size who had half her tenacity."

A puff of ashy dust, followed by a scraping noise, snatches Athena's attention. She gazes into the darkness on the far bank. Thor materializes like a Great Forest Spirit, dragging an burnt antelope. Moonbeams highlight streaks of soot on his face, making him look like a battle-hardened warrior. He drops into the ravine and releases their supper.

Thor dons a champion's smile, "On the bright side of all this carnage, hunting is easy. We might even figure out why humans are so infatuated with cooked meat. We'll stay here for a little while and let you and Nikita heal."

Athena's heart rate trebles. She brushes against Thor in a suggestive manner, "You know something? Even after all the years we've spent together, you still make my blood boil with desire."

"Easy now, girl. You're hurt, remember?"

"You can't come around looking all hot and primal and not expect a reaction from me."

A surprised look blankets Thor's face, "All I did was find supper."

"Yeah, well your natural animal charisma gets me going every time."

"I appreciate the attention, but I don't want to get romantic and end up hurting you. I'd feel so guilty I wouldn't be able to perform ever again."

"Oh, all right," Athena sticks out her lower lip in a playful pout, "but I still say you'd enjoy it."

"There's no doubt about that, but I still don't want to hurt you. When you're healed, I'll treat you to a romantic romp in the leaves. Until then, I want you to eat and get some sleep. The sooner you're better, the less I'll worry."

Thor runs off gathering the family. Athena and Shiloh walk toward the pile of meat their hunting party adds to Thor's antelope. There are: two prairie dogs, one small deer, and a couple of skunks.

Shiloh inspects the smorgasbord, "Our hunters have done well finding this much meat in just a few hours."

"I hope it tastes okay. Most of it looks crisped so bad I can hardly tell what's what." Athena pokes the antelope with her paw. Flesh falls away, exposing stark white bone.

Shiloh wrinkles her nose, "I don't know about this."

"Me either. It has the same sooty odor on the inside as on the outside." Athena takes a tentative bite, swallows, then flicks her tongue in and out. "Yuck-eew-blahh. I have no idea how humans can stand this crap. It certainly destroys a good meal. It tastes like ash." She wipes a muddy paw over her insulted tongue.

Thor returns from upriver, followed by Harley and Ella. He scolds them over his right shoulder, "so from now on, when you two want to take a bath, do it downstream. That way, the rest of us don't end up drinking the nastiness washed off your coats."

"Sorry, Father" The youngsters answer in unison.

The whole family gathers around Shiloh and Athena. Thor nuzzles Athena, steps back, and sneezes. He drapes a paw over his nose, "Wow, your breath smells burnt."

"I tried the prize you brought us."

"I get the feeling I'm going to regret this, but how is it?"

"It's horrible. Make sure you wolf it down so you don't have to taste it."

Shiloh scans the crowd, "Where's Phantom?"

The wolves look at one another. Demon speaks carefully, "The last I knew, he was with you."

A storm builds on Shiloh's face faster than a mountain blizzard, "Damn that boy. He **will** learn to quit disappearing. One way, or another."

She tromps down the shore. When she rounds the corner, a heart wrenching sight greets her. Phantom stands vigil over Nikita's motionless form. He laps up cool water and sprinkles it on her side. Her head lies on a pillow of mounded sand. Shiloh's anger dissipates like fog in the wind.

She pads to her son's side, "Phantom, you should eat now."

"I can't leave her, Mother. She lies here in pain because of me. It's not right for me to take comfort while she suffers."

"I thought Grandmother already has this conversation with you. Besides, what do you think Aunt Nikita would say if she heard you?"

Phantom hangs his head and lowers his defeated voice, "That I should go eat."

"Don't you think she'd feel guilty if she knew you were skipping meals to care for her?"

"Yes"

"Then go have your supper. I'll watch over her until you return. Oh, and just a warning, it tastes like skunk crap, but eat it anyway. You'll need it to keep your strength up."

Phantom turns and walks downstream. Shiloh watches him, shakes her head, and thinks, "My poor Phantom. You're capable of such great things. If only you can cast aside the guilt and allow yourself to reach your full potential."

CHAPTER 16

Night proves itself to be more comfortable than day. Smells of smoke and ash wafting down the ravine haunt the wolves' sleep. Sooty acrid clouds, floating on every breeze, wake the lupines many times; a palatable fear of restarting fires hangs about them. Thor hopes Nikita heals fast, so they can leave before their taut nerves snap.

Athena struggles to her feet sometime before daybreak. Singed spots in her coat burn and itch, "I guess I've got more blistering than Shiloh told me about. Not that I would've worried about it anyway." She does some cautious stretches, relieving her overtaxed muscles, and prowls in silence to check on Nikita.

Nikita lies close by camp, so she can be watched and cared for more easily. She rests in the cool trickle of water flowing by as it dances around stones jutting out here and there on its way to the sea. Phantom lies beside her. Athena can tell he's helped her roll over. A load of helplessness sits hard on her shoulders, weighing down her spirits, "Poor dears. They must be in so much pain. I have no doubt that Phantom's inner pain bites as severely as Nikita's outer. They share a lot right now. I hope Nikita can nurse away Phantom's suffering as well as he eases hers."

Tears meander down Athena's cheeks as she makes her way back to bed. Grunts and snores let her know the family gains some much needed rest. She scans each member, searching for tell-tale signs of nightmares. She sighs at the prevalence of whimpers and moans then lies down and drifts into troubled sleep.

Dawn breaks in ominous silence. No birds sing, no grasshoppers flit about, even the wind doesn't dare stir this absolute quiet. A gray-blue haze tops the mountains like a winter cap. Thick burly rain clouds creep in from the south; a waking Father Sun paints their bellies deep red and their edges fiery orange. A blanket of humid air smothers all creatures' energy.

Light tremors in the ground snap Thor awake. Nervous senses warn him of danger. He jumps up, leaps out of the gully, and scans the area. Distant thunder rumbles, its notes tickle his bones. Father Sun fights a losing battle against building rain clouds; meager daylight drowns in twilight. Lightning strikes somewhere near the mountains. Its vibrations reverberate through the earth.

Thor dives back into the streambed, "Everybody up, we need to find cover."

Athena rises onto her forelegs, sleep heavy in her eyes, "What-huh? Thor, what's going on?"

"There's a storm coming, we've got to find shelter."

"It's just rain, we won't melt." Athena slumps to the ground, flops her head down, and closes her eyes.

Thunder booms, sheet lightning crackles and sizzles over the prairie. Thor's hair stands on end; he can smell searing electricity in the sir, "This will be more than just s little rain. This storm is nasty. I don't want us caught in it."

The wolves rise slowly. Strain from fire, losing track of Phantom, plus Athena and Nikita's injuries has drained them. Outlaw and Goddess stumble around like newborns, run into each other, then plop their butts in the water. Their heads hang upon their chests as if they'll fall asleep at any moment. Lightning hammers the prairie. Its bright flashes are blinding even behind closed eyes. The ensuing thunderclap jolts the ground like an earthquake.

Demon leaps up, staggers, shakes his head to clear away the sleepy fog, and tries rallying the pack, "C'mon, everyone," he pokes Harley with his snout, "Father wouldn't be nervous for nothing. Can't you smell the heavy rain?" He smacks Ella with his paw, "Ella, get up."

Shiloh rouses her pups, "Up and at 'em, this is no time for dragging your butts." Getting no response from Goddess or Outlaw, she nips them in their front shoulders.

"Owww-we're awake, we're awake." They cry in unison.

Phantom helps Nikita stand. She blinks and stares off in an incoherent daze, "What, what's going on?"

"It's okay, Aunt Nikita, I'm right here. Grandfather wants us to find cover, there's a big storm coming."

"You're a good boy, Phantom. How are you feeling this evening? You're not still sad are you?"

""It's morning, and I'm fine. Come, we must be ready when Grandfather gives us the word."

"I'm ready, all I need is you steadying me. I'm a little weak. I think my leg fell asleep from lying on it. Where are we going?"

"All I know is we are looking for shelter."

"Your grandparents know best, follow them and you'll turn out fine."

"Okay, Aunt Nikita. Now please hush, we must listen to Grandfather's instruction."

Thor whips out his last minute plan, "Demon, Avalanche, go downstream, one on each side. Mother and I will go upstream. I want someplace where we can get out of the rain. Stay in the ravine, I doubt we'll find anything out on the flats." Thor looks at the darkening sky. A huge blast of wind, carrying ash and debris, forecasts a taste of the storm's fury. "Hurry, I have a feeling we're running out of time, fast. The rest of you stay here, but be ready to move in an instant. Nikita, can you make a quick exit?"

"Yes"

"Good, let's get on with it."

Shiloh gazes at Nikita, doubt on her face as conspicuous as Father Sun in a cloudless sky. She can't stand unassisted; she leans on Phantom so hard his knees quake under the strain. Nikita's eyes seem dim, her attention wanders from the conversation to lightning flashing overhead, to dust devils made of soot and burnt leaves winding their miniature tornado paths along the stream, to Phantom.

Nikita sounds lost, "Phantom, are we traveling again?"

"No, Aunt Nikita, we're finding a place to ride out this storm."

"That's good, the air smells wet and electrified. Dangerous combination. We could get struck by clouds."

Shiloh licks Nikita's nose, "Your fever is back. Maybe you should lie down and rest."

"Oh no, I'm fine"

"Your nose feels dry and hot, that means fever. Fever can lead to delirium. We sure don't want you wandering around in a daze. Please, lie down while we search for a safer place, take a drink, and rest."

"Very well, if you insist."

"I do"

Nikita collapses in a heavy heap. Lying on her belly, she stretches her neck toward the stream, and sips cool soot-tainted water. Her vision darkens until even blinding lightning flashes can't penetrate it.

Demon and Avalanche trot downstream, studying the banks for shelter. So far, they've had no luck. Loamy soil doesn't make for good shelters. It can withstand narrow cuts, but anything deep sends it crashing into the water.

Avalanche squints. A dark cylinder against the far bank, well away from the water builds hope in his strained spirit, "Demon, what is that?"

"I believe it's a fallen tree."

"I didn't think there were any trees in this open emptiness."

"Probably the last one."

"The hollow under it big enough for a good shelter?"

"Even if it were, it's in a bad place. The rain will raise the water level. It doesn't have far to go before we'd be flooded."

"I guess you're right. Let's keep looking."

"If we don't find something soon, we'll have to rejoin the others and hope Mother and Father find suitable cover."

Thor and Athena get discouraged. They walk 1/4 mile along rising banks and don't find a den. Fearsome clouds bear down on them. Flashes of sheet lightning seem closer. Thick static raises the fine hairs on their backs. Thunder rumbles and snarls louder with each outburst. Darkness settles in deeper by the minute. Athena's gaze wanders across the sky and down toward Thor on the opposite shore. Even though she's trying to stay positive, worry creeps into her heart.

"Thor, we've been a long way, maybe we should go back and see if Demon and Avalanche have found something."

"Let's go a little further, I want to make sure we've exhausted all our possibilities before we give up."

They round a switchback and Athena sees a tumbled boulder lying at the foot of the high inner wall, "Thor, up ahead. The hole above that rock could be just what we're looking for."

"I hope so. The stone will protect the soil under the den from erosion in case the water gets violent."

Dirt covering the rock forms a steep ramp on the downstream side. The pair scamper up its slope, stand on either side of the opening and peer inside. Past floods extended the cavern to twice its original size leaving plenty of room for the family. A mat of interwoven grass roots holds up the ceiling; even if the soil gives out, these roots will prevent a quick cave-in, allowing more escape time.

Thor's acute vision picks out every detail in seconds, "Except for the soft soil, this is perfect. Let's go get the others and move in here quick."

They hurry back to their family. Demon and Avalanche trudge upstream; they look dejected. Harley and Ella pace alongside Goddess and Outlaw. The upcoming storm keeps increasing everyone's agitation. Phantom and Nikita are the only ones unfazed by the impending weather. Nikita hovers halfway into her own little world and Phantom focuses his attention on her care.

Thor raises his voice over constant pounding thunder, "Mother and I have found a decent shelter. If we hurry, we might get under cover before Mother Nature unleashes her fury."

The wolves strike off for their new den as fast as Nikita can go. Phantom and Outlaw trot on either side of her, ready to catch her should she stumble.

"Don't wait for me, Boys, you'll miss supper. Run along, I'll catch up."

"It's okay, Aunt Nikita," Phantom's soothing voice comes out soft as rabbit fur, "we enjoy walking with you. Besides, you've spent so much time caring for us, it's about time we return the favor."

Nikita reaches the dirt slope just as the black clouds dump their burden. Paw sized raindrops hammer all around her. In the few minutes it takes to hobble up the ramp, she and her escorts get soaked. They give their bodies a vigorous shake, expelling most of the water in their coats before entering; Nikita shuffles in still dripping wet. A cloud of wet fur odor hangs heavy in the humid cubby-hole. Relieved, the wolves settle down. Their fatigue pushes them beyond performing their pre-bed circles. They plop down where they are, stretch out, and let their adrenaline rushes fizzle out. Stifling heat, mixed with a mind dulling staccato of rain on the roof, lulls the pack to sleep.

While the wolves search for shelter, an old beat-up Chevy pick up hammers and rattles over the prairie; an ash cloud marking its progress rises skyward as two humans race on in reckless abandon.

From its passenger seat, John studies what little bit of sky he can see, "Damn, Paul, we're gonna git soaked."

"Not if I cin hep it."

"Well don't git us in a wreck. I tolt Ma we shoulda waited ta do a garbage run. Now we'll probly git struck by lightnin'."

"If'n we hurry, we cin beat it. We're at the dump site now, all we gotta do is unload like madmen."

Paul whips his truck around and backs to the edge of a steep bank. Below lies a struggling stream choked by garbage, dead refrigerators and miscellaneous human discharge in a pile almost reaching the top of the bank. Thunder cracks and lightning sizzles.

Walking toward the truck's rear, John's heart leaps into his throat while his knees go weak, "Damn, I hate lighnin', 'specially when I'm the tallest thin' around. I make too gooda target."

"Then let's haul ass and git unloaded."

Paul drops the tailgate and both men jump into the bed. Green garbage bags flash by Paul's head as John heaves them out with all his might.

Paul stands back and scans the refuse pile with a critical eye, "It's 'bout time we git a big rainstorm. It'll wash away all this crap an' give us more room ta dump. Shouldn't hafta worry 'bout no more grass fires for a while neither. This last one come way too close ta the house fer comfort."

"You gonna hep me unload our you gonna run yer trap?"

"Alright, alright. Sheesh, take a Midol er sumthin'"

"Hey, I jes wanna git outta the weather 'fore I git fried or drowned."

John and Paul empty their truck in record time. Using their feet, they scuff out loose debris. A ground shaking thunderclap sends them scrambling for the cab. Raindrops half the size of a man's fist pound the windshield, turning its surface into a running quagmire. Paul instantly regrets switching on the wipers; they smear soot into an impregnable slime. He shuts them off until the rain cleans the goop out of his view, then drives cautiously back the way they came.

Water builds behind the garbage dam. As rain intensifies, small rivulets appear in every crack possible. Lightning flashes and thunder roars with an intensity that would send The Great Forest Spirits fleeing for cover. The blockade's front looks like a sieve once water reaches the top of its banks and starts spilling out onto the prairie. Intensifying pressure forces more openings; the dam weakens. Dark liquid worries its outer edges, an old dryer in the bottom shifts. Moving in slow motion at first, the whole dam soon plunges downstream.

A rumbling sound, much deeper than any thunder, catches Thor's attention. His head pops up and he strains his ears upstream; the smell of muddy, rotten water slaps his nose. It smells wrong in a big way. Alarm bells ring throughout his mind; something terrible bears down on them. Leaping upon his feet, he bounds to the lip of their den.

Athena pries open her sleep laden eyes. She pushes herself into a sitting position, "Now what's wrong?" she asks with a mouth that feels as if it's stuffed full of leaves.

Thor spins around to face his family, "We must vacate, **Now.**"

The volume and tone of his order wrenches the others from their dreams. They stand on instinct, but pins and needles poking their sleeping legs send some crashing to the floor. Thor circles his group, motivating them with light nips. He looks at the tiny stream on his way by; it's not tiny anymore. In a few short minutes the stream has become a creek. The water rises at an alarming rate. Soon it'll be a raging river.

Frantic, Thor screams, "Move, move, move, get out now. Climb to the top of the bank. We'll be flooded at any second."

A thundering wall of water ravages its way down the streambed. In narrow places, it spreads over its banks, stretches wide hands onto the prairie, and flushes unsuspecting victims from their burrows. Before they can recover, it plucks them from the mud and immerses them in a watery death. Bottlenecks also build pressure behind the wave. Dirt rips away in large chunks, sods and stones tumble like marbles in a washing machine. What few shrubs still cling to the banks are torn from their strongholds with the ease of a robin pulling worms. The roiling mass thickens into a muddy black soup. Debris and carcasses swirl in a kaleidoscope of death.

Avalanche feels the ground shake as he helps Nikita stand. Thor bellows at everyone to move faster. Phantom steadies Nikita, keeping her from crumpling into a heap. She has taken a turn for the worst; her fever burnt eyes squeezed to mere slits. Phantom and Avalanche shuffle her toward the outside. She stumbles and leans hard on Phantom's exhausted shoulder. Avalanche sees the strain on his face.

"Phantom, go. I'll help Nikita."

"I won't leave her."

"You've barely strength enough for saving yourself. I can handle it, get out."

"I won't leave her."

"Alright, fine, I don't have time for arguments."

Thor's twisted nerves vibrate him almost senseless. He can't help with Nikita and having just harried the others out, there's nothing left for him to do. He paces their entrance, watching the water rise, "Come on, you two, step it up. We don't have anymore time."

The liquid devastation rumbles nearly loud enough to drown out Avalanche's words, "Go, Father, we're right behind you."

Thor leaps atop the bank, Avalanche and Phantom struggle moving Nikita faster. Near the brim, she sags.

Athena looks upstream and notices the great surge pounding down upon them. She screams at the top of her lungs, "Run, run, run."

The wolves make a mad dash out of the hammering mass's way. Avalanche slips behind Nikita and heaves both her and Phantom out. Thor grabs Nikita's scruff and lifts her feet off the ground. Scrabbling, Phantom snags her tail, holding up her back end; the trio stumbles away.

Avalanche twist his foot while lifting Nikita and Phantom. He rolls back down the ramp-way then scrambles to his feet and does a three legged hop toward the lip of the bank. He never sees the great murky tide slam into him. A giant muddy hand slams him downstream. He rolls in the turbulence and loses his sense of direction. He fights toward what he hopes will is the surface; he finds a stone strewn bottom. Panic jams a splintered, thought-killing stick deep into his mind. He spins around and makes another desperate dash. His oxygen starved lungs shrivel inside his chest, replaced by two molten stones of pain. With no visibility in the murky morass; Avalanche can only hope he's picked the right direction this time. His mind drains, muscles tire, and he reaches the verge of surrendering to the deep sleep of death. All hope vanishes. His body makes one last involuntary push then he bursts into the world, weak as a newborn. He pants and gasps, fighting for breath. He tips his head back, barely keeping it above water. Fresh air somewhat replenishes his tortured body. The river bounces, whirls, and whips him around. Avalanche spies land as he spins out of an eddy, turns toward shore, then dog paddles with all his might.

A square timber charges along the swollen stream like a charging ram. It hurtles after Avalanche with a purpose. He catches movement in the corner of his eye and turns his head; t A deep resonating crack rings deep in his ears, an explosion of pain erupts in his skull then the world blacks out. The 6x6 deflects off his head and barrels downstream, hunting more victims. Avalanche's limp body floats at the water's mercy.

———————————————

Demon turns around from their retreat across the flats in time to see his brother swept away. Shock pushes him into a single-minded mission for saving Avalanche. Demon's whole being immerses itself in the tunnel vision of a twin's love. He splashes across the mire that seconds ago was prairie, screaming at the top of his lungs, "Avalanche, Great Forest Spirits, no-o-o."

Athena drives her head into his ribs on the third bound, knocking him down and forcing all the wind out of his lungs, "You can't go back there now, you'll get taken away too." Tears stream down her face in a flood rivaling the one they just escaped.

Demon lies shuddering in sticky mud, "Let me up, I have to save him, he's drowning."

"We must approach with cautioun."

Demon's stomach knots, "Mother, Ple-e-ase, let me help him."

"We'll handle it, don't worry."

Stress overpowers him; it spews forth in a heart wrenching cry.

Athena chokes on sobs, "I'm sorry, Son, but I can't risk losing you both."

Thor and Phantom ease Nikita down into the mud beside Demon whose anguished howl brings her back to the edge of consciousness, "Huh, what, what's happening?"

Phantom lies beside her, licking her face, "It's okay, don't worry, we just had to leave the den. Rest now, you will need your strength later."

Nikita settles her head on Phantom's shoulder and drifts into oblivion. The flood's rumble yields to the boom of thunder. Lightning snaps and crackles; high voltage fingers fry the air as they strain to reach the ground. Static leaves a tingly metallic taste in the wolves' mouths. Rain intensifies until it's a solid sheet of water beating the terrain into a cauldron of muck.

After the flood's initial fury calms a little, the family slogs through knee-deep water toward the stream's edge. Phantom stays vigilant at Nikita's side. Thor left Goddess and Outlaw the task of preventing Demon from charging downstream while the rest attempt a rescue. The pack proceeds with caution; the murky liquid allows no distinction between prairie and stream. Trees, popped like blackheads from the distant mountain's face, rush past. Their branches stick out like gnarled hands, threatening to snatch anyone who gets close into a watery death.

Demon paces a circle around Phantom and Nikita, "Damn Father, I should be helping. Avalanche is my brother. Why am I left as nurse maid?"

Outlaw answers, timid and nervous, "Easy, Uncle, Grandfather said you are too emotional for the search. He fears you will put yourself at risk by dashing into a dangerous situation."

Demon's eyes widen until they look like they'll pop out of his head. He stomps over and stands nose to nose with Outlaw. His lip curls up in a snarl, "Why shouldn't I dash in and save my brother? I would give my life for him."

Goddess' sweet gentle words float past Demon's rage, "Because, if you get injured or killed saving him, Uncle Avalanche will be crushed by guilt."

Demon's vision turns watery Outlaw's image doubles then triples. Demon drops head, "I suppose you're right." He resumes pacing slow circles around Phantom and Nikita, keeping his face away from the others lest they see his tears.

———————————————

Thor spots an odd looking lump atop a rock at the rippling water's edge. His heart hammers his ribs in anticipation.

Athena whispers in a quavering voice, "Is that him?"

"I hope so."

Thor works hard restraining himself from barreling through the quagmire to reach his son. An emotional outburst in this situation will have disastrous effects. The pain of seeing Avalanche lying helpless on a rock cuts a jagged slash in his soul. Sounding calmer than he feels, Thor calls out, "Avalanche, can you hear me?"

On top of the boulder, Avalanche hears a voice echoing from miles away. It's familiar, but he can't quite place it. The world swoons and sinks; his hind foot hangs in a cold sloppy morass flowing all around him. His island lies embedded in the lip of the stream bank. Swirling water eats at soil supporting the haven. A hole forms under it and his rock creeps toward the rushing water.

Thor detects a shift in Avalanche's position, "We've got to hurry, that stone is slipping into the stream. If it tumbles Avalanche into this torrent, we'll lose him. Harley, Ella, you two are our strongest swimmers. Do you think you can get him?"

"Easy as falling off a log, Father."

"Don't get cocky, Harley. There could be ankle breaking holes hidden anywhere between here and there. You must also be careful of the bank. The current could've undercut it, making it weak and dangerous. Be prepared to fall in and swim hard at any moment. Don't let this flood take you by surprise and drag you away."

Harley's arrogant grin falls from her face. Fear bubbles in her chest. Ella's calm assurance renders stability to Harley's wavering confidence, "We can accomplish anything as long as we work together."

Avalanche's haven continues inching into the water. His front legs rest draped over the top, preventing him from sliding into the soup. Muddy water covers his hind legs to the knees; there's not much time left before the pack loses him.

Harley and Ella take cautious steps toward their brother. They slide their feet along, checking the footing before putting their full weight on the ground. Their legs quake, one misstep could be their last. They stand apart, so if one falls in a hole, the other won't follow, yet close enough for one to save the other if needed. Harley grows impatient with their slow progress. She takes two quick steps and disappears.

Ella's heart slams into her throat. Fear races through her veins, "Oh no, Harley." Adrenaline electrifies her muscles as she leaps toward hersister.

Harley pops up, coughing and sputtering, "I'm okay, I', okay. The hole's not deep.

"Damn it, Harley, don't scare me like that."

Angry currents pull stronger by the minute. Avalanche's rock shifts; he slides into the stream. Harley and Ella disregard caution and charge after him. Savage water pins Avalanche against the stone, for now.

Avalanche slides to one end of the boulder. Harley lunges across the last few yards to the stream's edge and stumbles in. She expends most of her strength in a mighty surge forward. She snatches his tail just as his shoulders enter the rapids. She fights a deadly tug-o-war with the swift torrent to save her brother's life and she's losing.

Through clenched teeth, she makes a desperate call, "Ella—help me—I'm losing—him."

CHAPTER 17

Bit by agonizing bit, Avalanche's tail slips from Harley's grasp. She braces her feet as best she can against the slippery rock. Every muscle in her body screams out in fiery pain. Tears blur her vision, but she stays resolute, "I will not lose you. By all the Great Forest Spirits, I will not lose you." Her heart twists when her feet slide to the stone's outer limits. Avalanche's unconscious body turns downstream. Harley fights an imminent sense of failure. Her exhausted consciousness wonders, "Where in hell is Ella? This is a fine time for her to turn chicken." Harley's drenched lungs beg for a reprieve; breathing through her nose draws in almost as much water as air.

Ella blasts to the surface, energized with fear and pulling Avalanche's hind leg. Relief and joy washes over Harley. Combining their strength, they drag Avalanche out of the white capped rapids. A milder current helps hold him against his unstable stone. Harley grabs the loose skin on his rump, Ella his scruff, then using all their remaining power, pull their heavy, sodden brother across the undertow. The rock rolls into the stream creating a miniature whirlpool in its wake; riptides reach out and grasp at the rescuer's heels. Harley's joy gets swept away by Mother Nature's newest trick. Dread quickly fills the void, spilling out from her overtaxed mind.

Horror stricken, Thor watches a frightening scene unfold. The raging stream slowly drags Harley and Ella back towards its killer current. They hold Avalanche fast and strain forward. No longer able to stand by, Thor rejects his own advice and splashes into the brown soup at top speed. He dodges floating brush and carcasses on the way to his children. He reaches them as the girls gain the streambank and their feet scrabble on its muddy walls. He latches onto Avalanche's scruff, just above Ella, and takes some weight off the tired heroes. He advances three paces when tough stringy grass, swirling it's long stalks beneath the surface like dancing herons, wraps around both front ankles. Thor stumbles and drags the others underwater.

Athena's heart freezes. She prepares a mad dive when they erupt out of the water's killer grasp in a plume of brown spray, hacking and wheezing. Harley and Ella plod toward drier land, dragging Avalanche to safety. Gritty water runs off them in rivers. As soon as Avalanche lies upon safe ground, they collapse in a heap.

Being held down brews boiling anger in Thor's belly. He grits his teeth and pulls with every ounce of strength he can muster. The grass stretches; its roots cling to the soil for dear life. A snarling roar spews forth from Thor's lips and he heaves again. The tenacious anchors tear loose, sending him scrambling for balance. He catches himself then wades over to his panting daughters, a strand of grass still wrapped around his foreleg.

Harley and Ella lie on their sides, Thor drops to his knees beside them, "Are you okay?"

"Yes—Father" they wheeze.

Thor looks at Athena as she checks Avalanche's condition, "How is he?"

Panic pours from her words, "He's not breathing."

Athena stands on her hind legs and drives her front feet into Avalanche's ribs. No response. She beats his chest over and over in a desperate rhythm. Minutes stretch out like hours. Athena's nerves tighten to the point of snapping. Thor sits by Avalanche's head, licks his face, and checks his breathing, feeling helpless. He ignores the steady throb in his ankles. Blood trickles through the grass tourniquet and runs between his toes.

After what seems like an eternity, he nudges Athena's shoulder and whispers in her ear, "It's no use, he's gone."

"No, I won't let him go. Come on, Baby, don't leave Momma. Come on, you can do it, live damn you, live."

Thor places a gentle paw on Athena's shoulder. Her determination breaks his heart; they've lost so much. Where will it end? Athena sobs outright while she pumps Avalanche's ribs. Thor can't stand to watch her suffer, but he can't crush her hopes of saving their son either. He opens his mouth, searching his mind for the right thing to say, when Avalanche coughs, sputters, vomits a geyser of muddy water and gasps for air. Shocked and overjoyed, Thor jumps straight into the air.

Athena licks Avalanche's face all over, "My Baby, My Baby, I knew you wouldn't leave me. I love you so much."

Avalanche hacks, gags, burps, and vomits more water. Thor slides his snout under Athena's chin and lifts her head, "Athena Dear, give the boy some air."

Avalanche opens one eye and rolls it about, "Where am I? What happened?"

Athena flips her chin off Thor's snout, "You're safe, Baby, Momma's right here. You fell into the flash flood, we thought we'd lost you. Harley and Ella pulled you out and almost didn't make it themselves. Father jumped in and dragged you all the rest of the way out, but you weren't breathing, so I jumped on your ribs just like Demon did for me." Joyful tears course down her face like twin waterfalls.

Athena resumes licking Avalanche's face, making him wheeze and gasp. Thor gives her a gentle push, "Let the boy breathe, Dear, you're smothering him again."

A thought blasts into Avalanche's mind; the urgency of it overwhelms him. He kicks and struggles, trying to get up, "Nikita, Phantom, did they get out? Where are they? We have to help them."

"Easy, Son," Thor reassures him, "they're fine. You pushed them out of harm's way at the last instant. They're waiting for us upstream." Thor looks in the direction they came from, "I take that back, here they come."

Demon charges to his fallen brother, "Avalanche, are you okay? I tried helping, but they stopped me, some foolishness about me taking unnecessary risks. Please say you're okay." He vibrates in anticipation.

"I'm fine, just a little tired." A weak smile crosses his face, "I know one thing, though, I'll never take a bath again."

Demon's anxiety melts and he flops down beside his brother. Goddess and Outlaw creep toward Thor on their bellies, every move a submissive gesture.

Outlaw gathers his last shreds of courage and speaks in a quavering voice, "We're sorry, Grandfather. We tried stopping Uncle Demon like you told us, but he got so worried about Uncle Avalanche that he wouldn't stay still any longer."

"Did you try your best?"

"We gave our assignment every ounce of energy and wit we have."

"Then you've made me proud. Uncle Demon can be hardheaded and worry pushes a wolf into throwing caution to the wind. You kept him out of danger and prevented him from fouling the rescue, so you accomplished your assignment."

The pups spring upright, throwing their chests out in pride. Thor looks over the gathered wolves, "Where are Phantom and Aunt Nikita?"

With the threat of a nipping gone, Goddess finds her voice, "They are on their way. Phantom said he could tend Aunt Nikita alone." She looks over her shoulder, "There they are."

A little ways in the distance, Phantom and Nikita tread a slow pace toward their family. Nikita uses Phantom as a crutch and stops several times; even this quick bit of excitement takes its toll on her. When they finally reach the others, she slumps to the ground, exhausted.

Thunder grumbles, lightning flashes brief and bright. Raindrops shrink as the storm loses its fury. The wolves, look like a bunch of oversized, drowned rats. Thor knows that, once again, they must find shelter. Avalanche and Nikita are far too weak for traveling fast enough to stay warm and if the canines don't get dry and warm, they all run the risk of catching colds, chills, or pneumonia. Joyous feelings generated by Avalanche's rescue, dampen with their next crisis.

Thor drops his head, "Will the curses never end?" He pulls himself back from the brink of depression, gives himself a vigorous shake, and addresses the others, "As always, we need shelter. The storm may be letting up now, but I don't depend on it staying that way. Besides, Avalanche and Nikita need rest. Until the mud dries a little, travel will be hard."

"When has it ever been easy?" Demon mutters.

Thor tries ignoring the snide comment, but his eyes betray an anger bubbling inside him. Athena steps in front of him; her soft knowing gaze quells his fire, "We've all had a scare, Love. Such stress can make young ones forget their place. I'm sure he means no disrespect."

"I know. I can let it go, this time. I won't let him make a habit of it, though. I'll lose standing in the pack."

"You've gotten us through enough by now that I don't think you'll ever have to worry about losing any of your standing."

"Perhaps you're right, but I'd rather not take a chance. I'll pass on leadership when the time comes. I'll not allow it to be taken from me."

"You worry too much."

"That's what has kept us alive all this time."

———————————

Father Sun sinks low on the horizon, dragging temperatures down with him. The pack embarks on a desperate search. They haven't had a chance to dry off properly; chills may soon start attacking. Demon finds a dead deer at the receding river's edge. Full bellies will help stave off cold night air while the family rests. After gulping down a quick meal, they resume their search. Despite extensive carousing, they can't find anything resembling a den. The wolves gather back at their leftover carcass. They shake as much water out of their coats as they can then the group works together, licking Avalanche and Nikita almost dry. Athena makes sure Thor chews the grass tourniquet off his foot, lest the appendage swell beyond saving. After every conceivable preparation, the lupines curl into tight balls and press close together. Athena puts

Avalanche and Nikita in the warm center; with luck, no one will get sick.

Thor and Athena rise at dawn. The sky smears a red coating across deep blue—almost black—clouds lumbering over the prairie. Night changes from cool to hot and humid. Steam rising off wet ground reaches skyward, forming a streaky mist that obscures their view.

Thor drops his front shoulders, holds his butt high, stretching his front legs, then reverses the process, limbering his hind end.

He fills his lungs with moist, balmy air, "Well, Athena, I was sure we would freeze last night. Now we wake to another stifling sunrise. Back in the hills, looking at a red sky like that, I'd say we were in for another storm, but the weather here is so freaky, I have no idea what it will do. It could rain, hail, snow, or kill us with intense heat."

"It makes planning anything a real challenge."

"To an aggravating degree. The only thing I can say with any amount of confidence is we have to find a few days worth of food and shelter. Avalanche and Nikita need convalescence." Thor closes his eyes and raises his nose skyward, inhaling deeply, looking for clues about the coming day, "I hope they heal soon. For all I know, it'll blizzard tomorrow. I'm about ready to give up on figuring out the weather here."

"You're doing fine, Love. Don't lose faith in yourself, you're a good leader."

Thor smiles and licks Athena's face, "I'd be nothing without you."

Athena feels a hot flush fill her cheeks, "Oh stop, you'd do fine on your own."

Thor's intense loving gaze locks her gentle brown eyes. In this light, she looks like the young wolf he fell in love with so many years ago, "No I wouldn't. You keep me grounded. If not for your steady strength, I'd have overreacted myself right into a human trap long before now."

The mates smile at each other, enraptured in the mellow intensity of their love. They nuzzle for only a few moments before angry voices break their spell. They turn toward the pack then see Goddess and Outlaw locked in a fierce argument.

Thor leans close to Athena's ear, "Well that didn't last long, did it?"

"It never does."

Outlaw rages at his sister, "You stole my bone."

"The hell I did."

"You were the closest one to me last night and you admired it. I could see the jealousy in your eyes."

"Why would I be jealous of your bone? We have an entire deer full of bones, you idiot."

"Thief"

"Take it back"

"Never"

Thor's voice cracks the air like a killing stick, "What the hell is going on here?"

The combatants give a start. Anger drains away when they see the rigid set of their patron's stance. His every line and contour speaks authority. They crouch, side by side, in submissive postures. Rolling onto their backs, urine dribbles from weakened bladders.

"I asked you two a question, I expect an answer."

Outlaw rolls onto his belly, but keeps his chin on the ground as he looks up at Thor's looming figure, "Goddess stole a prize leg bone from me."

Goddess springs to her feet, "I did not."

"Yeah, well where'd it go?" Outlaw snaps, careful to maintain his submissive position lest he incur his grandfather's wrath, "It was right beside me when I laid down. I woke up, and it was gone."

"I don't know, but it wasn't me."

"Stop" Thor's deep bellow shakes the quiet morning, "Outlaw, have you hunted the entire area? Your bone may have gotten kicked around in the night."

Outlaw's response comes out soft and respectful, "I have searched everywhere, Grandfather. She must have chewed it up."

"Come, Grandson, let's make one last sweep before we take any rash measures."

The fracas rouses the whole pack. Avalanche opens one eye and groans; just lifting his head hurts. One by one, the members stand on tired, stiff limbs. In slow motion, Nikita struggles to her feet. Her eyes appear sleepy, yet coherent and brighter than they were. She blinks, yawns, shuffles to Thor, and asks, "What's going on?"

"These two are fighting over a lost bone."

"What kind of bone?"

"Leg"

"I know where it is. I don't know how it got there, but it spent most of the night jabbing me in the ribs. It's still in my bed."

Relief and shame tangle in Outlaw's heart. His mouth flaps several times, but no sound comes out. He looks like a fish thrown onto dry land. Thor fixes him with a riveting gaze, "Well, don't you have something to say to your sister?"

"I'm sorry, Goddess."

Goddess thrusts her snout into the air, "Humpf, I told you I didn't steal it."

"From now on, Grandson, you need to be sure of your facts before throwing accusations around. Leave that sort of thing for chattering squirrels. It is beneath wolf dignity."

Tucking his tail between his legs, Outlaw retrieves his prize and drops it at Goddess' feet, "A peace offering, Sister. I let my short temper get the better of me, for that I apologize."

"You are forgiven, Brother. If you like, I am more than happy to share your bone." She picks it up, grins, and growls playfully.

""Ha-ha" Outlaw bounces left, right, snatches the treasure, and runs; Goddess hot on his heels.

Athena lays her head on Thor's shoulder, "If only all our problems were solved that easy, life would be simple."

"Indeed. We should check on our family, see if they're ready to search for a den."

"Let's start with you. How's your leg?"

"A little sore, but if the others can get around, so can I. How about you, My Dear? You're not exactly in tip-top shape either."

"I'm healing well and my coat started growing back. I'll be good as new in no time."

Thor scans his battered family, "We sure are a rough looking bunch, aren't we?"

"Yes, but we've got each other. We'll get by. Come, let's see to our family."

They separate and visit each member, taking plenty of time checking injuries and providing encouragement. By noon, Father Sun glares upon the world in merciless contempt, killing all shade. Surface moisture burns off; humidity presses in on them like a vise.

Mud hardens; soon it will be dust. The raging stream falls back inside its banks in most places. Its muddy roiling debris infested water will not be safe to drink for a while. The wolves lie scattered about—either panting or sleeping—in whatever somewhat comfortable spots they can find. Thor stares at a tiny dark spot about a mile south of their position. Athena watches her mate, enthralled by his quiet dignity. She sees no worry in his features, but his narrowed, intelligent eyes show that his mind whirls, hard at work resolving their latest problem. Thor sits for hours before his expression softens. Athena notices the change and settles beside him.

When their eyes meet, she smiles, "Piece of liver for your thoughts."

Seeing her brightens his mood further, "Considering the condition of everyone and the weather's unpredictability, I'm convinced we'd better rest for a few days. I'm sure we have more rough weather coming, so we need good shelter. The question is, where? I don't want to waste all our energy searching. I want us off this damn prairie. I think our best bet lies in that dark spot down there. It could be a rock, but my gut says it's shelter."

"Then that's where we should go. Your gut has served us well thus far. I trust your judgment." Athena studies the doubt in Thor's eyes. "Should I get the others?"

He hesitates, mind twisting and turning in on itself. Mistakes weigh heavy on his memories. Trepidation in his answer rings in Athena's ears, "Yes".

"Don't worry so much, Love. After all we've been through, we're doing well. Without you, we'd all be dead by now. Stop doubting yourself."

"I'll try"

"Don't try, do it."

A new confidence clears the clutter of second guesses from his mind, "Very well, gather the pack. We head for that shelter before any more storms beat the hell out of us."

Despite their bruised condition, the determined lupines quickly cover the distance. They slow their pace as they get into smelling range of their next challenge. The dark lump takes on a more defined shape the closer they get. It has sharp unnatural angles and a strange metallic odor. Sunshine glints off reflective patches near its top. Bright, clear eyes, round feet, silvery teeth marked by dark flaky spots, and large red dots on its rear, render it a familiar look.

Demon stands rigid beside Thor, hackles up, senses taut, "Father, is this one of the human's metal beasts?"

"Yes"

"Do we fight or flee?"

Thor looks at the sky. Strange streaky clouds bustle past; the light exudes an odd quality, making it seem out of place, skewed. He stares back at the metal beast, remembering their last encounter with one, "Back at that camp those humans we frightened used theirs for protection." He looks at his son, "Maybe we can use it."

"How?"

"We may be able to shelter inside it the same way those humans did."

Demon sniffs the air, "The weather is about to do something weird, isn't it?" His face conveys perplexed sincerity.

"You feel it too?"

"Yes, what is it?"

"I don't know. It feels like a blizzard and a thunderstorm at the same time."

Demon tips his head toward the metal beast, "Do you think it's safe?"

"I don't think we have much choice. We'll approach it as a pack. We can protect each other better in a tight group. If it attacks, we fight. If it flees, we let it go."

One careful step after another, the pack works its way toward this weird creature. A cacophony of odd smells confuses them. Hot rusty metal, old dry rubber, evaporated gasoline, congealed motor oil, and moldering upholstery are new experiences. Thor slips ahead and stands inches from the beast's ribs. Stretching his neck forward, he lightly touches the strange thing's side with his nose. He flinches backward on contact; nothing happens. He repeats this process, bumping harder and harder, until convinced it's harmless. Rising onto his hind legs, he puts his front feet on the beast's side; his nails click on a hard, clear surface.

Looking through a window in the old station wagon, Thor confronts foreign stimuli. Torn seats—grass sprouting from their foam rubber—smell rank and musty. A moss covered floor littered with assorted human waste. A faded dash, cracked from years in Father Sun's glare. He scans the rear cargo space. Then the front and rear seats; there should be enough room to fit his pack in relative comfort. It exudes strange and potent smells, but if they can ignore them, the family will have shelter. Thor drops and begins walking around the front.

Demon strides at his shoulder, "What do you think, Father?"

"It carries no human scent, so I think this beast is long dead. Let's inspect that opening on the other side then I'll do a careful exploration and determine whether or not we can use it for cover."

"Maybe I should take Phantom, Outlaw, and Goddess around the back. I think we should cover all sides, in case it is feigning death.

It will be confused if it decides to attack. It'll also be good practice for the little ones."

"Good idea"

Demon calls the youngsters. Phantom lies beside Nikita. Outlaw nudges him, "Come, Brother, let's join Uncle Demon for some adventure." The blank stare Phantom gives him tells Outlaw he'll never coax his sibling from Nikita's side. Outlaw trudges toward Demon and shakes his head at the older wolf's questioning look.

Downhearted at Phantom's absence, Demon presses on, "You two follow me and do **exactly** what I do. I'll give you a lesson on investigating something unknown."

Heavy rain tumbles from the clouds as Goddess and Outlaw fall in at Demon's heels. They mimic his approach of: step, smell; step, look; step, listen. Long minutes pass before they converge with Thor and Athena at the open door on the beast's far side. So far, they meet no opposition from the odd creature. Wind increases; the sky turns more ominous. Thor noses his way in while the others wait, on high assert, for his signal. He inspects every inch of the interior then gets out shaking his head and sneezing.

"It's safe, but it's dusty and rank. I have a feeling it's the best we'll find, though. Better get under cover."

The remaining wolves join their vanguard. They help Avalanche and Nikita get in the back. The two hobble into the cargo area where they can stretch out in moderate comfort. As always, Phantom stakes his claim at Nikita's side; the rest of the younger generations crowd onto the back seat and both floors. Thor and Athena crawl into the front seat as pea-sized hail, borne on an aggressive gale, begins pelting them.

Athena turns on their narrow seat and faces Thor, "I'm glad your sharp eyes found this thing. We'd be getting hammered out there.

I can't figure humans out, most often they're trying to kill us, but every once in a while, they leave something helpful for us. Why do you think they act that way?"

"I have no idea. I'd like it a lot better if they left us alone altogether. Life would be much easier."

"I agree"

Hail size increases to as big as a paw then half the size of a wolf's head. Wind rocks the rusting hulk; ice balls beat its metal in a deafening drum-roll. The windshield cracks and bows—spraying tiny glass pellets everywhere—yet holds fast.

Athena snuggles closer to her mate, "Someone angered The Great Forest Spirits. I've never seen a storm this furious."

"Probably humans"

Ella peeks over the back of their seat and stares aghast through the broken windshield, "Father, what is that?"

Thor follows her gaze. He shakes his head in disbelief at the distorted image before him. In the distance, raging toward them from the west, a black twisting funnel cloud reaches from ground to sky. It pulls trees from the forest like quills out of a porcupine then heaves them ¼ mile onto the prairie. The astonished wolves watch this spinning mass of destruction cut a wide swath through the woods. It emerges into the grassland, plows a mile long furrow, then dissipates as fast as it appeared.

Thor looks from face to face, "Now I know where my sense of foreboding came from."

One at a time the pack steps into golden sunshine. A bright rainbow smiles on them as they inventory the damage. A long brown furrow stretches through forest and prairie for a total of about two miles. In just a few minutes ice chunks covered the ground, caved in their shelter's top, littered its exterior with huge dents, and smashed out the rear window.

Athena picks her way over large ice cubes and peeks into the station wagon, "Thor look at this."

Thor tiptoes to Athena's side, "What?"

"Look inside"

Inside Thor sees Avalanche and Nikita lying side by side, snoring. He slowly shakes his head, "I don't believe it. Those two are so exhausted they slept through the whole storm."

Ella stumbles on the frozen riprap scattered about, "Damn, this stuff sure will make for hard traveling."

Harley sits gnawing on an ice block, "Yea, but at least we have clean water for awhile."

CHAPTER 18

The pack stays at their shelter for several weeks ensuring Avalanche and Nikita time to heal. As Nikita gains strength, she tries helping Phantom lose his guilt and resume the normal activities of a young wolf. It's a long and trying process; fortunately, the old nursemaid has plenty of patience. She spends hours on end talking with him, consoling his fears. His need for her support decreases each day until he can function on his own.

Their battered den serves them well. The wolves have plenty of room inside, yet it is small enough for their combined body heat to keep it warm during the increasingly colder nights. Thor and Athena are thankful for their lucky find when the weather turns more vicious and unpredictable than they've ever experienced. The decrepit vehicle repels rain, sleet, snow, hail, and high abrasive winds that thrash across the grasslands. During days when temperatures turn stifling, everyone lays under it by way of a short tunnel Thor digs out of boredom.

Now Thor wants them moving; he senses winter coming. On a few hunting forays, a couple of lone wolves take time to visit these strangers from the east. They tell about bone biting cold and wind that'll whip the fur right off you. Their stories detail a harsh survival in the prairie winter. At first, Thor has plenty of time for trading stories. The hail caught many by surprise; dead prey animals lie strewn everywhere. As his wolves use up this unexpected bonanza, they must spend more time hunting. Often, Thor goes alone, giving himself a chance to think, plan for their uncertain future. Other times, he either hunts with his pack or teaches his grandchildren the many skills they will need for survival. He also spends extra time with Phantom, trying to pull the youngster out of himself.

On a bright, cold morning, Thor's pack strikes out for the furrow of destruction left by the tornado. Dozens of grasses and flowers, laid over by an early snow storm, fill the swale; it looks almost healed. They peer through the woods and see a much different sight. Awe inspiring in its ugliness, a fifty foot swath stretches for tens of miles, peppered with jagged stumps and twisted piles of mangled trees. Tough prairie grasses and blackberry bushes have begun taking over.

Phantom speaks in a hushed voice, "What a waste. Why would the Great Forest Spirits wreak such havoc?"

Thor answers in a reverent tone, "I don't know. Someone, probably humans, must have angered them. However, The Great Forest Spirits never totally destroy anything. Although it looks like a barren mess now, in coming seasons this area will be teeming with prey for our brothers and cousins to live on."

Colder weather brings more than snow, for as the day progresses, the wolves spot humans. Thor rages, "Damn humans. Can we never get away from them? We have to go, tonight."

Athena pipes up, "I don't think Nikita has grown strong enough for hard travel. She says she is, but I've seen her limping when she thinks no one watches. Let's wait them out. We can hide in your burrow by day and hunt at night. The last person into the shelter at dawn can use their tail to erase our tracks."

"I don't like the idea of being around humans, but if Nikita isn't ready for travel, we must do something. Your idea sounds workable. Let's give it a try. If any humans see us, we leave."

Several days later, on a crisp silent morning, Thor wakes to the sound of crunching snow. Dim light cast through the den gives his surroundings a gray tint. He strains his ears and nose toward the intruder. It smells like an elk, but has the wide footed tread of a bear, or man. The realization sends Thor's heart charging into his throat. He races down a mental checklist, "Is the entrance covered?" He cranes his neck around behind him. "Yes. Did Avalanche erase our tracks?" He squints to try and cut down on the glare from outside. "I can't tell. Damn. One, two, three, four, five, six, seven, eight, nine, ten, eleven. Okay, everybody's still here." Athena stirs; Thor leans over and whispers in her ear, "Sh-h-h, I think there's a human coming."

Athena's eyes snap open and Thor hears a sharp intake of breath. He tries easing her mind, "Don't worry, everyone is accounted for. Our only concerns right now will be waking everyone quietly and whether or not we've covered our tracks."

One by one, the wolves wake. Thor sends around a whispered warning. He catches Avalanche's eye, the question of their tracks written all over his face. Avalanche nods and Thor carefully releases his held breath. Everyone listens as the crunching snow advances on their position. The older wolves pick human scent out of the fake elk smell. The intensity of the situation makes their small chamber very hot. They work hard at keeping themselves from panting. Ears ring, blood pounds, adrenaline makes every member quiver in fear and anticipation.

When the human almost reaches their hiding place, Outlaw slips into a low pant. Shiloh thumps him atop the head with her paw. His chin smacks the dirt floor and slams his mouth shut, just in time. Shiloh looks at the entrance and sees a boot. She chokes down the lump building in her throat. A rifle butt settles beside the boot. A soft grunt rattles through the air and a bright orange knee appears. The sharp taste of fear sucks the air out of their den.

The human huffs and puffs as if he's run for miles. A strange crackling noise rips the wolves' eardrums, followed by a sloppy, smacking, chewing noise then an odd smelling skin flutters to the snow. The man groans himself upright, heaves an exhausted sigh, and moves on.

Thor listens, his packmates' hearts slow to normal. The intruder's trudging footsteps fade. Thor wriggles to the exit and pokes his nose out. Scanning the area turns up nothing. He slides out, checks again, still finds nothing, then studies the strange skin shed by the human.

Demon slips out behind him and stands at his shoulder, "What is it, Father?"

"I have no idea."

Thor bumps the alien object with his snout and a brown crumb rolls out. A cautious sniff, "Hmmm, smells sweet. The human ate it, so it can't be poison."

Demon guesses Thor's next move, "Father, no"

Too late; Thor flicks out his tongue and scoops up the strange crumb. A sticky sweetness coats his mouth. After a small swallow, Thor licks his chops, "I don't know what it is, but it's good. Now that the excitement is over, let's get back to bed."

The appearance of more humans turns out to be a mixed blessing. The wolves are forced to spend many hours crammed in their small den; however, most of these hunters prove themselves incompetent, careless, or both. In the two weeks men spend bumbling around the nearby woods, Thor's wolves cash in on an elk and two mule deer; the former shot for his horns, the latter are wounded then lost. An added bonus comes in the form of new snow everyday covering their tracks. It's as if The Great Forest Spirits see the trials of Thor's pack and reward them for their courage.

Thor waits until human signs disappear for several days then leads his group into the forest; heading once more for the Land of the Buffalo. Thor's spirits rise, he's full of hope. During their goodbyes, his new friends told him they are closing on their goal. They should reach their new home in less than a week.

The woods stand silent. New snow scintillates in bright light thrown by a full, pale, Brother Moon. Millions of shiny stars perforate an inky black sky. Frost glistens on trees like a coating of glitter. The wolves' muffled steps throw up puffs of powdery snow. White clouds of frozen vapor drift over the line of valiant hunters.

Demon increases his speed to run abreast of Thor, "Do we hunt tonight, Father?"

"No, that's why I encouraged you all to gorge for the last few days. I wanted us prepared for this trip, so we can put as many miles as possible between us and the humans. I plan on running all night. If anyone gets thirsty, they'll have to grab some snow as we run, because I'm not stopping until dawn."

Demon delivers Thor's message to the rest of his family. He circles around Outlaw, at the end of their line, and speeds back toward his place behind Athena. No one grumbles about the order; they've been expecting something of this nature since the first human sighting. Everyone is well rested and ready for a good, long run.

Temperatures stay just right for travel. It's cold enough to prevent overheating, but not so cold as to burn one's lungs with frozen air. Thor doesn't overwork his family after their long convalescence. He picks an easy, steady trot throughout the night. The Great Forest Spirits have looked out for this brave group in more ways than one. Not only did they provide the wolves with plenty of food during their rest, the Spirits sent the tornado from the direction the pack travels. For the length of this furrow, Thor's wolves have ample shelter. Twisted deadfalls and thick brambles discourage human encroachment where as wolves can burrow through this mess with ease. Thor makes a mental note to thank The great Forest Spirits for their generosity.

Night passes in an uneventful, almost boring, manner. All human scents and tracks have been erased by cleansing snows. Tall, thick branched, spruce trees prevent Father Sun from entering the woods. Dawn doesn't make its appearance until late morning. The pack stops at the forest's border. Thor and Athena study a rolling meadow interspersed with clumps of forest.

"Isn't it beautiful, Thor?"

"It'll make a nice home. If what our new friends told us holds true, we should be on the edge of The Land of the Buffalo. We could see one any time now."

"What do they look like?"

"Something like cattle, except bigger, hairier, and harder to kill. The lone wolf told me a story of his pack's last buffalo hunt. They were foolish and attacked a healthy bull. That bull killed every one but the story teller. In order to have any hope of success, we must go after the very young, the old, and the weak."

"Won't it be safer for us to hunt the prey we know?"

"We may not have a choice. The great herds push all other large prey to their outskirts when they come through. If we want a stable home, we must learn to hunt buffalo."

"I have my doubts about the wisdom in that, but we'll cross that river when we come to it."

"And, as always, we'll do it together." Thor nuzzles Athena's ear, "Let's get some sleep."

They crawl into a gnarled pile of spruce trees and join their pack. The matted green boughs keep out most of the melt water working its way to the ground. The day continues warming at a steady rate. Snow makes a slow retreat; by evening, only scattered spots of white hide in shaded solace.

Dusk outdoes dawn's display of color. Reds and oranges coat the horizon in wide, far reaching bands. The outer orange streak, pastels itself into the soft blue sky. The young wolves stand enjoying Mother Nature's artistic flair.

Bright curiosity returns to Phantom's eyes. He turns to his siblings, "Hey, you guys, we've got some time before Grandfather moves us. What do you say we look around a bit?"

Goddess and Outlaw gape at him in shock. Goddess regains her voice first, "Are you kidding? After all you've been through? Haven't you learned anything about wandering off?"

"I'm not talking about wandering away by myself. I'm suggesting you two come with me and explore a little. We don't even have time enough to get lost. C'mon, it'll be fun. We've earned a little fun haven't we?"

Outlaw perks up and grins, "He's got a point. We've all been so serious for so long, it seems as if we've lost our ability to have fun."

Goddess frowns, "As usual, I don't like it, but I'll go along. Maybe I can keep you two from killing yourselves."

Phantom jumps into the air, "Yes!" He bounds over to Outlaw, nips his brother's flank, and runs through the trees; Outlaw charges off, hot on his heels.

Goddess heaves a worried sigh, "I can already tell this will not end well." She follows her rambunctious brothers at a slower, safer pace. She finds the boys some distance away, playing and wrestling. "I thought you guys wanted to explore."

Phantom dashes away from Outlaw and knocks Goddess down. He bounces back, just out of reach, and stands grinning at her, "The idea is to have fun, Miss Snooty."

Goddess springs to her feet, "I'll show you snooty." She chases Phantom around a majestic spruce.

Outlaw joins the chase and a three way melee ensues. During their frolic, Outlaw rolls aside, evading Goddess' attack and crashes into a clump of small cedar growing around a fallen giant.

A sharp reprimand comes from inside the tangle, "Hey, quit wreckin' my house. What the hell is wrong with you?"

Outlaw jumps back in surprise. The youngsters circle the thicket, inspecting each and every cubbyhole. They find a huge cedar tree that toppled years ago. It pulled its root ball out of the ground, leaving a rounded stony hole on one end. Small replacements grow in every conceivable nook and cranny around their parent tree. The pups use their noses to find an entrance. Phantom gathers his courage then pokes his nose into the small hole. A sharp, eye watering scent burns deep into his snout. There's no comparison; it's the worst smell he's ever encountered. Being at the age of having more courage than brains, he continues pushing his way in.

He can't fit his head in far enough to see the foul odor's cause, so he calls out in a soft voice, "Hello?" He receives a cat-like hiss in return.

Phantom scrambles backward so fast he plows over Goddess. A small, black creature covered in white spots with a slim body and bushy tail strolls out of the hole. Stepping into the clear, this animal surveys his situation. The invaders form a half circle in front of him. He assumes a defensive stance, knees bent, leg muscles coiled. He turns first one way then the other, facing each trespasser in turn. He bares his teeth and snarls; building bravado stills his hammering heart.

He uses the brusquest tone he can muster, "Who are you and what do you want?"

Since the beast faces Outlaw, he answers, "We're part of a wayward wolf pack looking for a new home. We mean you no harm, Mr. Weasel, we are just passing through."

"Weasel? How dare you call me a weasel? I'm not one of those damned vampires. Do I look like a bloodsucker to you?"

"Well, kinda."

"For your information, I am part of a noble breed. I am a spotted skunk, not a dirty weasel."

"I'm sorry, but you do look a lot like a big weasel."

"Oh yeah? Can a weasel do this?"

The skunk raises his hind end off the ground. He steadies himself by spreading his front legs and putting his elbows down; his head keeps him from tumbling forward. Rolling a bushy tail down his back to his forehead, he points his rear at Outlaw then sprays strong smelling urine into the wolf's face. Outlaw's reflexes save his eyes. When the stream hits his snout, he clamps his eyes shut and dodges to one side. This foul liquid works like tear gas. His nose swells shut, his eyes water and he's having trouble breathing. He rolls around and pushes his face through the duff in an attempt to rid himself of the crippling smell. Five feet away, his siblings cough and gag. Phantom sneezes incessantly and Goddess vomits. Outlaw cries in pain, his nose feels like someone lit a fire inside it. No amount of rolling quenches the agony.

Phantom comes to his rescue, "Outlaw—cough, sneeze—over—wheeze—here—sneeze, gag."

Outlaw follows his brother's voice to the base of a spruce tree. Its thick needles hide a patch of wind blown snow from Father Sun's devastating rays. He drives his whole face into its cooling comfort. As the white crystals melt, it washes some of the debilitating stench from his eyes and snout. He even packs his nostrils full of snow. The cold numbs some of his hypersensitive olfactory nerves. It's a full ten minutes before he can speak.

Squinting at the skunk, he bellows in a nasal tone, "Why did you do that?"

"Cause you called me a weasel." The skunk jabs a pointy nose into the air, puffs out his chest, and stomps into the bracken.

Outlaw fumes, "Why you little . . . ." He charges after the skunk; a blind fury in his brain screams for vengeance.

Goddess blocks the entrance, "Outlaw, don't."

He stops and stares his sister square in the face, biting on his anger, "Get out of my way, Goddess. I'm going to teach that insignificant vermin a lesson in manners."

"Outlaw, think for a minute. If he can hurt you in the open, what do you think he'll do if you go smashing into that tiny hole? He knows what's in there, you don't. Being small, he can move in a cramped area better than you can. He could blind you, scratch you, bite you. Hell, he might even give you rabies."

Outlaw unlocks his rigid muscles as Goddess's wisdom seeps into his mind. He sits down and rubs his snout with a foreleg. "I hate to admit it, but you're right. I'd be at a huge disadvantage in there. For all I know, he's got an entire family waiting for me. They could do some serious damage."

"Now you're thinking. Come on, we'd better get back. I'm sure Grandfather wants to get moving before it gets much darker."

The three adventurers intend on getting back unnoticed. It doesn't work. Their relatives smell them long before they return. Shiloh stops her children a short distance from the pack. She sits as close as she dares and covers her nose with a paw. She sounds like she has a bad head cold, "What have you three gotten into?"

The adolescents hang their heads. Outlaw speaks up, "It said it was a spotted skunk."

"Why would you tangle with a skunk? Didn't we teach you better than that?"

"He didn't look like any skunk I've ever seen."

"You should've been able to smell him."

"We smelled something rank, but couldn't determine what it was,"

"Well, you'll have plenty of time to become acquainted with skunk scent. It could take weeks for that stench to wear off."

"Can't we somehow dull it a little?"

"No"

Thor walks up behind Shiloh, "Until the stink wears off, you three will stay separate from the rest of us. If any of that odor gets on a hunter, he can't sneak up on prey. They could smell him for miles. Every animal in the forest avoids skunks."

Thor and Shiloh walk away sneezing. Between bouts, Thor whispers, "That's one lesson they'll never forget."

Deep in a dark, moonless night, frost tosses a white blanket over everything. Shishing, crispy, meadow grass plays a soft lullaby. The air smells fresh and cold; green trails in the grass mark the carnivores' progress. Sharp air gives the pack a reprieve from their odiferous youngsters. Shiloh's pups get no break; the skunk scent sticks on them like pine pitch, so overpowering in its intensity that their eyes water constantly, blurring their vision. If not for frost making tracking easy, they would have a hard time following their family. A light wind picks up, blowing frozen crystals into their faces. Its cooling effects are a welcome treat for sore noses.

Up ahead, Thor stops and drops to his belly. An old, familiar scent alerts his senses. It worries him, it could mean trouble. Slipping forward, silent as a ghost, and laying his ears flat, he peers over the top of a knoll. He sees a wide, deep bowl covered in lush greenery. Low hills on all sides protect this dip from wind and frost. Packed side to side, nose to tail, stands a giant herd of cattle. Two bovine sentinels low at each other. Thor slides away from the lip and trots toward his pack.

"A hollow lies packed with cattle on the other side of this hill."

"Cattle?" Athena sounds bewildered, "But, I haven't seen any fences, have you?"

"No. I don't like this at all. Cattle mean humans. I don't know what they mean with no fences or human dens, though"

"Why not hunt one?", Harley suggests, "Cows are easy targets and it may be awhile until our next meal."

Thor shakes his head, "I've never seen cattle outside fences in these numbers. It could be some sort of trap. It's not worth the risk. We're going to swing south and sneak past them."

The wolves creep to the knoll's base, follow it until they gain sight of the cows then work their way around this strange herd. The rise sweeps down into a gully where a huge scrub forest grows in its wet bottom. Tall grass covers the wolves' approach. At the edge of the woods, they find a four strand, barb wire fence blocking off the swale. Thor stops and scans the surrounding prairie; except for cattle, it's empty.

Athena's feet crunch frosty grass as she pads to Thor's side, "What the hell is this all about? Why would humans put a fence around a clump of trees?"

"I have no idea, I don't like it either. Demon, Avalanche, Harley, follow this fence south. Mother, Ella, and I will inspect its north side. The rest of you lay low and watch our backs. Get those youngsters further away so their new scent doesn't give us away."

The canines set out on their assigned tasks. Thor, Athena, and Ella creep along the fence, headed straight for the cattle. At the valley's entrance, cows have the grass grazed short.

Thor hunkers, turns, and whispers to his companions, "Stay low, be extra quiet."

They sneak into the open; bovines stir and mumble in their sleep. Every disturbance freezes the wolves in their tracks. They creep toward the middle of the low grass. An errant wind picks up their scent and whips it to the sentinels' nostrils. A loud moo warns the herd of impending danger. Sleepy cows stagger to their feet and pass on an alarm, raising the noise level to deafening proportions.

This ruckus wakes five humans sleeping in a camper on the far end of the dell. They clatter and stumble out their door in various states of disarray. Some with no boots, some in their long-johns, no one has a hat, but they all have guns.

One short man squints as he fumbles putting on his glasses, "Whaddya 'spose it is, Boss?"

A tall man holding a .308 Remington answers, "I dunno, 'spect it could be wolves, or a grizz. Spread out and circle the herd. Jimmy, git everbody a lantern or flashlight. I don't want nobody stumblin' onta a grizz or shootin' each other."

The betraying wind doubles back, carrying human scent to the wolves. A quarter of a mile away, Thor freezes. He casts his head about, straining all his senses to pinpoint them. Cattle mill around on the verge of panic. Some of the outer cows spot wolves and try pushing their way through the herd.

Thor reacts on impulse, "Quick, take cover. If they stampede, we'll be trampled."

The three dive between taut strands of barbed wire. Sharp barbs rake their backs, pulling out hair and leaving bloody scratches. Once they're out of sight, the fugitives crawl through four inches of snow and regroup under the short, close growing cedars.

Thor lays out a new plan, "We've got to meet up with the others and get out of here. Stay together so no one gets lost. We'll catch Demon's group first, then join Shiloh's bunch and vamoose. Be extra careful in here, these humans are keeping their herd out for a reason."

They move low and fast through the thicket. Thor fixes his senses on finding Demon. His concentration shatters when he hears a loud, metallic snap and Athena's agonized scream.

CHAPTER 19

Jimmy works his way along the left side of their herd. He stays just below the ridgetop; with no idea what they're facing, he's not giving them a silhouette to shoot at in case it's rustlers. His nerves twist as tight as fiddle strings. The bobbing lights on the far side of the dale supply little comfort. He doesn't like having Billy behind him either. That damn fool is drunk half the time and more apt to shoot him than anything else. Jimmy gathers his courage, focusing it on the Boss's light up ahead. He draws strength from the man he idolizes. He wipes his sweaty palms on his pants, shifting his .32 Winchester rifle from one arm to the other.

Jimmy searches every inch of the herd for hidden predators. Out of nowhere, the eeriest scream he's ever heard rips the night wide open. Fear pins his feet down, his blood turns cold, and his heart stops. Billy restarts Jimmy's heart by flinching at the horrifying sound and firing a shot between his friend's feet.

Jimmy jumps, letting out a blood curdling scream of his own, "Got dammit, Billy. What in the hell are ya' tryin' ta do, kill me? Ya friggin' idiot."

"Sorry, Jimmy. Thet screech scairt the livin' bajesus outta me. I guess I flinched."

Jimmy stomps back and starts smacking Billy with his fur lined cap, "Flinched? I guess the hell ya flinched. Ya damn near kilt me, ya stupid idiot."

"Ow, ow, ow, ow, cut it out. I said I was sorry."

Light from their leader's lantern lands on Jimmy's feet. He stops beating Billy and turns to face the 6'5" beanpole. The Boss hisses at them, "Will you two dummies quit the shit? We got sumpin', most likely sumpin' dangerous, in the swale and you guys are out here goofin' off."

"Sorry, Boss" the underlings mumble, looking down and shuffling their feet like children.

"Git back on track an' pay attention."

The boys know better than disobey. The Boss may look gaunt, but he possesses a surprising amount of strength and quickness. They've seen what happens when someone goes against their leader. Their answer comes as second nature, "Yes sir, Boss, right away."

The Boss uses his light, signaling the others to continue on their route. They slowly comply; no one looks forward to whatever lies ahead. Tension and fear ride the wind like late fall leaves.

Thor thrashes against stubborn bushes getting turned around. "Athena, are you okay? What happened?"

"It's my foot. Something bit onto it and won't let go. Aw-w-w, it hurts like crazy."

Ella crowds to Athena's side and sees angry metal teeth clamped on her mother's hind foot. She attacks it, biting hard at the base of the strange mouth. She hears a dull snap and pain flares along her lower jaw, forcing her to let go. "Ow, I broke a tooth. What in the name of The Great Forest Spirits is that thing?"

Athena pulls and thrashes against the offender. A steel chain, leading to a stout bush, reveals itself from under the snow. She shakes her foot, "Thor, it won't let go. Help me,"

The fear in her voice cranks Thor's brain into high gear. His nerves tingle with dread, "Hold still, let's study this thing a second, maybe we can figure it out."

"The humans are no doubt coming. We don't have time for studying."

"Thinking for a minute is better than chewing your foot off, isn't it?"

Athena sits down and sighs, "Very well, but let's hurry."

The rest of the family charges out of the brush. Avalanche's breathless words quiver with dread, "What happened? We heard Mother scream."

Demon inspects the metal jaws full of spiked teeth, clamped on his mother's foot. A man-made cord connecting it to a tree seems unbreakable. His thoughts fill with foreboding, "If Mother's great strength can not snap that restraint, what can we do?" His worried eyes meet Thor's grim expression, "What is that thing, Father?"

"A leg catcher. Humans use these to hold us in place until they can come with their killing sticks. Damn cowardly way of hunting."

"How do we release Mother from its grasp?"

"I don't know."

"What do you mean, you don't know? There must be something we can do."

"Don't you think if there was I'd have done it already? Now shut up and let me think."

Demon reaches forward to gnaw on the trap when Athena stops him, "That doesn't work. Ella already broke a tooth on this cursed thing."

Athena yelps and screams when Avalanche chews and tugs on the chain, shaking his head violently, all to no avail. Shiloh gnaws on the shrub anchoring it. Every movement sends quills of fiery pain shooting up the pack matron's leg. Harley and Ella grab either side of its jaws, attempting to pull them apart. Athena's foot falls asleep from lack of blood. Her wound throbs and burns as if she's been bitten by a timber rattler. Precious blood coats the leg catcher's jaws; a half circle around her injured limb wears a red spattering on its white blanket of snow.

Thor watches the activity, his mind calculating their failures and trying to formulate a viable solution. Ideas twist and slide through his consciousness. A shift in wind direction smashes his concentration. An ominous odor finds its way into his super sensitive nose. Humans approach.

The men reach their barbed wire fence. They grumbled like crazy last spring when The Boss made them build it, but he didn't care. He knew this was the best place for wolves to sneak up on his herd. He also knew this was a perfect spot to set leg-hold traps and didn't want any of the cattle getting tangled in his modified traps. The illegal spikes he welded on their jaws ensure that a wolf won't get away and would do a nasty job even on a cow's heavy leg.

Inspecting the wire, The Boss finds fresh hair and blood on many barbs. "Hot damn." he thinks to himself, "I'm gonna git at least one a the little bastards. I'll have ta remind the boys ta shut-up about this. I sure don't need no damn game warden stickin' his nose in my business." Using his lantern, he signals the men on the far side to circle the swale. He closes his eyes and says a silent prayer, "Dear God, please don't let any of these idiots shoot each other."

Handing Jimmy his rifle, The Boss places a hand on a post and vaults over the fence. Jimmy hands both guns over then copies the leap. Billy's jump comes up short; a barb on the top strand catches his pants leg and he falls flat on his face with his left foot hung on a barb.

The Boss shakes his head in disbelief, "Jimmy, will you help numbnuts here untangle hisself?"

"Sure thing, Boss."

"And hold it down, both a ya'. Ya'll sound like a herd a buffalo thrashin' around."

Billy, still hanging upside down whimpers, "I think I done busted muh arm. It hurts like hell."

Jimmy frees Billy and throws his leg to the ground. "Yer lucky ya didn't break yer fool head."

Billy drags himself to his feet, rubs his unbroken arm, grabs his rifle from where it leans against a post, and stumbles into the thicket.

Man's ugly scent assaults Thor's nose long before the commotion that a stone can hear reaches his ears. Knowing their time runs short, he makes a snap decision, "Demon, take the pack and get out of here."

"Wh-what?"

"I said, take the pack and get out of here. There are too many humans with killing sticks coming, we can't fight them all. I'll work on getting Mother free while you run." A hard lump builds in Thor's throat, tears blur his vision, "If we don't make it out, you have leadership."

The shock of Thor's words knocks the wind out of Demon's lungs, "No, Father, I can't. You're our leader."

Thor pushes his forehead tight against Demon's; he stares deep into his son's soul. A frightening rumble starts in Thor's chest, "Damn you, Boy, don't argue with me. You get your ass out of here, and you do it now. Otherwise, you'll have the decimation of our pack on your conscience. Do you want to be responsible for the death of your family?"

A tear forms in the corner of Demon's eye. He shivers as a cold wave of sadness blankets him, "No, Father."

Thor's tone softens, "Then gather them and lead them to safety. I love you, Son. I've always been proud of you." He turns toward his pack and uses his most commanding voice, one that leaves no room for debate. "Listen up. Follow Demon out of here and do exactly what he says. Mother and I will meet you on the other side of these hills."

The weight of their situation crashes down on the group like a felled tree. Sadness strangles arguments as Thor's heavy hearted family picks their way through the bracken. Nikita, leaving last, ventures a look back.

Tears roll down her cheeks and her lip quivers, "Please hurry, Father."

Thor and Athena listen to her soft sobs as she disappears into the brush. Thor wastes no time. He attacks the anchor tree, releasing some of his fear in a more acceptable, violent manner. Next he chews the chain hard enough to bend its links.

Athena's fear almost overwhelms her, "Thor, Thor, what are you doing? You have to get out of here, go with the pack."

"I will not leave you."

"I don't want you to die because of me."

Thor gives the deep gash on Athena's foot a tender lick then nuzzles her; love pours from him like a waterfall. It hangs around them in a bright nimbus. He gazes into the farthest recesses of her being and asks, "Would you leave me?"

Tears treble Athena's vision, "Never"

A twig snaps. Thor whirls to face five humans breaking cover in a half circle around the valiant mates. Thor hunkers, raises his hackles, curls his lip, and looses a bone chilling snarl.

The humans' bowels turn watery. The Boss keeps a tentative hold on composure. He masks his fear with false bravado, "Well looky here, Boys. Them's some fine lookin' pelts, 'specially on the big 'un. I could pritnear make a whole coat outta that 'un."

Thor and Athena stand tail to tail, watching the humans form a circle around them. They can't understand his words, but they feel the hate emanating from The Boss. Fear oozing from the other humans' pores mixes with The Boss's malice and charges the air with a disconcerting aura even the men can feel.

Knees shaking, berating himself for cowardice in the face of danger, The boss raises his .308 Remington to his shoulder. His heart hammers, rushing blood pounds in his ears, and his hands tremble as he puts the scope to his eye. Thor sits very still; all his muscles coiled as tight as over-wound springs. Inner vibrations of fear and anger heighten his senses to new peaks.

The Boss sucks in a startled breath and his heart stops when he gets Thor in the cross-hairs, "Jesus Christ, that critter's eyes is blood red. That just ain't natral." Terror immobilizes him.

Thor leaps; his trajectory takes him under the line of fire. He drives his head into the gun's forestock, sending its barrel straight up. The Boss flinches and pulls the trigger. The bullet sails over Athena and strikes a man facing her square in the chest. The lead tipped missile destroys his sternum and splatters his spine all over nearby bushes.

"Holy shit," Billy screams.

He turns to run and slams into Jimmy, who's shot gets thrown off, striking Athena in her haunch. She yelps in pain as the bullet's force knocks her legs out from under her, gets up, then hunkers close to the anchor bush. A man beside Jimmy steps in front of him to gain a clear firing lane. He raises his shotgun as Athena charges. She latches onto his crotch; his screams rip through the air like a dull circular saw. He grabs Athena's ears, and tries pushing her back, but she clamps down as hard as she can. First she hears cloth tear then blood pours into her mouth; its coppery taste excites a beast within her. She shakes her head violently, ripping off his genitals. The man sinks to his knees, whimpering for Mommy, as his life seeps into the half frozen ground. Athena spits out the offensive human meat and grabs a quick mouthful of snow to get its disgusting taste off her tongue.

Athena's pained yip drives into Thor's brain like rabid adrenaline. He attacks his fallen opponent with a viciousness seldom seen in nature; it's almost human in its hatred. The Boss screams for help as Thor's jaws snap like a threshing machine just inches from his nose. Fear pours into the man's blood like rattlesnake venom. He throws up an arm to protect his face. Thor latches onto the limb with an iron bite, crushing it with unforgiving force. The bones crack and shatter like dry branches. He shakes his foe senseless. Blinding pain immobilizes The Boss; he lies there, vacant eyes staring at purple and green stars floating across his vision. Thor strikes the man's throat. Blood sprays out in a crimson plume when sharp teeth slice flesh as if it is butter.

Athena pulls against the leg catcher with all her considerable power. She shakes it, jumps, thrashes, then pulls some more. Her skin peels away from the flesh bit by agonizing bit. The trap's red coating deepens; her pain fades away. Fear, anger, and a fierce determination to protect her mate block out all other sensations.

Billy and Jimmy recuperate from their stumbling long enough to realize that the biggest wolf they've ever seen is about to pull free. They both aim their rifles at her head, then fire. Blood and brain matter shower nearby brush. Thor turns in time to see his soulmate's last twitches.

Horror, heartache, and fury rush through him like stampeding cattle. His snarling howl freezes the men in their tracks. Thor's heart shrivels into a worthless black lump. He has nothing left to lose, vengeance becomes his only solace. Driven by unmatched hatred, he rushes behind these murdering humans, snips an Achilles tendon of the closest one, and disappears into the brush.

Billy screams, his rifle tumbles from his shock numbed fingers, and his knees unlock. He crumples into a bleeding, crying bundle of fright. Jimmy blanches at the sight of his friend's leg. Ligaments and bone show through a jagged tear pumping blood onto the ground.

"Hang on, Billy, you're gonna be okay, I'm right here." Dropping to his knees, Jimmy lays his rifle beside him, takes off his black, leather belt, wraps it around his friend's thigh, and uses it for a tourniquet.

"Damn, Jimmy, it hurts, it hurts real bad."

"Yer gonna be fine. I'm gonna git ya outta here."

"What about the wolf? Is he still out there?"

"Naw, I think we scared 'im off."

Jimmy gets on one knee, slides an arm around Billy's shoulders, and the other under his legs. He sees movement in some bushes to his right. A gray blur flashing sharp, white teeth bears down on him. He throws an arm in front of his throat just in time. Thor hits him with the force of a speeding truck, rolling him over. On impact, Thor clamps a vise like grip onto the human's arm. Blood flows into his mouth; it tastes of revenge. Bone disintegrates, grating and grinding in a joyful tune. Horrible cries from his enemy add a happy accompaniment in Thor's ears. He feels the power of vengeance course through him as he doles out payment for wrongs put upon his family; a kill for a kill. Pure hatred floods the wolf leader's every thought, every feeling. It creates an insatiable hunger for pain and suffering.

White hot agony erases Jimmy's mind. The wolf chews on his arm like a left over ham bone, mangling it beyond repair. His screams excite his attacker as if the creature gets high from inflicting pain. The wolf shakes its head, trying to rip off what little remains of Jimmy's right arm. He punches the crazed predator over and over; Thor doesn't even feel it. Blood loss drains Jimmy's strength. He can't get out from under this savage beast. In desperation, he reaches up, grabs its ear, and using the last of his energy, raises his head while pulling the ear down and bites as hard as he can.

A sudden, shocking jolt surprises Thor. He loosens his grip and the human pushes him off. He rolls and lands on his feet shaking his sore ear in bewilderment. The wretched creature tries scuttling away.

"Oh no you don't," Thor snarls, "You're not going anywhere." His leg muscles bunch as he crouches into an attack position. He springs with all his might. A loud crack splits the air just before a hard thump slams his left shoulder. It pushes Thor sideways in mid-leap. He crashes into a small tree and thuds to the ground; whatever hit him hurts like hell.

Billy rests on one elbow, teeth gritted, Jimmy's smoking gun in his shaking hands. Tears of relief build in his eyes. He watches the gray lump, making sure it doesn't get up again. The world gets dark; he swoons and drops onto his back.

Jimmy's not sure if this is real or a nightmare. It must be real, because he wouldn't hurt this much if he were dead. An alarming amount of blood drenches his coat. His arm hangs mangled and useless at his side, while his brain screams at him to stop the bleeding. Fighting a massive struggle, he rises into a sitting position. He keeps a wary eye on that deadly figure at his left. Scooting the few feet to Billy's side takes forever. Any movement sends fresh waves of molten agony up his destroyed arm. He checks Billy's pulse then pulls off his friend's belt and wraps it around his own arm, pulling it as tight as he can in an attempt to staunch blood streaming from the wound. Holding one end of the belt in his teeth, Jimmy turns his attention onto Billy's tourniquet.

The wolf stirs.

Thor's dark world becomes gray and fuzzy; it's as if false dawn approaches. His left shoulder feels numb and unresponsive. Breathing hurts, he feels like he's drowning. He turns his head and spots Athena lying limp and lifeless in a red pool. His physical pain washes away in a flash flood of emotional anguish. His soul withers and blows away like a dead leaf in a cold fall breeze. His whole life lies destroyed in blood soaked snow. Using his right leg, Thor pulls his wrecked body toward Athena. Shrapnel lodged in his left shoulder locks the joint in place. His hind legs slip on blood slicked ground, sending bolts of jagged agony ripping through him. Tears stream down his face as he gains his mate's side. Falling beside her limp form, he looks to the sky and cries a gut wrenching howl. The stricken leader settles his head across Athena's neck, whispers in her ear, "Wait for me Dear, I'm coming to join you." then, grimacing at the pain running rampant through his body and soul, heaves a blood flecked sigh, and dies.

Jimmy ties off his tourniquet while working to catch his breath, "I can't believe I'm still alive. Smashed to hell, but alive."

Billy groans and struggles to sit up. "Where's that psycho wolf?" his voice quavers in undisguised fear.

"Dead"

"You sure?"

"You cin hobble over an' check 'im if ya want."

"No thanks, I'll take yer word fer it. We best git to the camper or we're gonna be in the same boat."

Jimmy grabs a small cedar tree and cries out in pain as he pulls himself up. His head swims, balance falters, the world dims, then refocuses. He takes several deep breaths orienting his spinning head. Once his senses begin working the way they should, he helps Billy off the ground and they begin a slow, painful trek to safety.

CHAPTER 20

Demon paces, the pack gathers behind a short, brushy knoll. Anxiety coursing through his entire body radiates off him like a deadly fever, infecting anyone who comes near. He tramples a path in coarse, sharp smelling, swamp grass until the saturated soil squishes between his toes. He ignores both wet and cold. Everyone feels agitated, nervous, and unsure of what they should do next. The chilling crack of a killing stick echoes off nearby rolling hills. Demon stops, curses his helplessness, and paces again.

Shiloh tries soothing her children, "Don't worry, Grandfather and Grandmother are the craftiest wolves in the forest, they'll be joining us in no time." She turns and faces the direction they just came from, hoping her pups don't see the lie in her eyes.

Avalanche makes an attempt at catching his brother's attention as he paces by, "Demon, listen, we're not far enough away. Father wanted our pack well away from the humans. There will be hell to pay when he shows up and sees you've disobeyed him."

Demon stops, ponders Avalanche's words, then almost gives an order to go further when Thor's anguished cry rolls across the land. "That's it. Avalanche, keep the family moving, I'm going back, Mother and father need help."

The wolves balk, they gather around their temporary leader. A cacophony of objections assaults Demon's ears. He can't sort individual complaints, but the general attitude holds the same for everyone, "You may be leader, but we won't let you do this alone. We do what we should've done in the first place, we face those humans together."

"Alright, alright. settle down. I can't spare the time or energy arguing this issue, so let's make a quick plan. We'll return to the swale's edge, then spread out, and come at them in a semi-circle. Maybe we can scare them into scattering."

Cold, heartless moonlight casts an ominous glow on the meadow. Dark, stealthy forms slip along the woods' dim outer limits, taking advantage of its tall grass. Smells of blood and death saturate the air. Normal night sounds have ceased, adding a tinge of doom to the atmosphere. Pounding hearts batter rib cages and send blood hammering into overtaxed brains. This fear soaked setting makes thinking hard. Paws shake, ears twitch, noses fill with disturbing scents of death, and eyes water in anxious expectation.

Demon breaks out of the brush onto a gruesome scene. His stomach twists as if someone kicked it. His jaw drops. He stops breathing, his knees go weak, and his feet freeze in place. Gasps of disbelief and pained whimpers mark the pack's arrival. Their sense of loss hangs around them like a fog. The family encircles their dead leaders and cry in soft strangled sobs. Demon's shredded emotions congeal into something ugly. He sees the world through a red haze as his anger builds. He turns his head and his glare lands on a human body. Anger thickens into a black rage; he attacks the corpse.

Demon bites its calf muscle and shakes his head until meat tears free of bone. He heaves it into the brush then rips and tears the rest of the body with a frightening fervor. After stripping meat from its limbs, his powerful jaws crush the bones beneath. A bloody, mangled, unrecognizable mess lies at his feet. He severs the head, turns it face up and urinates on it.

Demon's hatred infects his pack. Even the youngsters attack corpses while engulfed in an uncontrollable fury. They rip open dismembered torsos and scatter inner organs. Arms and legs get strewn about the brush. When the wolves finish, they leave a halo of carnage around their beloved leaders The family sits, leaning on one another, panting. As their anger cools, pain slips in to squeeze tears from their eyes.

Demon steps toward his parents. His heart slowly crushes under the weight of his anguish. He grabs the leg catcher on Athena's foot, twisting and turning it to no avail. His teeth grate against the steel creating a high pitched squeal; the more he struggles against this evil contraption, the more frantic he becomes.

"Somebody help me."

Avalanche approaches his brother with great care, "Demon, we must go. When the humans see what we've done, they'll come for us."

"No, I will not leave Mother and Father to the humans. You've heard stories told by stray wolves about how humans pull fur off animals and save it as some kind of trophy. I'll be damned to hell before I let that happen to our parents. How can you even suggest leaving them? Mother and Father gave their lives so we could get away. I will not abandon them to such vile degradation."

"But the humans will come en masse. They always do when there is a confrontation between us and them."

Quick as a striking rattlesnake, Demon turns and crouches into a fighting stance. his eyes bloodshot from the power of his hatred. The fierce look in them forces Avalanche to take a step backward and suck in a surprised breath. Demon's voice rumbles, full of fire and ice, "Let the bastards come. Leave if you are afraid, I'll kill them all myself."

"Easy, Brother, easy. As you said 'Mother and Father gave their lives for us.' Let's not waste their sacrifice. I will help you in whatever plan you have for saving them from human defilement, but we must be quick about it."

Shiloh joins the brothers, "I want to help as well."

After several failed attempts to free their mother, Shiloh and Demon each grab a jaw of the leg catcher and pull in opposite directions. Avalanche moves Athena's leg clear.

The ice cold hand of guilt squeezes Demon's heart, "Damn it, why didn't I think of that sooner? I could've saved them." He forges through the swampy emotional morass, "Everyone, dig a clearing through these disgusting human remains so we can get Mother and Father away from here without contaminating them."

In no time, the wolves scrape a shallow trench free from every fleck of human remains. Demon, Avalanche, Shiloh, and Nikita drag their heroes through the swale while the younger lupines race back and forth making as many tracks as possible, thus obscuring their trail. A quarter mile away, they find an area littered with criss-crossed, fallen trees. Woven into this landscape grows a mixture of blackberry bushes and nettles; a frightening mixture humans will surely avoid. The pack scours this bracken until Nikita finds the perfect resting place for their parents. Phantom, Outlaw, Goddess, Harley, and Ella use their bodies to hold back brush, creating a hole deep into the thicket. The adults reverently carry Thor and Athena through, then the young ones release the brambles; their passage disappears.

Sad pall bearers nestle the corpses side by side beneath a tangle of dead trees and thorns. They lie panting in a rough circle. Hard work and emotional stress take their toll. Every member hovers on the verge of collapse. They gather the last scattered pebbles of their energy for one final task, The Death Song.

Dawn's first dull rays color the horizon a ghostly steel gray. The forest sits silent in a gentle twilight between the workings of night and day creatures, creating an eerie effect. In their thorny haven, the pack lies in an atmosphere as dark as the death around them. Demon starts a low mournful cry. One by one, other members add their own sorrow until the song reaches a chilling crescendo. They harbor no fear of humans now; The Death Song freezes the bravest souls. None will come while the wolves sing.

Their song withers after many hours. The woods still remain quiet when Father Sun wriggles his way into the burial site. Each wolf says a final good-bye then struggles into a bright late morning. Demon hangs back, his sadness driving a dull stick into his soul. He has no more tears; he cried them all during the singing. He stands over his parents, head on chest, quivering in dry sobs.

He forces enough control to speak, "Father, Mother, you will be missed. A piece of every soul in the pack goes to The Astral Forest with you. Please keep watch over us, guide us on our way. I can never match your wisdom, but will try to honor your memory in all my decisions. If only I didn't have to start my leadership with such failure. I am so sorry." He leans down, licks Thor and Athena's faces, then joins his pack.

Demon stops beside Avalanche, hangs his head and sighs. Avalanche's tone carries deep concern, "Are you okay?"

"As okay as I can be, I suppose."

"What now?"

"First, we find a place to sleep. We need rest until our strength returns and our sorrow fades a little. When we've recuperated, we finish Father's journey. We'll find The Land of the Buffalo, start a new life, and enjoy some happiness."

Shiloh's soft voice enters the conversation, "May I make a suggestion?"

Demon looks at her through tired eyes, "Please do."

"Well, I think we should move away from here, quickly. The humans will soon regain their courage and come looking for us. I'm sure they heard our singing, so it stands to reason they'll start in this vicinity. If we move on, they're less apt to find us or your parents."

"Sounds like a wise idea. Any suggestions on where to go?"

"I think we should follow these blow downs. If the bracken stays thick, we'll find a perfect hiding spot."

Demon nods his head, "Let's round up everyone and move on."

They follow the deadfall jungle to a steep ravine with a small brook running along its bottom. Both banks lie covered in fallen, twisted trees. A layer of thick, green moss grows on each trunk. Beefy stalked, blackberry bushes criss-cross into a painful latticework that guards the perimeter. Demon finds a small opening and wriggles between these sentries; his heavy coat protects him from their dagger like thorns. He works his way through a maze of tiny holes and clears obstacles with an agility handed down from generations of athletes. He crawls over one log then under another. In front of him lies an immense pine top; its branches covered in light brown needles. Twisting berry bushes intertwine the branches, forming an impenetrable wall. Demon follows His nose until he finds a rabbit tunnel leading into the tangle. Carefully, keeping his senses alert for any danger, he slips his nose into the burrow. It holds no threats and even carries an enticing scent. Making himself as small as possible, he pushes through the vegetation.

Demon squirms for two body lengths before reaching his goal. The tunnel opens into a large, dark den. Berry bushes arch together above the pine tree; grape vines meander through everything, their tenacious broad leaves forming a watertight roof. The floor impresses him most. Large, flat stones lie together as if it has been tiled. Over that grows the shaggy, green moss he could smell from outside. This carpet makes a comfortable, wall to wall bed big enough for all nine wolves to sleep in. A search of the room's inner perimeter reveals a rear exit leading deeper into the blackberry jungle. One last tour of the den and Demon returns to his pack. When he emerges from the brush, he finds Avalanche in a lookout position atop a nearby boulder. Avalanche notices his brother and joins him.

"How does our back trail look, Avalanche?"

"All clear."

"Good. Okay, everyone, I found a cozy den for a change." Demon backs into the berry bushes and holds a hole open. "Just follow my scent and you'll find an old rabbit trail that leads inside. I'll be right behind you."

Avalanche leads the way. Each wolf passes Demon carrying an expression of mixed sorrow and admiration. Shiloh—who walks last in line—carries a different look about her. Is it respect, or something more? Demon squashes a strange flutter in his stomach like stomping on a giant butterfly. He scans the immediate area, taking note of every rock and tree; nothing moves. He turns and disappears into the bracken like a ghost walking through a wall.

John can't believe the carnage before him. His co-workers' bodies lie strewn and mutilated beyond recognition. "Dear God, what could've done this?"

"Looks like wolves" Bob, their best tracker, crouches, studying clues that cover the ground. "Damn strange ones at that." He looks around, making sure none of their six hired hands stand within earshot, then lowers voice, "If I didn't know any better, I'd say they were werewolves."

"What makes you say a crazy thing like that?"

"Wolves don't mutilate, they kill to survive. This is an act of hatred and retribution."

"Animals don't have feelings."

"I know, but look at the tracks. There was a huge one caught in the trap. Here's where another one laid beside it and bled out. Now if both wolves are dead, where are they? There are no drag marks to indicate that the pack milling around here later took them. Makes you wonder if they were carried, and if so, by whom, or what? Their trail leads through the brush, but not in a typical straight line. They work their way back and forth over the main tracks like they tried covering their trail on purpose. You ever hear of wolves being that smart?"

"No"

"Me either. I don't like this one bit"

"What do you suggest we do?"

"We gather the remains, return them to their families, then forget all about this weird ass shit."

"I guess this proves Jimmy and Billy weren't babblin' fairy tales about psycho wolves."

"No, and if we tell anybody else what we found, they'll think **we're** babblin' fairy tales. I say we tell them the guys were attacked by a rampaging grizzly that we later killed and left for the scavengers."

"I don't like lying."

"If you tell them the truth, they'll put you in a loony bin. You'll go alone too, cause I ain't backin' you up. This is too weird. I just wanna forget it."

"Alright, but I still don't like it." John sighs, "C'mon, Boys, let's clean up this unholy mess."

Demon twitches and whimpers; nightmares dripping with guilt and regret race around his exhausted mind. His mother's agonizing scream echoes through his memory. He sits bolt uptight, casting frightened eyes about the den. No one sleeps well; sobs and anguished cries keep silence at bay. The fog in his brain slowly clears. A dark form looms on the den's far side. Shiloh's concerned face wavers into focus; the strange flutter returns. He dips his head and picks a path past restless forms around him as he moves toward the entrance. A moment later, he emerges into a graying world. The rustle at his back doesn't concern him, he knows Shiloh's light step.

Demon draws air, drenched in the scent of blackberries, into his lungs, holds it a second, then pushes it out in a rush, "Hello, Shiloh."

"Hello, Demon. Are you okay?"

"Not really, can't sleep."

"Me either, the loss of your parents weighs heavy on all our souls."

"I could've saved them. I should've stayed and fought. I should've figured out that leg catcher sooner"

"No, you did the right thing. Your father knew we didn't have time to save your mother before the humans came and slaughtered us all.

Being a faithful mate, there's no way he would leave her side, even facing certain death. That's why he entrusted you with protecting us and leading us to safety. We would've died without your leadership. You saved us."

Demon stares at Brother Moon's faint half face, "I suppose you're right, but I can't help feeling guilty."

"I think we all feel a twinge of guilt for living while our leaders died. We must remember the one thing they wanted us to do, keep on living. They are in The Astral Forest now, traveling alongside their ancestor, and meeting The Great Forest Spirits. They hunt there together and will be happy for eternity."

"That's not much comfort right now."

"It will be."

She turns to rejoin the family. She reaches the bushes when Demon calls, "Shiloh?"

She stops and looks back, "Yes?"

"Thank you. I felt so incompetent and alone. Your encouragement really helped"

Shiloh's smile makes his heart skip a beat; her soft voice weakens his knees, "I'm glad I could help. I'm always here if you need someone to lean on."

After she fades into the tangle, Demon curses himself, "What's wrong with me? My parents have just died and I'm acting like an adolescent pup toward my brother's widow. If this is a test from The Great Forest Spirits, I doubt I'll pass. Maybe if I tour the surrounding area, I can divert my scrambled brain from thoughts I shouldn't entertain."

Shiloh finds her spot beside her children, contemplating emotions as mixed up as Demon's. "Am I truly over Bandit or am I reacting to this latest trauma by reaching out to Demon? Is this acceptable?

He is my mate's brother." She lays her head on her paws and drifts into a troubled doze. Dreams, nightmares, and visions of disturbing romance form a dizzying display in her mind. She stays in her pool of confusion until Demon returns.

Demon's jaunt did little good at distracting his thoughts, but it wasn't a total waste. He did find a stray calf to vent some frustration on. He drops its shredded carcass in the lee of a boulder and gets the pack. Worry for their new leader's sanity flits through their guts when they see the damage he has done to their meal. They eat very little; sorrow and fear extinguishes appetites. Demon prods the young members to eat a few bites.

"But we're not hungry." Phantom whines.

"I know, but you can't miss a chance to eat. One never knows when another opportunity will present itself, especially during a journey as torturous as this one."

The pack grieves for three days, each in their own way. Some become angry and hard to live with while others become aloof. Nikita's nurturing instincts reach a pinnacle of frenzied proportions. She spends all her energy moving from one family member to another, soothing everyone's pain while hers goes untended. Demon and Shiloh soon realize they can't ignore the emotions roiling inside them; something must be done. Even the angry and isolated wolves know an attraction builds between the pair. They feel their intimacy and confusion crackling in the air like lightning before a storm. None are surprised when the two leave together under the pretense of finding food.

Shiloh and Demon cross a brook and climb the opposite hill, dodging brambles with ease. They stop at the ridgetop where they have a good view of their area. Still concerned about human presence, they blend themselves into a background of gray stone that sticks out of the knoll like a finger pointing west. A setting Father Sun hangs low over distant mountains, painting the sky blood red. The orb itself mimics a deep orange iris in a sleepy eye. Below them sits a small, tangled wood bordered by open, rolling hills. At this vantage point, they can smell cattle and smoke from the human's camp. Anger and shame twist around Demon's guilty attraction to Shiloh. A faint west wind tickles their noses with a fleeting scent. Not dangerous, just strange and distant.

They sit in quiet contemplation for some time, waiting for the right words to come. Demon breaks their silence. His nerves fray, his stomach alternates between knots, nausea, and butterflies, "Shiloh, something strange is happening to me and I hope you feel it too." He prays he doesn't trip over his tongue or make a fool of himself with his next words, "I—uh—think—I'm developing feelings for you, but I don't know if it's right or not. I mean, you're a great wolf and you were a perfect mate for my brother, but that's the problem, you're my brother's widow. Is it wrong for me to feel the way I do, especially so quickly after my parent's death?"

"Is love ever wrong?"

"It feels right and wrong at the same time."

"That's because you feel guilty about it. You've spent so much time and energy denying your feelings that you've lost track of what they truly are."

"Why now? After all this time, why do I have these feelings now?"

"Perhaps the pain of your parents' death forces you to realize just how lonely you really are."

"Do you share my feelings, or was I wrong about that?"

"No, I have them. I've struggled with them for a while now. I think mine stem from the strengths you share with Bandit. You sometimes remind me of him very much. I thought I might be betraying him by allowing myself these emotions, but now I think falling for someone so like him would be a tribute to his memory. He would want us to be happy."

"Where do we go from here?"

"I say let our feelings run and see where they go."

"What do we tell the others?"

"I don't know. I doubt we need to tell them much. I suspect they already have a good idea of what's going on."

"Then I guess all that's left is preparing the pack to restart our journey."

CHAPTER 21

The pack creeps up on an elk herd using tall grass for cover. A shifty wind causes Demon to abandon their typical approach of spreading out. He decides staying together will prevent their scent from being dispersed too far, thus alerting the group. Their own acute sense of smell helps the wolves pinpoint a sick cow on the vast herd's eastern edge. A deep green scent of fresh-cropped grass tells the true majesty of this group; few gatherings generate as heavy an odor as this one.

Demon decided earlier, they should take time out for a hunt since they've had little to eat for several nights. Their first attempt at a bunch of antelope failed miserably. The northern wolves have no experience chasing those speedy, high jumping mammals. The antelopes' keen eyesight picked out the pack before they even had a chance to start running; the bounders disappeared in seconds.

Now the hunters stalk a prey more known to them. Although elk have excellent vision, their night vision is nowhere near as good as a wolf's. The pack comes forward at a slow trot; turbulent wind may betray them at anytime, but it does cover the sound of their approach. The lupines converge on the sick cow before she can rise out of her bed; the main herd bolts for safety. Demon makes the lethal throat bite—severing the carotid artery—then dives away from thrashing hooves. The cow's death comes quick and almost painless.

Considering everyone's hunger, Demon dispenses with the customary hierarchy and lets all members eat at once. In response to his generosity, the others save him the choice liver and tenderloin. They've gotten themselves a very large cow; when the famished pack finishes, leftovers still remain.

While they relax, chewing on various bones, Avalanche asks the question on everyone's mind, "So, Demon, what have you and Shiloh decided to do?"

"About what?"

"The feelings you hold for each other and have been suppressing."

A shocked look crosses Demon's face, "How long have you known?"

"Nikita picked up on it a long time ago."

Nikita chimes in, "I've always been nursemaid for everyone, Demon. That makes me more sensitive to the pack's emotional state than anyone else."

"No one objects?"

"Of course not, you fool." Avalanche cajoles, "Every Alpha Male needs a mate. Who better than Shiloh? We all know and love her, besides, she has a good head on her shoulders, she'll keep you from doing anything too stupid. The two of you will make a great couple."

Demon looks across the circle at Shiloh, who lies gnawing on a leg bone, "So much for letting our feelings run to see where they take us. These guys have us mated already."

She gives him a coquettish smile, "That wouldn't be all bad either."

Ever curious, Phantom breaks into the conversation, "If you mate Mother, will you still be Uncle Demon or Father?"

"I'll always be Uncle Demon. I can never take your father's place. I won't even try. You never got a chance to know him, but I don't want you thinking any less of him by calling me Father. He was always a better wolf than me and he is the only father you will ever have." Demon's eyes meet Shiloh's; she smiles and nods her head in approval.

———————————

After a long night of travel, the wolves end up far from any forest and must settle for sleeping in the lee of a grassy knoll. Father Sun's first rays peek out of the east. While their family rests, Demon and Shiloh lie with their heads on the hillcrest, looking west. That strange scent rides the air once again. Thick, dirty, almost familiar, but not quite.

Shiloh leans close and whispers in Demon's ear, "What do you suppose it is?"

"I don't know. It's frustrating, I feel as though I should be able to identify it, yet I can't. It's like cattle, but it's not. Do you have any ideas?"

"I'm as frustrated as you are. Should we be worried?"

"I think we should be cautious, we'll save worried for when we identify it."

"In that case, let's get some sleep."

"Alright, I'll let everyone in on it. We can take turns scouting the area every few hours."

They return to find Avalanche watching their back trail. Demon can sense his pacing brother's agitation. Avalanche sees the two then meets them beside the pack.

Demon addresses his family, "I've decided Avalanche, Shiloh, and I will take turns getting up every few hours and checking our surroundings. I'm sure you've all picked up the strange scent by now, but no, I have no idea what it is."

"Then we should post guards all around us." Avalanche breaks in.

"There's no need. It just smells strange, not dangerous. It carries no hint of predator."

"If it's an enemy covering his scent, like humans for example, we could get caught unaware."

"I've detected nothing. It seems to me one of us would've picked up at leas a whiff of trouble by now. Has anyone found anything they've yet to report?" Demon waits several seconds for an answer. "In that case, I see no reason to tire everyone by standing watch. I'll check first, everybody get some sleep."

Shiloh leans close and whispers, "Are you sure we have nothing to fear? I mean, we don't know what kind of creature exudes such a strange scent. What if it turns out to be a new kind of enemy?"

"We'll be fine. Come, we need rest."

Demon doesn't feel the confidence he projects. He circles the pack a few times then lies down, his fitful sleep plagued with questions brought up by Shiloh and Avalanche. "Are you sure we're safe? What if it's a new kind of threat? What if it's an enemy covering his scent? We could get caught off guard." He tosses and turns, willing his wandering mind to settle down.

The temperature climbs with Father Sun; it's turning into a hot day. The wolves lie panting in their sleep, unconsciously wishing for shade. Demon's fragile doze shatters when the ground trembles. He springs to his feet, all senses peak in a split second. He joins Avalanche at the knoll crest. In the distance a copious dust cloud rises skyward. The strange scent hangs so thick they can taste it. It's flavor holds a combination of musk, hair, and mud. Guttural lows and bellows mix with a deep rumble shuddering through the quiet afternoon. The menagerie of dust, noise, and heavy odors heads straight for them.

Demon's jaw drops, "Great—Forest—Spirits. What do you suppose it is?"

Avalanche slowly shakes his head. "I have no idea."

"How long has it been coming?"

"Half an hour, I guess. The dust cloud doesn't disperse in the distance either; that means there are feet stirring the ground for at least a mile from end to end. Whatever that thing is, it's colossal."

The pack gathers around the brothers. Questions hammer like a woodpecker's drilling staccato, "What is it? Is it coming here? Why aren't we running? Is it dangerous?"

"I don't know." Demon sounds hypnotized, "I just hope it's a herd and not one creature."

An awe inspiring brown mass tops a rise facing the wolves. Relief washes over the canines when they see it is indeed a herd; the strangest they've ever seen. Its members resemble oversized cattle; each one dark brown with large muscular shoulders reaching six feet in height and a small rump. Thick, curly hair covers their immense bodies; rugged, black horns protrude above beady eyes and take a short curve upward. Considering their size, these animals are fast; their running black hooves create a blur. Long tails, sporting a tuft of hair on the end, fly straight out behind them like trailing flags. The dust cloud rising from millions of hooves hides most individuals, preventing an accurate guess of their numbers.

The herd leader, a wizened old bull, notices wolves sitting in plain sight and changes course; his column turns as if it shares one consciousness. The rumble soon becomes a deafening roar. Demon spies smaller, lighter colored legs in the middle of the herd straining to keep up.

Shiloh shouts to be heard over the din, "Do you think it's their young in the center?"

"It appears to be. I wonder how any hunter could get past the adults. These creatures must be invincible."

"At least we know where the strange scent comes from."

"I wish I knew what these creatures are, though."

The lupines must settle back into their hollow to get below a rolling wall of choking dust that makes breathing impossible. Several family members cough and sneeze. Ella's eyes water, Harley rubs her snout with a forepaw, Phantom rolls his face in the grass, Outlaw and Goddess shake themselves vigorously dispersing dust trapped in their coats. Nikita moves from one to another, tending everyone's needs. It takes an hour for the thundering herd to pass; another twenty minutes for the dust to settle. The wolves can still feel a tremble in the pads of their feet as they re-climb the hill.

None can prepare for the sight awaiting them. The grass filled gully no longer exists; it now looks like a trail humans use for their metal monsters. Not a single blade of grass survives. Closer inspection reveals an uncountable number of hoof prints in rich black soil. The earth lies dug up as if a farmer attacked it with a plow. Manure, grass, and dirt are mixed and pounded together. Phantom sticks one foot in a track and sinks halfway to his knee.

"Holy smokes, Uncle Demon, how heavy are these things?"

"They must be heavier than a moose to make tracks that deep."

"What now?" Shiloh asks.

"We finish resting for the day then head out tonight."

Avalanche freezes, "Strangers coming."

Demon whirls to see three wolves approaching; one grey, one black, and one white. The pack forms a defensive concave half circle, stemming from Demon at center. Muscles tighten and they crouch in anticipation of trouble. The electric force of adrenaline charged nerves leaps from one to another. Hearts beat faster, snarls tremble under tense lips. The strangers, sensing hostility, pull up short.

The large grey steps forward, "Ho, Brothers, where are you from?"

Demon tosses a suspicious glance Shiloh's way before answering, "What makes you think we're not from here?"

"No one in these territories shows hostility toward other wolves, we've learned to co-exist, co-operate, and prosper."

"You have our apologies." Demon relaxes a bit then winks at Avalanche.

Avalanche catches this subtle signal and takes a couple of steps left, gaining himself a better angle to flank the strangers should a fight break out.

"My name is Streak," the gray continues, "these are my litter mates. This black beauty is my sister, Diana and the white wonder here is my brother, Eros."

"I am Demon, leader of this pack, my mate Shiloh, my twin brother Avalanche, first litter sister Nikita, our third litter sisters Harley and Ella, my nephews Outlaw and Phantom, and my niece Goddess."

"We are honored to make your acquaintance."

"To answer your question, we are from the northeast, land of the moose and white tailed deer."

"Welcome, Friends. If you'd like, we can show you around the area, perhaps we will run into the rest of our pack. We can also go to the boulder we call Yellowstone. We should see some of our friends there. It's the social spot for our neighborhood."

"You allow other packs into your territory?"

"Of course. As I said, we've learned co-existence, co-operation. When game gets scarce in one territory, that pack asks permission to hunt on their neighbor's. We respect each other's range by not killing more than we need. This way there is always enough food."

"Interesting concept. You have no quarrels?"

"On occasion. If we can't resolve it amongst ourselves we go to the elders of a neutral pack and let them settle the dispute. Our system works quite well. It saves on bloodshed and pack members don't get so worn out from fighting that they can't provide for their families. When we heard of this place, we left our old pack to come here. We escaped vicious competition for game that killed several family members over the years. We just got sick of warring and starving all the time."

"What about humans?"

"Humans don't hunt here. I don't know why, but the few we do see only watch us. There are some ranchers around. They'll kill you on sight, so stay away from them. Fortunately, we have enough game to keep our bellies full without risking confrontations with humans."

"Sounds like paradise."

"It is"

From the center of her pack, Goddess watches Eros. He carries a fighter's markings. His right ear lacks its tip, he is blind in one eye, a long scar runs diagonally down his ribs, and he limps on his right front leg. His otherwise bright shiny coat dazzles her. She wonders if someone sporting his own scars will overlook hers. She tilts her head at a coquettish angle when he looks her way. His immaculate smile makes her heart flutter like a hummingbird.

Their progressing conversation abates Demon's suspicion in small degrees. While listening, he contemplates his next move, "Perhaps I can trust these strangers. It would be the first trust I've extended to someone not related to me in a long time." One final question burns in the back of his mind, "Streak, what do you know about The Land of the Buffalo?"

"You're standing in it."

"Don't jest."

"I'm not. You are standing in The Land of the Buffalo."

"How far into this land are we?"

"Coming from the northeast, I'd say you've been in it for at least a hard day's run."

The news washes away all of Demon's agitation. Smiling, he turns to Shiloh, "That means Mother and Father made it. Father found his Land of the Buffalo, he just didn't know it."

Shiloh leans on Demon, "I'm sure they know now."

"It soothes my soul to know that Father's dream came true. Now we can finally live in peace."

EPILOGUE

Both packs bond quickly; Streak and his family teach their new friends how to hunt buffalo. Demon and Streak become inseparable. Streak's pack gives Demon's a corner of their territory to call home. The new arrivals excavate a den in the side of a grassy knoll overlooking a small brook. Over several years, shishing grass and babbling water lull many litters of pups to sleep while they escape a blistering Father Sun.

Demon and Shiloh live long, happy lives together, producing many strong pups. Nikita enjoys her nursemaid duties for several more litters before passing away in her sleep, a very gray and happy old wolf. Harley and Ella work together carrying on Nikita's legacy. Phantom and Outlaw mate a pair of sisters from a neighboring pack and bring home pups of their own. Phantom has three with his inquisitive nature who give him the kind of scares he used to give his mother. Goddess and Eros begin a tentative courtship born of self consciousness. In time, they heal each other's scars and enjoy a long happy relationship.

Avalanche doesn't mate; instead he follows an old pack law which states, "Only the Alpha Male and Female are allowed to mate." He finds contentment in his job as Demon's advisor and training his many great nieces and nephews. His wisdom solves many day-to-day problems. However, a conflict often brews in his mind. On one hand, his heart fills with pride watching Thor and Athena's descendants come into the world, living tributes to their great leaders' memory. On the other hand, he holds concern about overpopulation. Mortality rates for wolves in The Land of the Buffalo stay minimal. Add the fact that most packs let all members mate, and it's only a matter of time before game becomes scarce. These problems will inevitably lead to confrontations with humans, and that always lead to decimation.

Avalanche sits atop a grassy knoll; Father Sun sets at his back, painting the sky a lustrous pink. Watching his soon to be massive pack, he wonders, "How long will it be until the humans force us into moving again?"

His eldest great-nieces and nephews break his reverie by calling from below, "Uncle Avalanche, Uncle Avalanche, come play with us." He smiles, thinking, "What the hell, why worry about the future? Life is good." Then bounces down the hill, tail high in the air, to wrestle the youngsters.

.